THE HOLD OUT

AN ENEMIES TO LOVERS ROMANCE

MICKEY MILLER

Edited by SUE GRIMSHAW

Edited by ELAINE YORK

Illustrated by LORI DESIGNS

NOTE FROM THE AUTHOR:

T*he Hold Out: An Enemies to Lovers Romance*, is the second standalone in the Brewer Brothers Series. It is an interconnected series of standalones. Each book can be read separately with no spoilers.

BREWER BROTHERS BOOKS:

Book 1: *The Lake House* (Maddox & Sherry)

Book 2: *The Hold Out* (Emma & Everett)

Book 3: *FDF* (Jocko & Allie) - Releasing November 8th! Cover Reveal in October.

HAPPY READING!

Love,

Mickey

1

EMMA

You can tell a lot about someone by the way they order a hot dog.

This is one of the many amazing things I've learned working at the hot dog stand this year.

As my grandmother might have said if she were still around, *'It sounds like a great character-building job, Emmy.'*

"I've got seniority over you," my co-worker Ken reminds me early on this Sunday morning as we're trying to decide what music to play. "I've worked here for a full year and a half. You've barely been here since spring. So we will be playing *my* playlist. And that's final."

Before I can protest, he changes the song to "*Go Loco*" and turns up the volume. I check to make sure there's not a customer waiting at the window, then cross my arms and give Ken my best dead eyes.

"Ten on a Sunday is just a little early to be blasting gangster rap."

He makes an exaggerated, pouty face. "Oh, yeah, are you offended? Can't listen to gangster rap on the Lord's day, but here you are working on the Sabbath?"

Still with dead eyes, I shake my head. "You're not even a gangster. You don't even *know* any gangsters."

Ken pauses, a little flustered. "Sure I do."

"Name one gangster."

"Al Capone."

I roll my eyes. "One gangster who's *alive.* You don't have to answer, because I know you can't do it. You're from the northern 'burbs."

Ken takes a sip of his coffee. "I'm sorry, Em, but we are just not listening to your crappy 50's and 60's go-go music. It's just horrible."

"You bite your tongue," I spit back. "The '50s—and especially the '60s—were a golden era of music."

He blinks a few times and stares at me, slack jawed, but doesn't say anything. So I continue.

"Not convinced? In the '60s, you've got Elvis, Beatlemania, and Johnny Cash, all on the popular charts. Not to mention artists like Nat King Cole, Louis Armstrong, and Sergio Mendez mixed in. Can you imagine having a jazz trumpet song on the Top 40 these days? No, you can't. It would never happen. Half of the music that's playing now is made by computer algorithms, anyway. It's just crack for our ears."

After my diatribe, Ken says nothing, and I notice his eyes seem a little wider than normal. Maybe I'm actually getting through to him.

"Shall I continue?"

Ken tips his head toward the window, a little sheepishly, and I wonder what's behind me.

Someone clears their throat, and to be honest, it sounds almost like the low rumble of an animal growling. I turn around and my eyes widen when I see who it is—and I'm not exaggerating—the guy is the most muscled man I've ever seen in the flesh. He's tall with a solid chest, chiseled jaw, and chestnut hair...and without his shirt, I'd imagine he looks as if he's a Spartan warrior who just dropped out of the movie *300*.

I get the nagging feeling like I should recognize him, but I don't. Ken steps to the side, manning the brats, cat all of a sudden got his tongue, apparently.

"Uh, hello?" the man outside our window says. "Can I get some damn service here?"

I flash my best smile, though I'm suddenly self-conscious of how I look in my uniform, which is an unflattering red polo, black pants, and a red and yellow visor.

"Of course," I say. "Welcome to Wade's Weiner Shack. How can I help you?"

"I'll take three double hot dogs."

"Three doubles?" I recoil. "That's a lot. You sure you want three?" Of course, I'm assuming he's eating them all himself, which may not be the case, but that's where my assumption went.

"Look, Miss, if I wanted diet advice, I would have gone to my personal trainer. Just take my money and give me what I want. Spare me the commentary."

Ha! I was right, he *is* planning to eat them all. I knew it. A rush of adrenaline pours through me because I am a little annoyed at his snotty response.

"Yes, sir," I say.

The man pays without another word, or a thank you, and takes a seat at the red picnic bench in front of the hot dog stand. I notice he's got a pen and he's writing something down on a napkin while he waits.

"Dude," Ken whispers. "That's Everett Brewer."

"Who?"

"You don't watch football?"

I shake my head. "I know Aaron Rodgers. That's about it."

Ken chuckles. "Figures. Well, Everett Brewer is the star running back for the Chicago Grizzlies. He sat out last year, though."

"Did he have an injury?"

Ken shakes his head. "Nope. He and the owners disagreed on how much Everett should make. He refused to sign a contract."

I stare at Everett. He's still writing something intently on the napkin. Hasn't he heard of the Notes app on his smartphone?

After putting his *three* double hot dogs on a tray, I call his order number.

"Number sixteen," I say into the microphone.

He looks around. There is absolutely no one else in the vicinity, and I'm sure he's wondering why the mic announcement was even necessary. I chuckle, gotta get my fun in somewhere working at a hot dog stand.

Slowly, he gets up and comes over to the window.

"You know, you could just open the window and say, 'your order is ready.'"

"Just following procedure," I inform him dryly. The man has a monster of an attitude.

"Right. Because someone might steal my order if you don't," he says, begrudgingly showing me his receipt.

"If you have suggestions, you can put them in the box," I point over to the little box near the condiment stand. "Also, you are welcome to leave a tip."

I gesture toward the tin can on the silver ledge, aptly named *student loan fund.*

Everett scoffs. "This is exactly what's wrong with the world today."

My brow furrows. "Tips are what's wrong with the world?"

I notice Ken takes out his phone and points it at Everett.

"Yes. Everyone wants a handout these days. It's absolutely mind-blowing," Everett nods.

"I work a lot of hours. We're on our feet all day. Sure, maybe this isn't the most intellectually demanding profession, I'll give you that. But dealing with customers all day can be...emotionally draining."

"Customers...like me? Are you calling me an asshole?"

"I didn't say that at all. I'm just giving you the rationale for the tip jar, since you're so anti-tip. Aren't you...pretty well off? What's a dollar to you?" Honestly, I would never speak to a customer this way, but no one else is around, and he just really got under my skin.

Everett's nostrils flare, and his jaw hardens. My heartbeat doubles under my red polo just watching the negative emotions burning through him. His brown eyes turn orange and fiery.

"It's not about me having money to tip or not. It's about the principal of the matter."

"And what is the *principal* of the matter?" I ask, though I get exactly what he's saying but won't give him the satisfaction, but I have this odd feeling and I want to antagonize him. Again, this is so not me.

Ken takes a bite of a potato chip, still pointing the camera at us and apparently enjoying just being a spectator. I don't think Everett sees it, and I'm not going to let Ken use his video in any way. In fact, I'll smash the damn phone if I need to.

"The principal of the matter, sweetheart, is that there are tipping professions and non-tipping professions. For example, when I sit down at a nice restaurant or a bar, a server takes care of me for an hour or more. The server waits *on me* so I don't have to get up and move. I just enjoy myself. I will gladly tip twenty, twenty-five percent in that case. But now, everywhere you go, you swipe your card and they ask do you want to tip? It's like, *no, buddy*! You just swiped my card and hit one button for a tall latte. I hate to break it to you, but that is not worth an extra twenty-percent tip."

My expression flummoxes, though I'm grinning inside when he leans in.

"Same goes at a hot dog stand. You wanted a tip? Well, here's the best tip you'll get all day. If you want to make more than eight dollars an hour, you should probably change professions. Because you won't make more than that working at Wade's Weiner Shack."

I lean in and lower my voice. "Yeah? Well, you're welcome to your opinion. But it doesn't mean you're not an asshole."

His eyes widen. "What did you call me?"

I challenge his brown-orange eyes with my blues. "You heard me. Oh, and one more thing." I pause, making sure I've got his undivided attention.

"What's that?"

I get as close to his ear as possible, leaning over the counter through the window. "I'm not your sweetheart. Not sure if you got this memo, but it's 2019, not 1950. And I don't give a shit if you're a star. You don't call a girl who isn't your sweetheart, *sweetheart*. Especially when you're not tipping them. Got it?"

He stares me down, and I wonder if he's going to get the last word in. I wait for it.

But instead, he takes a deep breath, turns around, sits down and eats his hot dogs.

"Holy shit!" Ken says when I close the window. "You just laid a verbal smackdown on Everett freaking Brewer!"

Ken is ecstatic. "For that, I give you Bluetooth privileges. Play whatever music you want until noon. You earned it. Here, connect your phone."

"Were you recording that?" I ask.

"Oh, yeah," he says, tapping his phone. "I'm posting this to Twitter."

My hair stands on end because I'm not going to allow that. "Please do not post it anywhere."

"Why not? This is our big chance to go viral."

I glance over at Everett. "He looks miserable. Maybe he's not normally like this. I don't think it's our place to post a video of a private interaction—for which he could be skewered by the online mobs."

Ken fixes his glasses and puts his hand on my shoulder.

"But you were the one who called him out. You literally called him an asshole! You're the hero in this video! Don't you want to be an online hero?"

"Ken. I'm serious. Do not post that video. This is not what I want to be known for."

"Fine," he grumbles, putting his phone away. "But you're making a big mistake. We could be famous for this. Famous."

"I have a feeling that fame isn't all it's cracked up to be," I say, now feeling a little smarmy for being such a bitch to him.

~

WITHIN THE NEXT TWENTY MINUTES, three separate customers literally compliment us on the music, and I give Ken a *see?* eyebrow raise which he pretends he doesn't notice. I decide I'll put an anonymous note about the stellar choice of music today as a customer in the suggestions box on the off-chance that management actually reads those. I have my doubts.

When I go to pick up Everett's tray, I notice he left the napkin behind that he had been writing something on. Curious, I pick it up. To my surprise, it's a letter…a *love letter?*

I shouldn't read it, but curiosity pulls at me:

Dear Samantha,

I love you and I hope you know that. I want you to understand, I think about you every single day. Many times a day. Every minute, sometimes. I wonder what I could have done differently, but the thing about life is there are no takebacks. No do-overs. Someday, maybe you'll find it in your heart to forgive me. Until that day, I'll keep writing. I'll keep hoping. And I'll keep loving you how I can.

Love you always and forever,

E

Chills wash over me as I finish reading. I can't help but wonder who the woman is he's writing this to and what they mean to one another. Was she tall, smart, beautiful and caring, or a ruthless, thoughtless person since she's not accepting his heartfelt apology? Or apologies as this doesn't sound like the first letter he's written.

So, Mr. Asshole…is also a hopeless romantic? With feelings… I never would have guessed this was what he was writing while simultaneously berating me.

"Hey, Foster, how long does it take to clear a table?!"

Smartass Ken yells from the window. "Can't you see we've got a line, here!"

Oops, I hadn't noticed the gathering crowd, "Sorry, be right in," I sing, folding the napkin neatly and putting it in my pocket.

I'll probably never see him again, but regardless, I'll make sure that Ken deleted that damn video off his stupid phone.

2

EMMA

My heart thumps abnormally hard as I ride the train home after my shift. It's peculiar to me that a man like Everett, who clearly has a hardened exterior, could have a soft spot for women. Or at least *a particular* woman. His two disparate actions—writing that note and giving me a verbal lashing—seem like the personalities of two different people.

Is it possible he has a lover who scorned him? Or, the way the note reads, perhaps he scorned?

My gut sinks a little as I remember my ex, Troy. We broke up last winter, but you won't find me writing love notes to him any time soon. He was as emotionally unavailable as they come. I wonder if I have a thing for wounded guys, like my friend Rachel has told me in the past.

Now that I think about it, I haven't been on a single date since Troy and I parted ways. And I haven't really felt like going on a date, either. I've been too busy tending to my family situation.

Something inside me stirs as I think of Everett. Despite our argument, I have a brief fantasy about him getting so angry he jumps over the counter of the hot dog stand and rips off my visor and uniform so we can have a hot make-out —and maybe more. I wonder how the weight of his muscled body would feel on top of mine.

Record *that,* Ken, you poser.

Yikes. Clearly it's been too long since I've been laid if I'm having thoughts like this. But when I use my phone to google and find some pictures of Everett during games, they don't help matters. He's all brooding and serious looking in every single photo. And I find that hot as hell.

Note to self: start going on dates before the summer's over.

I take the napkin out of my purse and read it one more time. It appears that Everett wants to get back with the woman he's writing to, though that isn't working out well for him.

I mean, I know unrequited love is a bitch, but a guy like Everett — multimillionaire, celebrity sports star — can have any woman he wants, right? So why would he get all down and out about one girl unless he was head over heels in love?

I get off the train and walk to my sister's house where I'm currently living. Due to financial issues, I just graduated college this past winter, late, at age twenty-four, and now here I am working at a hot dog stand.

Full time. If it were part time, maybe I could justify that.

But full time?

Maybe Everett's words cut into me so much because there is a lot of truth to them. I should be shooting higher.

After I received my diploma this past winter, I researched jobs, but so far nothing has piqued my interest. Or maybe I'm searching for some perfect unicorn of a job that doesn't even exist, instead of just starting somewhere. So Everett's assertion that if I needed money, I should change my career, was accurate and that's why it struck a nerve.

On the other hand, it's been a tougher year than normal. I've been living with my sister Pam since her husband passed away unexpectedly and tragically this winter in a car accident. With a ten-month old daughter, and a son due in September, Pam needs all the help she can get. I'm doing my best to try and help her make ends meet, and watch Eve whenever she needs me. But I know for a fact I need to up my game and put myself in a job that makes more money, or at least has a trajectory of upward growth.

"Thank goodness you're here," Pam says as soon as I walk through the door. "Can you watch Eve for a little while? I need to run some errands."

"Of course I can."

"Thanks, Em. You're the best. She's down for a nap right now. But she'll be up soon."

"Got it. What kind of errands are you running?"

"Can't talk. Gotta run. See ya!"

She heads out the door, practically running, and I heave a sigh. It's been like this, more or less, since Jack died. She's closed off and pretends she's fine when I know she's not. Then when I try to ask her where she's going, she evades the question. Our dad used to do that all the time. Maybe Pam inherited the penchant for secrecy from him.

She hasn't come back drunk or high, so I don't think she's going on a bender. Which would be unacceptable, obviously. Still, I worry about her.

After Pam leaves, I check on Eve and then make myself a mac and cheese TV dinner. It happens to be one of my favorites because you get a yummy little brownie with it for dessert — just enough for a healthy taste, but not too much to put on the pounds. Looking at the food, my mind begins wandering back to Everett's words. Again.

If you want to make more than eight dollars an hour, you should probably change professions.

Ugh. Money has never been especially important to me, because I don't believe it buys happiness. But seeing the stress — specifically, financial stress — that has befallen my sister this year, my view has shifted. While I don't need to live in a house made of gold, I know I certainly don't want to be poor my entire life.

My phone buzzes, and my best friend Rachel's name shows up on the caller ID.

"Hey, Emma bean," she says. "I just got off my shift at the bar. What are you up to? Want to hang?"

"I'd love to...but I'm watching Eve tonight." Rachel is a lot like me. We've got great degrees on paper, but sadly, our occupations don't reflect that. And although that bothers us both, we haven't dwelled on it much...well, until now, for me.

"Again? Well, okay. Are you watching her *all* night?"

"I'm not sure," I say truthfully. "My sister ran out as soon as I got home without saying where she was going."

"She doesn't have school tonight?"

My sister is studying to be a nurse, while working all the part-time hours she can as a Certified Nursing Assistant at a community-based residential facility. "She doesn't have class on Sundays. I honestly don't know where she went. She's been ducking out like this at least once a week lately."

"Where do you think she's going?" She pauses. "You don't think there could be a man in the picture that she doesn't want anyone to know about, do you?"

"I have no idea. She swears up and down she won't have another man in her life until the baby is a toddler or older.

We'll see, though. How was your shift?" I'm more than happy to change the subject away from my sister's strange behavior.

"Great. Everybody is obsessed with Carter Flynn and Chandler Spiros who were playing this big game this afternoon so...let's just say, tips were good. Drunk bros are surprisingly generous when their team is winning. Especially when I let the girls out to play."

I laugh. "Your girls are good to you. Speaking of tips..."

I let her in on the whole story about Everett Brewer's commentary today, leaving out the details about the love napkin.

For some reason, I feel like keeping that little bit of information private. Which is a little ridiculous, considering odds are I'll probably never see him again.

"That's a little harsh," she says, after I've told her the story.

"You think he was being harsh? I thought he was, too, but then I also kind of think he has a point about there being tipping professions and non-tipping professions."

"No! I mean *you're* being a little harsh on *him.* As the top tip-getter at Country Mike's BBQ Barn, I have an opinion on this. And the fact is, you're not going to get a tip if you chastise guys who call you 'sweetheart' or 'honey'. Although, there is the occasional creep. For a lot of them, it's just the way they talk and they're actually trying to be nice. It's no big deal, really."

"Oh. My. God. You're...taking his side completely?" I protest, which is odd because even I was coming around to Everett's point of view. I just figured Rachel would side with me. Then again, she's never been one to suffocate her point of view just because someone wouldn't like it. That's one of the reasons I like being friends with her, what you see is what you get.

"Bean, I've got your back all day long. And I love you. I know your situation is tough with your sister and Eve and the baby on the way, and I empathize with you. But you've got to set your sights higher! Everett's right in *that* way. The summer is hiring season downtown. And you've got a college degree. Get your résumé out there."

I let out a heavy sigh. "I know. It's just..."

As if on cue, Eve starts crying. I walk over to her room, and put the phone between my ear and shoulder.

"It feels selfish of me to be applying for jobs when my sister needs me."

I pick up Eve out of her crib and bring her to the playroom.

"You're quiet," I say.

"I know this is difficult for you. But you've got to apply now. The longer you wait after college, the more questions people will ask. They'll think you couldn't find a job because something is wrong with you. Hey, I'm no expert, but I can take a look at your resume if you want."

"Thanks." Deep down I know what she's saying makes sense. It's not like we haven't talked about it in the past.

"And if you ever want a job as a cocktail waitress..."

"I just don't think that's my jam." Though I know the tips Rachel makes are amazing.

"Okay. Well, there *are* tips involved. *Especially* when you let the girls out."

I laugh, wishing I was as well-endowed as my friend. "Somehow, I don't think my girls would get the same tips your girls do."

"Please. It's not about the size of the ship as much as it is about your attitude, confidence, and energy. I've seen you when you want to flirt. And when you turn it on, guys can't resist you."

My face reddens a little. "You're exaggerating."

"Am I? Remember when I brought those two guys back from the bar, and I decided I didn't want to hook up with the one, but after you talked to his friend, he wouldn't stop calling you for two months?"

I giggle. "I was tipsy that night. Plus, he was a little weird."

There's a pause on the phone until she finally says, "Ah, college roommates. The glory days."

"I know. Anyway, I just can't picture myself as a cocktail waitress. It sounds like I'd have to put up with a lot of assholes."

"Sounds like you're already doing that at the hot dog stand," she says, "Might as well be paid fairly for it."

Eve starts to cry again.

"Gotta run," I say as a waft of pungency hits my nose. "Diaper time. We'll talk more later. I'll text you sometime this week so we can make plans to get together, K?"

"That's fine. Just think about what I said." she yells into the receiver before I hang up. "Love you, Bean!"

When I hang up, I notice Eve has a silly smile on her face, and I smile back. Babies are so cute and love you unconditionally. I love that, want that...one day, have to get a decent job first, oh, and a man. But back to matters at hand. As I'm quickly getting the fragrant diaper into the diaper bin, my mind continues to wander. If I were to go to a job fair, what would I even put on my resume anyway?

Communications major with versatile skillset? Can cook hot dogs *and* change diapers?

I used to be the sort of person who knew what she wanted to do, who had goals. I was the seventh grader who had one, three, five, and yes, ten-year goals. And I achieved them. It was after college that I seemed to lose sight of that ambition, motivation. Gah! What happened? My record collection catches my eye, stacked on a shelf in the corner. I haven't had time to listen to Ella Fitzgerald, Dolly Parton, or Billie Holiday since I moved in.

Or, maybe that's a lie. I just haven't *made* the time.

Rachel is right. I'm losing sight of myself at a critical juncture in my life. Maybe there's a way I can be a good sister and do all the things that I want, too.

And those things don't involve working at a hot dog stand.

I can't believe I'm actually mentally thanking Everett Brewer for the kick in the butt I needed.

3

EMMA

Work at the dog stand continues as is with no sign of Mr. Snotty Pants in sight. Ken wonders if we'll see him again, teasing me that I scared him with my sweetheart rant. But—I'll be totally honest—that doesn't mean the man doesn't make a couple of appearances in my late night fantasies.

I admit that my sex drive has been in remission since my breakup. Troy and my parting combined with the responsibility I've been taking on with my sister this year put me into a strange new headspace. But Everett's rant—even though it pissed me off—sparked some feelings that had been dormant inside of me for a while. I feel like I'm coming back out of my shell, slowly but surely.

As part of this new energized headspace I'm in, I dust off my résumé and think of the best action verbs to market myself with. I hop onto LinkedIn and peruse through the various links in my field to see what it is that makes *you* stand out as the person everyone wants to hire. I must have written, rewritten, and tossed ten résumé drafts when Rachel stops by and helps me tweak it until it's done. She's a fabulous friend; together we look at all of the jobs and I submit my résumé to every job and job search site I can, canvassing the Chicago area. All done while scarfing down one pizza and a bottle of rosé in my room.

Within the next couple of weeks, interview requests trickle in, and I set up four interviews on one day, each two hours apart, all downtown. I planned it that way because I figure I can get warmed up as I go from one to the next.

Five hours and four interviews later, I'm in the John Hancock building, my final interview of the day having just ended.

"Thank you, Miss Foster. We'll let you know about the position."

I shake hands with everyone and thank them for their time, then head out of the office suite. The elevator pings on my floor and opens. I step on and pull out my phone to check if anything's come up while I've been radio silent.

I've got four missed calls from Rachel. Odd. She knows where I've been all day and that I wouldn't be able to take any calls. I wonder what was so urgent.

I'm about to call her when I look back up from my phone and realize the elevator is going up, not down like I intended, because I forgot to press the number for the floor I wanted. I try to press the button for the lobby floor now, but the light doesn't register. All of a sudden, I find the doors opening on the fifty-fifth floor of the building.

What I see astonishes me. There are gold-plated glass doors in front of me with a seal that says CG.

In a sort of trance, I walk down the hallway toward the doors and run my fingers over them.

Behind me, I hear the voices of two men talking.

"He's good, but twelve million dollars good? Give me a break. There's no one player on this team worth that much."

When I turn around, two suited men, one older and one younger, are looking at me. Knowing I'm not supposed to be here, I freeze up like a deer in headlights.

"Can I help you?" says the older one. He's got white and grey hair and looks to be in his sixties or so.

"Holy shit. It's *her*," says the younger one.

"Um...what's *me?*" I ask, my palms starting to sweat.

"Yeah, what do you mean?" the older man asks.

The younger man takes out his phone and plays a video, turning it toward me so I can see.

My stomach churns at what I see:

It's the video Ken took of me giving Everett an earful at the hot dog stand. And it has gone viral with the title, *Hot Dog Stand Girl Buries Everett Brewer in Epic Rant.*

I'm going to kill Ken. That little shit played me, and Everett, too. "Three million views?!" I smack my forehead in disbelief. "Jesus," I mutter, feeling the heat of embarrassment and shame build, and forcing back the moisture accumulating in my eyes. This is not what I want to be known for.

The two of them laugh as it gets to the end of the video where I tell him not to call me sweetheart.

"You really gave it to him," the younger one says. "I think he had it coming."

"Wait a minute now," the older one furrows his brow, now realizing my intrusion. "What are you doing on this floor?"

My cheeks may have even got redder as I feel like I've just stepped onto private property. "I just had a job interview in this building, and the elevator came up to this floor by accident. I got off, and, well, I was curious what was up here, to be honest."

They both look at me suspiciously, then nod at one another.

"I'm Rich Davis," the older one says, sticking out a hand for me to shake.

"And I'm Cal Davis," says the younger. "Rich's son."

"Ah. That's why you two look so much alike."

Rich pulls out a business card and hands it to me. It says *Chicago Grizzlies Football, majority owner.*

I try to play along like this is normal, and suppress how shocked I am to be meeting the owners of a professional sports team. "Uh, well, I'm sorry about eh, all that," I say, waving a hand to the phone he's still holding and trying not to stammer while looking for my closest escape.

They both laugh. "I should probably be mad at you for the bad PR that is going to ensue from this video," Rich says. "But my daughter sent it to me and thinks you're hilarious. Everett's been in need of a stern talking-to for a long time. And you weren't afraid to give it to him. And as we sometimes say in the biz, any publicity is good publicity."

I swallow, still utterly humiliated by this turn of events. "I'm not sure if you're joking, but I'm sorry. I told my co-worker not to post that video. I don't believe in online shaming. I think we should try to sort things out person to person."

Cal, who I realize is also tall and handsome, arches an eyebrow, and Rich nods.

"Say, how did your job interviews go today?"

"Alright, I guess," I shrug. "All of them said they'd let me know. I had four interviews, total. Hopefully one of them works out."

"What sorts of positions are you applying for?"

"My degree is in communications with a minor in psychology, so I've applied for a couple of sales jobs and internal support. Technology companies are the ones hiring these days."

Rich clears his throat. "How'd you like to interview for the Chicago Grizzlies organization?"

My heart flutters, he can't be serious. "In what capacity would that be?"

Rich steals a glance at his watch. "Look, it's late. We're heading out to a business dinner. Call the number on my card and my secretary will set you up with a time to come in and talk about the details."

Rich whispers something to Cal, and I don't know if I'm hallucinating, but I swear I hear Everett's name muttered under their breath.

"What position...would this be for?" I ask again, ever curious and concerned this is not going to have a good outcome. Somehow I feel like I'm getting in over my head.

Cal purses his lips. "It would be for Everett Brewer's personal assistant."

My lips part, and I try to swallow down the nerves that populate inside me. Squashing them down because anyone would kill for an opportunity like this — but that person isn't me — so, I respond.

"Let me get this straight. You're considering hiring me to work as an assistant for the guy who already hates me?"

"Yes."

"Alright," I say. "I'll be in touch."

No need to tell them now that's not gonna happen. No way am I going to work for Mr. Snotty Pants. I'm desperate, but I'm nowhere near that desperate yet.

~

THE FOLLOWING week I find myself heading to the John Hancock building and entering the same elevator that had a mind of its own.

I press the fifty-fifth floor, and the elevator moves up and pings when it slows to a stop. You may wonder why I'm here, not being desperate and all quite yet — well, a girl's gotta work, and so far, all of my interviewing last week got me *nada*. So, yes, I'm eating my words and what I once thought would never happen now *needs* to happen, very much.

With my earbuds in, I listen to Dave Matthews with today's mantra going through my head: *take these chances.*

I feel nervous putting myself in a position to take a job way out of my comfort zone. On the other hand, what do I have to lose?

Stepping off onto the floor, I see the gold-plated glass doors from before and cautiously walk inside. Before you know it, the interview is over and it all goes surprisingly well. I'm getting a feeling of success, one I didn't have in any of the previous four.

Which I think is good, since I've exhausted other options.

After the appointment comes to an end, they ask me if I have any questions for them.

"I have been wondering why the two of you are interviewing me. I'll be working with Everett, right? Shouldn't he be the one I interview with?"

"Told you she's a sharp one," Cal winks at his dad.

I squint, now wondering if this was a setup. I'm not a total idiot, and his comment seems like he's pandering to me. "What's that supposed to mean?"

Rich folds his hands and leans toward me. "Here's the thing, Miss Foster. Everett has had some issues this past year."

"That's an understatement," Cal adds.

"The only thing I heard was that the organization couldn't sign him last year. But wasn't that more due to negotiations? He wanted more money and you didn't give it to him," I say.

"There was that, but what you read isn't always the entire truth either. We've noticed something more with him, and luckily we were able to keep most of it out of the press," Cal replies.

"So...there's more to it?" I ask, narrowing my gaze, and a chill washes over me as I think about the napkin note.

I know something I bet you don't know, Rich.

Although it feels unlikely that Rich and Cal could be taking note of Everett's love life. However, they're being especially vague in describing what the true issue is that they're referring to.

Rich leans in and steadies his gaze on me. "That's the thing. At the end of the day, we never figured out what happened with him. Part of what you'll be doing as his personal assistant is giving us weekly reports. Cal and I think that since you clearly aren't afraid to stand up to him, as evidenced by that video, it makes you a truly perfect candidate. And you'd be doing this all as his personal assistant, so maybe after warming up to the idea of you as his PA, he'd be more open with you."

My first instinct is that there could be a relationship between Everett's unrequited love and his holding out. He doesn't seem like the lovesick type, but maybe under that hard masculine exterior there's something I can't see.

A ball of anxiety jumps up in my throat. I knew this was too good to be true! This is manipulative and sneaky and totally not something I'm interested in doing.

"You want me to *spy* on him under false pretenses?"

"It's not exactly spying. More like keeping an eye on him and just making sure he's okay."

"Sounds a lot like spying," I say, realizing I added a lot of snark to my tone.

"Miss Foster, we will compensate you more than adequately. And look, you'd be doing a good thing here. It's written into the contracts of all our athletes that we will contract a PA for them if they require one. As such, you'll be reporting to us, first and foremost, with Everett's habits. And hopefully providing some insight on his lifestyle."

Anxiety swims inside me because I'm not cool with this.

"Sounds like it's the same thing as spying, just with dollar signs attached to it." Tapping my finger against my leg and waiting for his reply, I realize I'm out of yet another job, and frustration and stress start to set in.

"You're just keeping an eye on him," Rich says, but the tone of his voice doesn't sound innocent in the least.

"And reporting back to you?"

"Right."

I'm not letting this go, I want them to know I know their intentions. "And *how* is this different from spying?"

"It's...complicated. It's not spying, though." Cal's father now chimes in.

I glance back and forth between the two men, gather my things, then stand up. "I'm sorry. I think this position isn't for me. Thank you for your time."

I start to walk toward the door when Cal's voice stops me.

"It's for his own good, Emma." I freeze, and he continues. "I know how this must seem to you. But believe me, we're the good guys here. We're worried he might do something ... well, bad."

I spin around, primarily to see their composure, and it does worry me. "What do you mean, bad?"

Rich speaks this time. "We're concerned about what he may do to harm his reputation and the organization. And for Everett himself! If he has nothing to hide, he'll be fine."

I put my hand on my hips — it's all about the business and not about him, of course. "If I were to agree to this position, couldn't we just tell him?"

"No," Cal says. "That would sort of defeat the purpose. He'd have his guard up around you at all times."

I rub my forehead with my thumb and forefinger.

"This is, just...I don't know. I feel like I'd be a double agent and selling my soul. I don't like lying."

"Miss Foster, you've met him," Cal goes on. "He's Everett the grouch right now. Distant, despondent, and we want to get a grasp as to what is going on. We also can't have any off-the-field issues bleeding into his performance on the field. As you know, he held out all year last year — even refused to sign a contract. The sports world is abuzz with conspiracy theories, and we need to put an end to those for the good of the rest of the team. You aren't doing this just for us, but for the entire Grizzlies' organization."

My heart palpitates, and I remember the napkin note again. Natural curiosity wants me to take the job, purely to find out more about this girl who has stolen his heart so I can solve the mystery that's been plaguing me ever since I found that note. But I don't want to hurt Everett in the process; though, maybe I could help him. Even though he's grouchy, he is a handsome man, so hanging around him wouldn't be a hardship.

But moral ambiguity has always made me uncomfortable, and this sounds like a textbook example of it.

"And, of course, we haven't discussed salary yet," Cal says.

"Oh. Right." I nod. I've been practicing salary negotiation all week with Rachel so as to not get screwed. "I've thought about it, too."

I move back to the table and sit down.

"Oh?" Rich says. "And what have you decided?"

I clear my throat. "I won't start for anything less than fifty-five thousand a year."

Nervousness coursing through me, I let the words linger in the air and revel in the awkward silence of the first bid.

Cal and Rich look at each other and chuckle, which makes my cheeks flush.

"Emma, I'm sorry, that's not going to work," Rich says.

Anger swirls through me, but I stay calm and take a deep breath. Rachel and I planned for this.

"I won't go any lower than that," I reiterate, looking right at both of them.

"We didn't mean lower," Cal says. "We meant higher. How about one-hundred-twenty thousand? That way, it's an even ten thousand a month."

My jaw drops. "You're offering me more? Why?"

"Let's just say, the last assistant he had — over a year ago — didn't exactly last. Everett's not the easiest client to deal with. Plus, with your keeping the extra eye on him, it would be well worth the salary," Cal pauses and winks, "and we want you to be happy."

"Ohh. I see. Because of the moral ambiguity of what you're asking me to do."

Rich tightens his face. "I'd prefer it if you didn't use that term. There's nothing morally ambiguous about this."

I look between the two of them, twisting my face up.

I consider my current job at the hot dog stand. I consider

the dumb luck I have right now to even be in this position, most likely for a short time. And the fact that I would instantly be making over five times per year what I thought I would make out of college.

Doing some quick math in my head, I realize I might be able to pay off the majority of my student loans in *one year*. Not to mention, I could move out of my room that doesn't feel like home, but still help my sister out financially from the comfort of my own place.

An old saying my grandmother used to say runs through my mind: *If it's too good to be true, it usually is*.

I'm leery about the prospect of reporting back to them. But then I remember the mantra with which I started my job interviews.

Take these chances.

What if this is a win-win situation, where I can help Everett out and never let on to Rich and Call what I find out?

I look Rich in the eye. "I'll do it. I'll be Everett Brewer's personal assistant."

"That's what I'm talking about!" Cal says, and shakes my hand. "You start Monday."

4

EVERETT

Monday morning. I'm putting my work-out clothes on when I get a call from my agent, Chip. He's letting me know about the *assistant* who will be coming to my house today.

"My house?! Seriously? You know how I feel about people coming here! I'm going to fire her. Can you take care of that? Or should I?"

"You can't fire your assistant, Everett. She hasn't even started yet," Chip barks into the phone.

"Sure, I can."

"No, you can't. It's written into your contract. The Grizzlies are paying you twelve-million dollars, so they *own you* for the next year, remember?"

"I don't care. I don't need an assistant, Chip."

"Have you signed the boxes of merchandise that came into your house yet?"

"What merchandise?"

He grunts. "How many charity events have you done this year?"

"None."

"And you've gotten many an invite! Now that you're done holding out, you've got to start showing your face in public in a positive way. And sign stuff. You do realize an assistant would just make your life easier, right?"

"I'll start handling my own events," I protest. "What do I have to do, answer an email or something?"

I can see Chip rolling his eyes over the phone. "When's the last time you logged into your email? Be honest."

I pause for a moment, because he's right. But still, fuck him. "Championships aren't won on the goddamn Internet."

"Just give her a chance. Please? I'm not going to be riding you all season and keeping track of your schedule. That's below my pay grade. Why are you so against having an assistant anyway?"

Even Chip doesn't know the *real* reason I held out last year.

While the money was part of it, it was more about the mental block of anxiety I couldn't get over. Staying focused has been an issue for me, one I hope I've overcome, but I won't know until I'm back in the game.

"I don't want someone at my house all the time. I like my privacy."

And I *definitely* don't want anyone snooping around my place. Who knows what an assistant might find?

And I have secrets. The kind of secrets that get you kicked out of leagues.

"You ever think that maybe it would be good for you to have a little social interaction in the off-season?"

"I work out plenty."

"I mean, besides the working out. You've been a recluse this entire year, Everett! Look, if you're doing something shady that I need to know about, please let me know right now so at least we can be proactive when everything goes to shit."

"It's nothing like that," I croak. I hear a noise, then peek my head out of the window of my office. "Gotta go. She's here."

"Alright. Just...give her a chance, man. Please? For me. For my sanity."

"I'll give her the tiniest of chances. How's that?"

"I suppose that's better than nothing."

I hang up and glance down from the window.

Something stirs inside me when I see her.

She's got on a blue pencil skirt, a white blouse, and sports sunglasses with long blonde hair cascading over her shoulders.

I look at the name I wrote down on my notepad when Chip mentioned it...

Emma Foster.

Not a bad name. A good name, really. A strong name.

I watch as she fumbles with the key in the door downstairs. When she's finally inside, I hear, "Hello! Anyone home?"

Oh yes, Emma Foster.

I'm definitely home.

I smirk.

Welcome to my world.

5

EMMA

On this gloriously hot-but-not-too-hot day of mid-July, I'm driving my new company car, a Prius that Rich and Cal loaned me. The perks of this job are fabulous and I haven't even had my first day yet. As I pull into Everett's U-shaped driveway and park, I admire a cute little yellow sports car in front of me. All this doesn't overshadow the fact that I feel like I'm playing the part of an assistant-slash-undercover agent. The blonde hair I'm sporting today adds to that feeling, even though it was a spur of the moment decision to dye it, very much aided by Rachel's suggestion.

Everett lives in Wilmette, on the north side of Chicago, and it is the polar opposite of the neighborhood where I grew up and currently live. The mansions close to Lake Michigan are so big here, it's rumored that F. Scott Fitzgerald even based *The Great Gatsby* on one of these places.

Everett Brewer lives just a few doors down from Michael Jordan's mansion.

I'm a poor girl from the south side of the city. I've only

seen houses like this in movies. Not real life. And I've never, ever been in one.

This whole job thing seems surreal, actually. I pinch myself, and yes, it hurts a little, but it reminds me of exactly where I am and what I am doing.

I get out of the car into the sunlight and quietly shut and lock the door.

I'm wearing the brand-new blue, pencil knee-length skirt that pairs beautifully with a tucked-in white blouse. And then there are the metallic heels that round this outfit out so well.

Yes, I went a little *Devil Wears Prada* and charged it, something I've sworn I wouldn't do after seeing how badly my mother used to get hit with credit card interest. My rationalization is that *confidence on your first day* has no price.

Especially when you're dealing with a man like Everett Brewer, who, according to all the news media reports, and of course my own personal experience with him at the hot dog stand, is basically the biggest asshat of a boss you could have.

My hand trembles as I turn the key in the doorknob of the mansion where my new boss lives. I remind myself over and over again that I've got to be the one to set the tone.

I don't care what this man throws at me because I have more at stake here than he even knows. I just cannot mess this up. And honestly, I'm hoping my being here will help benefit him, too. He's obviously had some tough times and I want to be cognizant of that and as supportive as I can be.

Pausing in front of the main door, I take a deep breath and remember the instructions from the owners of the team.

Just open the door and head inside. He'll be expecting you.

It's still a little weird to me that I'll be with him on a weekly basis, but this whole profession is new to me.

"Hello? Anyone here?" I call out, but no one answers.

I go inside and look around; after all, Everett knew I was arriving this morning.

I have to say the place is gorgeous. He must have had a top-of-the-line decorator, and it's all just...wow. Although I hesitate to use the word 'mansion,' because that makes it sound old and this home is so modern. But I wouldn't be surprised if that show *Cribs* would love to get a tour of the place.

There's a big, open-concept kitchen, and a dining room, too, that takes up literally half of the ground-level floor. The white marble counters and stainless-steel appliances sparkle in the distance.

I move a little farther inside, and I jump when I hear the loud, growling noise. I recognize it as a human man's voice and it's sounding eerily similar to the one I heard at the hot dog stand.

Everett.

I follow the direction of the growl into the living room, and see a very muscular, very shirtless man stirring on the couch.

He looks like Everett, except...not.

I squint.

The man smiles broadly.

"Well, hello there," he says. "I didn't know Everett hired a...cleaning service?"

My eyes widen. "Do I really look like a cleaning service?"

"Or an angel, maybe?"

The man sits up and rubs the sleep away from his eyes. I'm a little dumbfounded at this very good-looking, seemingly alternate version of Everett.

"I see you've met my brother, Jocko." A voice booms over my shoulder.

The man who I now know is Jocko's smirk broadens, and he wiggles his eyebrows. "That's me."

I jerk my head around to see Everett standing in a t-shirt and shorts with his arms folded.

"I'm Emma," I say, sticking my hand out for Everett's. "Your new assistant."

He stares at it for a moment, and doesn't shake. "I figured. Cal said they were sending someone over today."

"Oh, come on, that's no way to treat a lady," Jocko says, jumping to his feet. He takes my hand and kisses it like he's a prince and I'm a princess. "I'm really sorry. My brother's not himself this morning." He leans in and whispers in my ear. "Or any morning lately, really."

Everett steps closer to us. "I'm sure the lady would prefer not to be hit on during her first day on the job, jockstrap."

"Oh, he wasn't hitting on me," I say.

Jocko purses his lips, and winks. "I was, a little."

Everett gives us both a satisfied expression...one that's not quite a grin.

"Do you play football, too?" I ask Jocko.

I know he doesn't play, but it's a good conversation starter.

Also, I'm not beneath a little flattery to the brother of my new boss, who seems like a decent guy. I could use a possible ally if Everett's as much of an ass as his last assistant said he was.

"I don't play football," Jocko says. "I did play basketball in college. Actually, I came really close to beating Steph Curry in the final—"

"Bro, how many times you gonna tell that story?" Everett cuts in.

"You're just jealous because you picked the wrong sport," Jocko retorts, flashing a charming smile my way. "No, I do not play sports any more. I work for a technology company, and was out late last night wining and dining one of my biggest clients, a school district right here in the northern suburbs."

He walks over to the armrest of the couch, grabs hold of a t-shirt, and puts it on. "Plus, my big bro has been in a sour mood lately, so I wanted to cheer up old Grumps McGee here."

Cal and Rich's notes on *Everett the grouch* jump to mind.

Jocko slaps Everett on the shoulder, and Everett gives him a death stare in return.

"You just logged a twelve-million-dollar contract," Jocko says. "I don't understand why you're walking around like you've got such a stick up your ass."

"Whatever," Everett says in a low voice. The same tingles that surged through me at the hot dog stand return. The guy has a way of sounding like he just does not give a crap what anyone thinks. "How's doe-eyes doing, by the way?" Everett asks.

Now Jocko is the one who seems tense.

"Who is doe-eyes?" I ask.

Jocko stumbles, and Everett is quick to jump in. "Oh, just one of Jocko's coworkers whom he wants to get with. And from the way she was staring at him last night, it might just be mutual."

"Erroneous!" Jocko belts out, pointing a finger at Everett. "Erroneous on both counts. She was *not* shooting me googly eyes. And I definitely don't have a crush on her."

"Oh? Then what do you call it?"

Jocko seems defensive all of the sudden. "Allie has a boyfriend, okay? There's nothing going on there."

"Oh." Everett shrugs. "Coulda fooled me."

"She does have a boyfriend. And even though he's an asshole — homewrecker isn't my style." Jocko turns to me. "I'm sorry you have to witness this, Emma."

"No, go on," I say. "I'm fascinated. So this girl has a boyfriend, but was shooting you doe eyes?"

Jocko shakes his head. "You were imagining those googly-eyes. We have a *very* platonic friendship."

"Was, too," Everett interjects, with the hint of a smirk.

"Although I'll give it to you, she has..." he clears his throat, and lets his sentence trail off. "Shit, never mind. Forgot the lady was here for a second."

"Has what?" I ask, putting my hands on my hips.

"She just has a great smile, okay? And pretty eyes, too. Yes, I've noticed both of those attributes, fine. I'd have to be blind not to notice her. But that doesn't mean anything is happening between us. Because it's not. And it won't." He cocks his head to the side a little and narrows his eyes at me curiously.

"Hey, aren't you the tips girl?"

I freeze.

"Tips...?"

"Yeah!" Jocko's mouth drops open a little, and he points at me astonishingly, then makes eye contact with Everett. "That viral rant of yours about the tipping and the sweetheart stuff...that was you, wasn't it?"

My heart does a tumble. I knew this would probably happen at some point.

Jocko heads to the bathroom, grabbing a suit that's hanging up on a hanger.

Everett's head snaps to me. "Holy shit, *that's* where I recognize those dimples from!"

I lift my shoulders in a little shrug, and decide the only

move here is to own it. "That's me! The tips girl. I took your advice and got a different job! Pretty cool, eh?"

Everett crosses his arms. "Do you know how much shit I've been taking online after that little ditty went live?"

"I try not to look online, personally. The comments get out of hand. You know how people are when they don't feel like there's an actual face on the other end of what they're saying."

I want to tell him the truth, that I told — no, threatened — Ken to delete the damn thing, but I just don't think he's gonna believe me, and really, I probably wouldn't believe me either. On a side note, Ken apologized profusely swearing a friend of his got ahold of it, and the rest is history. Everett's nostrils flare, and he takes a few steps toward me, so that he's so close I can feel his body radiating heat. He touches the tiniest locks of my hair — which are now blonde. "You didn't want me to notice, did you? You wanted to slide under the radar."

"It was mostly coincidence, to be honest." My heartbeat starts to speed up, and I decide to redirect the conversation, instead of explaining to him that Rachel convinced me I needed to lighten my hair a little last night. Which is true. Another coincidence that doesn't reflect so well on me. "So, do I have an office?"

Jocko pops out of the bathroom in a suit and tie now and looking quite dapper.

"Glad to see you two are off to an amazing, storybook start," Jocko says with quite a satisfied smile. I can tell he gets off on starting trouble. "I wish I could stick around, but I have a meeting with another school this afternoon."

"Nice to meet you," I say.

Jocko shakes my hand. "You, as well." He pulls me in and

whispers, so Everett can't hear, "Keep an eye on him, will you?"

He heads out the front door, closing it with a bang, and I hear the start of a car as I stand with Everett still in the foyer.

For some reason, the vibe changes with the two of us alone. I feel my heart pounding, and the realization sets in that my boss is staring at me because I basically pissed off an entire army of Twitter trolls who are now cursing him online.

"You did have a point about the tips thing, when I stopped and thought about it," I say, trying to ease the sting for him. And, you know, not have my boss already hating me before I've even sat down at my desk on the first day in my new office. Though I've yet to find out if I actually have a desk...or an office.

Heck, I might get tossed out before I find out.

"Oh?" He raises an eyebrow. "So now you're a flip-flopper?"

"Not a flip-flopper, I'm just saying...I think people are blowing what you said out of proportion. Anyway, do I have an office here? Or should I just sit on the couch or at a table?"

He turns and looks at me for a moment, as if considering his words carefully.

"Why did Cal and Rich hire you?"

Not what I was expecting. He catches me off-guard, and I start to stumble over my words.

"I, um, guess...I got a little lucky."

"Do you have experience as a personal assistant?"

"No, but I have a college degree."

"In...?"

"Communications major, psychology minor." I smile proudly because in my world that is a big deal.

He crosses his arms over his chest, and gives me an up-and-down from head to toe.

"That's an interesting combination." A chill rips through me as his eyes seem to bore their way through me. Somehow the innocuous comment feels like an insult. "Why don't I give you the tour, then?"

I nod. Somehow I feel as though I've earned his disapproval just by my simple presence. It's a very unnerving feeling as I follow him around.

"There's the living room, where I watch football game film, the pool deck, and the kitchen. I have a workout area down here, but I almost always go to Midtown gym."

We stop at the stairs. "What's up there?" I ask, tipping my chin upward. Clearly, this mansion is massive, and that means there must be many rooms up there, too.

"Guest room. My room. Trophy room. My office. Which you're not allowed to see."

I pinch my eyebrows. "You have an office? What do you do there?"

He stares at me coldly and drums his fingers on his forearm just like you would a desk, and for some reason that little movement makes me think about other things his hands could do.

Like write.

And he writes love notes to someone named Samantha.

Suddenly the napkin note — for some reason, I've been carrying it around in my purse since I found it — seems like the tell-tale heart, louder than any other noise in the room and I'm a bit rattled thinking about it.

Technically, he's right to be suspicious of me.

Let's call a spade a spade: I'm a spy. Even though I have no plans whatsoever to indulge Cal and Rich with updates.

He leads me to a different area of the downstairs and points. "Your office is the white door next to the bathroom, toward the back. I've gotta run. Workout time."

I turn to head to the office before he calls me one more time.

"Oh, and Emma."

"Yes?"

"Good luck."

"Good luck with what?"

"Keeping this job. I'm going to work you into the ground."

6

EMMA

The next day in my new office, I arrive to see a handwritten list of 'To-do's' on my keyboard, written out by Everett. The list reads:

Emma – Assistant - To do's

-Water Everett's Plants

-Water Neighbor's garden (Mrs. Diedre is so nice)

-Pay bills

-laundry

-Buy jugs of specially ionized water (Only from Clean Canteen water shop by the lake)

-Other food (will email grocery list to you)

-Clean pool surface

-Call Spa, set up infrared sauna appointment

A minute or so later, he appears leaning in the door frame, shirtless and with a cup of coffee in his hand. "Morning, Sunshine."

"Morning!" I say. "This list looks great. I'll pick everything up. If not today, then tomorrow."

He squints. "You better. Especially the ionized water. Really important to stay hydrated in the summer heat."

He disappears, and I log into my email and see a note from Chip, Everett's agent and manager. After my first day on the job, he called to ask how everything went. Chip seems like a nice guy and it seemed that his concern for Everett was genuine. Apparently one of my duties as Everett's PA will include responding to fan mail, both digital and snail mail.

It feels kind of strange to do this, I mean, this could get kind of personal, but Chip swears that Everett rather I deal with it than him. But let me tell you, my eyes pop out of my head once I log into his public email.

SUBJECT: *You*

Body:

Hi, Everett, are you looking for a good time when your team comes to Seattle? I'd love to help you.

Signed,

Yazmin

TO TOP IT OFF, there's a scantily clad picture of her on some beach in only a bikini bottom...with her hands covering her voluminous breasts.

Well, her nipples.

"Jesus," I mutter, thinking why would someone want to be so desperate. But to each their own, right?

I draft a *tasteful* response:

Hello, Yazmin. While I appreciate the offer, as you know I'm all business this year after signing my new contract. No girls allowed for this guy! :) Hope you come to the game!

Everett

. . .

After I craft a few more of those types of emails, I decide perhaps this is something I should be asking for Everett's input on. He still hasn't come down to the first floor, so I go to the stairs and call his name.

"Hey, Everett? I mean, uh, Mr. Brewer?" I correct.

No answer. I head up the stairs to the second floor, which was not part of the tour. I call his name again, and he doesn't answer.

Seeing a wide-open door at the end of the hall, I walk toward it, still calling out his name, albeit a little quieter.

For some reason, I'm drawn to the room. It's a giant office with huge windows and a hulking, oak wood desk in the very middle of it.

In a trancelike state, I approach the desk. Now, looking down, I see a piece of paper with a letter written in black ink. I swear I see the words *Dear Samantha* at the top.

But before I can confirm that hunch, a voice behind me gives me the chills.

"What are you doing in here?" Everett's tone is cold now, and huskier. The trace of friendliness from our earlier encounter is gone.

I spin around, and he deftly maneuvers in between me and the desk, blocking any chance I have at reading anymore of what he was writing.

"Excuse me, I didn't mean to interrupt, but when I called for you and you didn't answer..." God, I'm just stumbling all over my words, "Well, anyway, I just had a question for you."

He raises an eyebrow, and that feeling of disapproval comes back ten times stronger than yesterday.

I hate to admit that it's mixed with a warm feeling of arousal that courses through me. It's been too long since my last date.

"So why would you come in *this* room if you had a question for *me?* Clearly, I'm not in it." He has a sleeveless workout shirt on now. A vein in his neck threatens to pop out. Jeez, he's built.

"Sorry. Is that not okay?" I say, trying to play dumb.

He nods toward the door, then pulls it shut as soon as we're both in the hallway. "No, it's not. I guess I didn't make it explicit on the initial tour yesterday. So here goes: you're not allowed to come into this room."

"Is this an outright ban on the second floor, then?" I just want to be clear. I'm not interested in invading his private space.

He shakes his head. "Just my office. It's private, for me only. Understand?"

I nod. "That's fine."

He leans in and lowers his voice. "Now head back to your office. And if I catch you in there again, there's going to be trouble."

"Oh? What kind of trouble?" I have to ask since his threat almost had a playfulness to it.

"You don't want to know."

I bring my hand to my forehead, my fingers pinching between my eyes. "Why are you acting this way? It was an honest mistake, I didn't know the layout of the rooms up here, if you recall."

He grinds his teeth together and glares at me, which causes my skin to prickle.

"I'm late for my workout," he says. "What question did you even have to ask me?"

"These women," I say as we head down the stairs. "The ones who send you all the emails of the..." ugh, I hate to say it, but I might as well. "The sex proposals. What do you want me to do with them?"

"The groupies who want to sleep with me?"

I nod.

He gives me a strange look. "Can you fuck them for me?"

My stomach tumbles in shock. "Uh, excuse me?"

We get to the bottom of the stairs. "Yeah, I have a strap on in the basement...go to their houses, and fuck them."

I search his face for a trace of sarcasm, but I can't find any. "Mr. Brewer, are you out of your mind?!"

He stares at me seriously for a few moments, then finally lets out a loud belly laugh and touches my shoulder. "I'm kidding, Emma. I don't care what you say to them. Tell them to buy a jersey or something if they're that into me."

I bust into nervous laughter, and where he touches me, a surge of energy enters my body. I swear his hand lingers just a second longer than I think it should.

And what bothers me about that? I don't mind it.

He grabs some sort of protein shake from the refrigerator, shakes it up, and heads out without saying goodbye.

Back in my office I answer more and more ridiculous offers from women — and men, too. Like this one.

Hello, Everett,

I am a sculpture student at Green State University. I am writing to humbly request that you come in to be a model for our final exam. I've run this by my professor, and we can work around your schedule, and we've even secured funds from the school to bring you in. Think about it, you would have the chance to see yourself immortalized forever!

You are welcome to stay with us in the I-House. (That's international House.) We're a diverse group of students from all over the world and I'm sure this would be something much out of the ordinary for you, maybe it would even be fun!

Lots of Love,

Joseph Santeroni

THE LETTER IS SO SWEET, I almost want to ask Everett if he'd attend, but I see his unsmiling face asking me *really? In the middle of the season I'm going to take time off for that?*

So I craft Joseph an easy let-down, instead, and tell him maybe he should try again next year, or in the off-season.

Before I know it, the day is almost at an end. When Everett gets back from his workout, he heads upstairs while I'm still typing away at my computer, sorting my way through the thousands of unanswered emails.

Then, I hear the noise.

It starts out as a faint-sounding voice, maybe headbanger music.

Heading out of the office, I close the door. It gets louder, and I realize it's coming from Everett's bedroom.

He's *screaming* at the top of his lungs.

I run up the stairs and down the hall to his bedroom, then knock frantically at his door. "Everett! Are you okay?"

I knock, louder this time.

No answer, and the scream gets louder.

My shoulders tighten and my palms sweat. I try the doorknob, and it's unlocked so I head in.

"Hello! Are you hurt, Everett?" I ask.

He's not in his bed. I hear water running in his bathroom. He's screaming.

"Oh, no," I mutter. What if he slipped or something and he's injured for life?

I rush into the bathroom and come to a full stop at what I see.

His shower is a glass cube in the middle of the bathroom, and what I see sends goosebumps all over my body.

My lips part, my body warms, and heat rushes all over my skin.

He's not injured at all. Nope. Not. At. All.

But he's got his arms spread wide, like he's some sort of warrior doing a chant, and he *is* yelling at the top of his lungs.

I blink a few times, wondering if this is some sort of optical illusion. A hologram, maybe.

But it's not.

Everett Brewer is totally naked, and I can see every last rippling muscle on his body.

And yes, I also see his...ahem...package.

My body slackens, and I try to move, but my feet feel suddenly heavy, frozen to the ground as my heart palpitates through my chest.

With every breath, he continues his primal scream, and even turns around in the shower to give me a full view of all sides.

"Everett!" I manage to call out. "Are you okay!?"

His head turns to meet me, his jaw drops, and his eyes widen incredulously. Turning the water off, he gets out of the shower and steps out, soaking wet.

"What the hell are you doing in here?" he snaps.

I make sure my eyes stay steady on his. *Eyes.*

"I heard yelling and I thought you might have fallen or something? Are you okay?" I stumble over my words, and clearly, he's fine. But I feel the need to over-explain myself so he doesn't think I was just stalking him in the shower for no apparent reason.

"Are you insane?" He takes a step forward, and puts his hands on his hips.

"Are *you?* Who *yells* like a caveman in the shower? I thought you were hurt."

He grits his teeth. "I was taking a contrast shower with freezing cold water, then hot, then freezing again. It's part of my routine."

"A hot and cold contrast shower? I have never heard of that."

My body heats from the core and my eyes can't help but run over Everett's body, which is dripping with water. With every breath he takes I can see the lines in his abs ripple.

"Now you have." He wiggles his eyebrows, his eyes following my line of sight. I do my best to stay focused straight ahead. But my boss is not making this easy. "Anything else you wanted to tell me?"

"Don't you need a towel?"

"Why would I need a towel? I'm not done with my shower. I was rudely interrupted. By you. And you're still interrupting me so I figured you had something important to say."

"Oh," I swallow. "It can wait." I shake my body out, turn around, and head out of the room.

I walk quickly down the hall, totally dumbfounded on so many levels about this man.

And with the image of Everett Brewer, gloriously naked and screaming like a wild animal seared into my head forever.

7

EMMA

"Constrast showers? Yes, I've heard of those," Rachel says, shoveling a nacho into her mouth. "My ex-boyfriend was obsessed with them. He said apparently, they are good for your testosterone."

I take a swig of my much-needed glass of rosé. "That man does *not* need any more testosterone. I'm already afraid he's going to like, explode or something. He's like an angry bear twenty-four-seven."

Rachel furrows her brow, and shakes her head. "I hate it when I have bosses who are all uptight and angry for no reason."

I giggle. "Is it weird that I find it kind of...hot."

"You find it hot that Everett is angry? Or do you just find it hot that he's, you know, shredded and has a huge package and you saw him in the shower? And obviously wasn't taking the cold shower when you walked in. And he just *happens* to be angry, as well."

I damn near spit out my drink, choking up laughing. "Maybe a little of both?" I manage to say.

"And how did you know that he has a nice package?"

She wiggles her eyebrows. "I could see it in your eyes. You were picturing it...and him."

That's what happens when you have a best friend like Rachel. We've known each other since high school, and I'm fairly sure we share a hivemind.

I shrug. "What can I say? I have a sexy boss...who hates me."

"Well, at least he's not indifferent like Troy was."

My nostrils flare at the mention of my last ex, Troy. He was a few months younger than me, and when Jack died last year and I needed a shoulder to cry on, someone to be strong and help me through a tough time in my family, all Troy could do was complain that we weren't having enough sex and that I wasn't emotionally available for him.

To be fair, we were already on the rocks before Jack died, but crisis has a strange way of putting things into focus. I broke up with Troy and never looked back. But since then, dating hasn't been on my radar at all. My life has been all about being there for Eve and Pam. When I broke up with him, he just shrugged it off, and said, 'Okay, see you around!' and I haven't heard from him since.

"I'm pretty sure Troy was just in the relationship with you for the sex," Rachel continues.

I nod and have a sip of my wine. "In retrospect, you're probably right. Clearly, he wasn't interested in being 'friends' with me after the fact." I giggle. "The difference between Everett and Troy could not be more stark. Everett's like a lion, and Troy is like a..."

"Chipmunk," Rachel says, and we both start laughing.

A couple of guys come up to us in the bar and start talking to us. Unfortunately, they aren't that cute. "Hi," one says. "We saw you from across the bar and we couldn't help but wonder what's so funny?"

Rachel rolls her eyes. "No, sorry. We're not interested. Not tonight."

"Why not?!" the other one says.

She shrugs. "Well, me, I just got off an eight-hour shift, so I'm not in the 'converse with a stranger' mood. And my friend here? She's got a crush on her boss and can't think about other guys."

The two of them sigh, turn, and walk away, dejected.

"I do *not* have a crush on my boss," I contest.

"Is that what you call it when you find it hot how angry he is?"

"Maybe after how indifferent Troy was, it just feels nice to have a man whom I make exude some kind of reaction."

"Even if that reaction is hate?" Rachel asks, then leans in. "Have you ever had hate sex?"

"Ew! No. Why? Have you?"

"Yes. With my ex, Jared. He was the worst. But so hot. And we did it a couple of times...anyway, I'm rambling. You have a crush on Everett, it's okay. You can admit it. Hell, if he were *my* boss, I'd be flirting my little tushy off with him every chance I got."

I picture Everett's brooding face from earlier today, arrogant with his hands at his sides as he made no effort to cover himself when he exited the shower. Just stared at me, gauging my reaction.

He's definitely an asshole. And I'd probably not be so drawn to him if not for one thing:

The note.

I still can't help but wonder if underneath his brooding veneer, he's a man capable of caring deeply for a woman. And *that's* the piece of him that really turns me on about him.

I will get to the bottom of this man's dual identity. I will figure out which side of him is real.

And maybe get to see him naked again, if luck's on my side.

A FEW UNEVENTFUL weeks roll by, and it almost seems like Everett is either making lists of ridiculous things for me to do, or avoiding me. This particular day starts out innocuous enough.

Everett sits out on the pool deck, in sunglasses, staring out at the water. I see him and head outside. The sun is blazing bright and my sunglasses are in the car. Great place for them at a time like this. Walking along the pool deck, squinting so I don't run into anything. Everett comes closer into view.

"Big plans today, eh?" I joke.

I try not to focus on his abs. Especially as it's not yet even noon, and I'm trying to keep things a modicum of professional. Even though I make a mental note that if the washer breaks down, instead of going to the laundry mat to wash his clothes (one of my responsibilities as a PA), his abs could serve as a hard surface on which to scrub out some clothing.

As his assistant this summer I'm learning that one of his favorite things to do in the world is sit out on his deck, hands behind his head, and relax.

He doesn't move.

"This is what I have an assistant for. So I can do nothing all day."

"Did you get a chance to look over the RSVP list for the party the weekend of the first exhibition game?" I ask. "I think we might have a packed house."

"Don't worry," he says flatly. "Most people won't show."

"You keep saying that, but I have a hard time believing you."

"Happens every year. People say they're coming and then they bail at the last minute. Besides, we always make room."

"I'm going out to the store right now to pick up a few extra air mattresses and sheets, just in case."

"You do that. I'll keep an eye on things here," he winks. As if there's something actually going on here.

I turn to walk out, thankful to get out of the blazing sun, and turn back. He's covered with a layer of sweat, and it serves to make his already defined muscles look even sexier.

"Can I ask you a question? It's sort of a strange one."

"What's up?" He's been fairly agreeable the last week or so. I'm starting to get the feeling that even though he might not admit it, he may actually appreciate my presence. Not that he likes me or anything, but maybe I'm a comfort, since he doesn't seem to have many visitors? Or maybe I'm reading into something since it's me who's really started to enjoy this job.

"That day when you came to the hot dog stand...what were you doing in that part of the city?"

I want to dig away for clues about the Samantha note. Not so much for Cal and Rich — funny because up to this point, I've told them nothing...no, this is for me.

He shifts in his lawn chair. "Nothing."

"Okay. So you were doing *nothing* in the lakeview area of Chicago at ten a.m. on a Sunday?"

"I told you. Nothing," he snips. "Out for a drive and I wanted a hot dog."

Who is Samantha? I want to ask him, desperately.

But I feel like bringing up the napkin he left behind

would open up a can of worms that would make him close off to me just when I think we're making a bit of progress — at least I consider it progress because I'm still here.

I feel a slight quiver in my stomach, I have no right to ask him anything — it's just my own curiosity.

"Sorry," I say. "I'm just interested, Everett. You're a little mysterious, in case you haven't noticed."

"Are you kidding? I'm all out in the open." He spreads his arms out, as if that implies openness.

Just then, his phone buzzes on the table next to him. He glances at it, then puts it back. It buzzes again, and he picks it up again with a huff. After reading a message, he puts it back on the table face-down and shifts his eyes to the pool.

"Who was that?" I ask.

"How is that your business?"

"You *just* said you're all out in the open. I'm not trying to pry."

"Yes, you *are* prying. And I don't get what's so mysterious about me."

"You sit around all day, except for when you workout and eat. I don't know, it's just not what I pictured a professional football player doing with their time."

He pushes his sunglasses up and turns to me.

"Do you know how lions hunt?" he asks.

"What's that got to do with anything?"

"Just try and answer. Work with me, Foster."

"Fine...lions hunt...in packs?"

"Right. And when they're not hunting, lions sit around for twenty-three hours of the day. Does anyone bother them?"

I shake my head. "No. Of course not."

"Right. No one bothers them, because the king of the

jungle only has to remind the rest of the jungle every once in a while how powerful he is."

"So you're...a lion."

"Yes. I do nothing most of the time. I'll have to report to football training camp a week from next Monday and I'll go back into lion mode. So I'm taking it easy right now."

"Well, okay, then."

The man is speaking to me in animal metaphors, and I resign myself to the fact that I'm not going to make headway with him today when it comes to the napkin note mystery.

I turn and walk back inside the house to grab the keys to the Prius. As I pull away, it feels amazing to get away for a moment. Even if it's for Everett's errands.

Halfway to the store, I realize I forgot the damn company credit card, which is next to my computer in the office. So I turn back, no way I can afford to foot the bill without it.

When I'm almost back to the house, however, I notice Everett pulling out of the driveway.

He doesn't see me, and I make the decision to tentatively follow him at a distance.

My pulse ratchets up as I wonder where he might be going since he just told me that he wasn't in lion mode yet. And with the way he was lounging poolside earlier, I figured he would be there all day.

My desire to investigate is stronger than my desire not to get caught. So I follow him, staying back as many car lengths as I can without losing sight of him as he pulls onto the highway, my pulse racing.

I can definitely add that amateur sleuth part to my name tomorrow. And oddly it's not because it is part of my job, but it's because I'm really starting to care about this man. Yes, maybe I even have a tiny little crush on him. I'll own up to that.

He takes the highway to Lakeshore Drive, then exits eerily close to the hot dog stand. The hair on the back of my neck stands up. It's nothing but a hunch at this point. It's based on a silly napkin note, and Everett's defensive body language when I asked him about that day. But I've never been more sure *something* is going on with him. I just need to figure out *what*.

I take pains to stay out of his sight, since he'd definitely recognize me if he saw this car.

He finds a spot to park close to Lake Michigan. I whiz by him and park on the other side of the street, then duck out of the car as fast as I can.

Yep, I am definitely deep into snooping territory and well-entrenched in my spying abilities.

Everett is acting shady. He's got a big baseball cap of the local Jaguars team, sunglasses, and a NAPLETON jersey, the name of a local baseball star — to confuse people, I assume.

I notice which way he is walking, toward the lake and heading north. In order to get ahead of his path, I quickly rent a scooter and take the long way around the block.

Right as I get off the scooter, I notice he's walking directly toward me, not even forty feet away.

My heart pounding, I duck into the closest shop, and watch from the inside window as Everett walks by.

He seems to be far into his own little world, and didn't even notice me. Probably because he would never suspect I would have gone to these lengths to find him.

I breathe a sigh of relief, leaning against the wall in the shop, and wonder why Cal and Rich don't just hire a dang private detective if they're so interested in Everett's off-the-field activities. Clearly he's up to *something*.

As I'm catching my breath, an attendant from the store appears next to me.

"Hi, can I help you?"

I take a few quick breaths, and he squints. "You're not... running from the cops, are you?"

He goes to unlock his phone, and I put my hand on his forearm.

"No! I mean, no, of course not. Not the cops, anyway." I glance around the store. "I just like to...run for fun sometimes."

"On your way to the vintage clothing shop?"

"Yes. When I arrive tired out, I can think more clearly. I'm a total weirdo, I know."

"Oh. Well, in that case, what can I help you with today?"

I glance around the room.

"I need something that's great for summer, but that I can move in, if I want to."

"Ah," he says. "Something you could run from the cops in?"

"You're funny one," I say without laughing.

"My name's Josh. Don't wear it out." He winks.

Not sure why I decide to share this little fact, "I dated a Josh once."

"Oh, yeah? Well, second time's the charm." This kid is literally trying to put the move on me, ugh.

"Let's stick to the clothing."

I quickly get into a light blue romper, stuff my other clothes into a bag. I also buy a big hat and some new sunglasses. I note I need to have another, more planned-out shopping spree now that I'm making non-hot dog stand money.

On the way out, Josh writes his number on the back of the receipt and gives it to me.

Not wanting to dismiss him so easily because he could've ratted me out at any moment, and because I don't want to cause a scene, I take the receipt, ready to follow my boss.

Now I head out on the scooter again. Everett would never recognize me in this getup.

Lady luck is with me, because I go in the general direction Everett was headed and come upon him, sitting on a bench looking out at the lake. Keeping a safe distance, I park the scooter out of sight and peer from behind a tree. He's talking with a man in his forties or so who is wearing a polo shirt and sunglasses.

I notice Everett now holds a manila folder in his hands, and I wish I had binoculars. I'm not quite ready to ramp up to that level of snooping, though. Obviously, I'm more of a fly-by-the-seat-of-my-romper spy.

A few moments later, the man in the polo gets up and walks away.

I watch as Everett pulls out a notebook and writes something down for a few minutes.

Then, he stands up, rips the paper from his notebook, and balls it up. He walks toward the water and throws it into the lake.

Folder in hand, he walks a beeline directly toward *me*.

My eyes widen, and I turn to pull away from the tree I've been using to block his view of me, but my hat gets caught on one of the branches and now I'm sure I'm making a scene but I have to get out of there before he sees me.

I pull away, hard, and take off running to where I left the scooter, never looking back.

I ride the scooter back to where I parked my car, get in, and speed back to Everett's house north of the city. I'm so out of breath and I know it's a mixture of my fast getaway and the adrenaline of my spying activities. Trying to calm my breathing, I have to take a moment to focus and think about what I just witnessed. I'm no closer to knowing what's going on than I was before I started this job, and that thought is a bit defeating.

Feeling the adrenaline dissipate, I'm starting to not like myself and what I just went out of the way to do. If I'm going to find out anything about this guy, I've got to change tactics. Maybe start befriending him in the way he'd want to be friends with me.

I MAKE it back to Everett's house, change and hide my romper before I hear Everett's car pulling up.

I lean back in my chair like I've just been answering emails for the past few hours, when I hear the door open and shut, and Everett's footsteps moving around downstairs. He heads upstairs for a moment, then knocks on my office door.

"Hey, there," I say nonchalantly. "Where did you go?"

"Just popped out for a little bit and met up with a couple of the offensive linemen on the team to go over game film. How was *the store?*" he asks accusatorially.

My mouth goes dry. He *knows. He saw me come out of the vintage clothing shop or saw me and my big hat stuck in the tree.*

I clear my throat. "The...store?" I'm at least going to try and play dumb. If he caught me, so be it. But I'm going to make him work for it.

"Uh, yeah. Wasn't that where you were? Picking up the air mattresses for the party or whatever?"

I press my palm to my heart. "Oh, yeah...that. Fine. It went fine."

Note to self: Pick up air mattresses tonight, off the clock.

"What about you, how was film watching?" I ask.

He shrugs. "We kind of got distracted with video games, to be honest. It's always fun to be able to be yourself in a game."

Liar, liar, pants on fire.

I want so badly to call him out on his lies when my eyes zoom in on a piece of jewelry he's holding, and I squint.

"What's that in your hand?" I ask.

He forces a laugh. "Oh, this? Just some random piece of jewelry I found on the ground as I was *leaving* from my meetup."

I rub the place on my neck where my necklace usually is, and my chest tightens when I realize it's gone. I look up at him, now seeing he noticed my movements. God, I'm so screwed.

Everett has the necklace my grandmother gave me.

"It's kind of unique, isn't it? I mean, who has a jaguar necklace? Seems older, too. Like it could be an heirloom."

My heart throbs, and I thank my lucky stars that I'm pretty sure Everett isn't observant enough to notice that *I've been wearing a jaguar necklace.*

Unless he's screwing with me.

Is he screwing with me?

"Totally unique," I agree. "Where did you find it?"

"Found it on the ground, by my friend's house."

"Oh. Okay."

"Yeah. I actually saw the girl who dropped it, but...she was running away for some reason."

My heart skips over a few beats. Well, that's the end of that. Now I'm curious as to what he's going to do.

"Scared of you, maybe?"

"Yeah, that's possible, I suppose." He steps into the office and looks out of my window for a minute, then turns and glares at me. "I can be a scary guy sometimes, you know."

My heart just might combust. "Haven't noticed."

Act normal, just act normal, I have on repeat in my brain, but I'm forgetting what normal is.

Just as I'm trying to coerce myself into calmness, he glances at the receipt on my desk, "Who is Josh?"

I realize he's staring at the number the clerk gave me after I bought the clothing and hat.

"Oh, just some guy who gave me his number today." I snatch it out of his hand so he doesn't see the time stamp and possibly the name and location of the place on the other side.

"Really? He just...gave you his number unprompted?"

"No, he flirted with me first." I put the number in my purse out of his sight. "That's none of your business, anyway. So, who do you think this mystery necklace belongs to?"

He leans in closer to me. "I don't know, but I like a good *mystery*."

He turns to me, clenches his jaw, and I think he might be about to call me out in my lie, right there. Because he knows and I know he knows and he knows that I know and shit, shit, shit...

But I'm not about to give myself up.

"That's good," I say. "Because so do I."

We stare each other down for a few moments, my heart beating like wild.

"Can't believe it's almost Friday," he smiles. "See you tomorrow."

My head almost snapped right off my neck at how quick he changed the subject. But when he leaves the office, I know this isn't over. I just have a feeling that tomorrow, Friday, is not going to be a very good day.

8

EVERETT

Emma's playing some oldies music when I walk into her office the next morning.

"Nice tunes," I say.

"Thanks," she smiles. "The Kinks. Ever heard of them?"

"Yes."

I inhale a big breath. If I was a nicer man, I'd probably feel bad for her. But I'm not. So I don't.

"Emma, we've got to talk for a moment."

"What about?"

"Turn around, please."

She does. "Yes?"

"Get your stuff out of here because you, Emma Foster, are fired."

"Excuse me?"

"You heard me. You're fired. So you can pack up and leave. It's definitive. You have been let go."

"Fine," comes her only response. The way her eyes glisten as she packs up her stuff, I almost feel bad for her. Plus I admit that over the past few weeks, I was starting to enjoy having her warm, welcoming presence around the house. Not to mention, she is absolutely gorgeous, and has taken over my night-time sexual fantasies, but I'd never admit that to anyone.

At the end of the day, I just don't like people poking their heads around my business — can't have them doing that — especially when the stakes are so high.

More importantly, with Emma. She's smart, and bound to find something out that she's better off not knowing. She's gotten to me in a way no one else has. Since she's been here, she's touched something that's been dead inside of me, and it's ignited a feeling I haven't felt in a long time. And that scares me.

As I watch her walk out to her car with a box of the few items she has accumulated at her desk, the tiniest smidge of remorse pulls at me, reminding me that I am indeed human.

Not only did I fire her, but, I *will* miss seeing her around.

I knew that necklace was hers. I'm a guy but I'm not that clueless, and I had noticed it hanging around her lovely neck, usually when I was checking out her tits. And there was no doubt in my mind that that long, flowing blonde hair that was blowing in the breeze as I headed to my car was that of my assistant's. I know she never made it to the store to buy whatever it was she claimed we needed for the party. The question that remains in my mind is why she felt the need to follow me? There must have been something she was onto.

Hey, it's not my fault Cal and Rich decided to hire a smoking-hot assistant for me, who apparently likes poking her nose in my business. Emma did a good job, too, but at the end of the day, I'll be fine without an assistant. I'll use one of those fancy new apps for grocery delivery my brother Jocko keeps telling me about, and besides, training camp starts a week from next Monday so I won't be needing as much help.

I head upstairs to my office, and look outside through the window as she drives off.

My stomach clenches a little thinking what I would do if she found what was in here, what I'm hiding, what it is that is haunting me and I would have to explain everything. Not an option.

I'm not going to be explaining myself to *anyone*. Least of all some personal assistant. My little secret is going to have to go to the grave with me, most likely.

I head back downstairs and flip on some game film to prep for next week. Since I didn't play last season, I want to make sure I'm completely up to speed on all the new players and their tendencies. It's hard to believe that it's almost August already, and that we'll be down at our training facility in central Illinois in less than ten days.

Shit, in about two weeks we'll be playing our first *game*. Preseason, but still. And we're facing off against last year's Super Bowl Champion, Peyton O'Rourke in the Thursday night special. The first game of the year.

An hour later, I hear the screech of a car pulling into my driveway, causing me to furrow my brow.

I get up from the couch and walk around to the foyer so I can observe who it is who just used my driveway as a pit stop on a NASCAR track. Emma Foster flings the door open, and her eyes are full of fury.

"You!" she yells, pointing. "How could you?!"

"What are you doing back here?" I ask, figuring she found out what I'd done. "Forget something?"

She stalks toward me. Her cheeks are a deep red hue, and her hair is a little messy the way it falls to her shoulders.

I'd be lying by omission if I didn't say her anger makes her look even hotter to me.

"I did forget something," she says when she stops in front of me, hands on hips. "I forgot that you're an asshole."

"How could you forget that? I wear that badge like a neon Vegas sign." I turn and walk to her office, and do a quick scan. "Looks like you got everything."

When I spin around, she pokes me so hard in the chest, I almost fall back.

Almost.

"You think I'm some dumbass assistant you can manipulate like that? I do a great job for you and you know it. I'm the most dedicated PA you could find. I did your *laundry* this week. Your fucking practice jerseys are all hung up for you. And how do you repay me?"

"You're getting confused," I retort strongly. "This is nothing personal, Emma. I just don't want a PA."

"And I don't want to get *fired* for no reason. Especially by someone who doesn't even have the *power* to fire me."

My smirk turns to a frown.

Shit.

I was betting on her being so flustered — as people are when they get fired — she would just take this lying down.

My throat clenches when I think about her *lying down*. When she gesticulates with her arms, all angry, I have to admit, I find it arousing watching her rack move up and down like that.

God, you're fucked up, Everett.

But it's true.

Why am I always so damn attracted to women who hate me?

She continues. "Yeah, that's right. I *called* Cal and Rich."

"You got through to them? I'm surprised."

Why would she have a direct line to the owners? I file that fact away under 'suspicious.'

She scoffs. "You *are* a fucking dick. But you know what? I don't care. I don't care that you mostly avoid me when I come in here every day. Or that you seem to make a game out of coming up with tasks for me to do, like getting ionized fucking water from some boutique nutrition shop. I'll do it. I'll go all day."

I fold my arms. "What about invading my privacy in the shower?"

"You were screaming so loud, I thought you were being skinned alive."

"Oh, come on. What's going to kill *me*?"

She shrugs. "Who knows? A stubbed toe? A bathroom fall? Household injuries are a thing."

"They're a thing when you're like seventy years old."

She steps so close to me I can feel the heat from her body. She's so angry right now, there's a layer of sweat on her skin. Might also be the heat.

"I'm not about to let my boss *die* on my watch," she says. "What are you saying, anyway? Was I sexually harassing you by seeing you naked or something?"

"There's an argument I could make to Cal and Rich."

She throws her arms out. "Yeah, well, it's a pretty weak freakin' argument."

"What," I ask, "were you doing in my office?"

She averts her eyes. "I *told* you, I just didn't know I wasn't allowed up there. Won't happen again. I really don't see what the big deal is, though. Are you running some sort of secret drug ring out of there or something?"

I swallow. "Even if I were, that would be none of your concern."

She shakes her head. "You think I'm...trying to *out* you or something?"

"Well, you did record a video of you *burying* me and post it all over social media just for some cheap fame."

"I didn't record that video, and I *told* my coworker, Ken, not to post it. I'm sorry about that, it was dumb."

Her eyes and lips are hypnotic. Even just *thinking* about my secret makes my anxiety creep in. She fixes her hair, and I secretly wish it could stay messed up because I like it that way.

I notice her eyes are starting to gloss over.

She walks over to her desk and picks up a picture frame.

"You see this?" she says, pointing to the picture. It's Emma, a brunette who looks a lot like her, a little baby, and a man with a red and blue Cubs hat.

"These are the only people who matter to me. My sister Pam, her daughter Eve, her unborn baby, and Jack — may he rest in peace." Her hand shakes a little as she holds the picture up for me. I take it from her.

"Her husband passed away?"

She nods. "Car accident. You asked me on the first day how I got this job. My honest answer is, I don't know. I got really fucking lucky. Sometimes, I wonder if Jack pulled some strings as a final act of redemption before he moved on to the next world."

My skin prickles a little, and I decide not to ask why it was an act of 'redemption.' I'm not superstitious, but any talk of the afterlife has always given me the willies.

I clench my jaw and stare at the photo. The man is weathered, and his wife just looks tired to me. Emma has the biggest smile of them all.

I look back up at her, and some new feeling crops up inside me. It's not attraction — that was there already. From the first moment I saw her, even at the hot dog stand, I felt a connection I couldn't fully explain.

When I don't say anything, she continues. "You want me to put it all out there? Think I'm hiding something? Fine. The pay is very good for me in this job. It's much better than I could find anywhere else. And if you think I'm just going to go back to the fucking hot dog stand without a fight, when the money I make now is going to help me raise Eve and my pregnant sister's soon-to-be-born son, well, you can just go fuck yourself, *Boss.*"

My jaw hardens. "Excuse me?"

She pokes my chest. "That's right. What's the matter with you, anyway? You think I'm going to, what, find out some secret about you and let it out to the world? Why would I do that? Then, you would surely have reason to fire me. I'm all in on your top-secret world, Everett, as fucked up as it could be. I don't want to lose this job. If something goes down with you, everything goes down with me, too. I don't want that."

I focus my eyes on the picture. Looking at — what was the little one's name, Eve? — especially makes my heart flutter.

And it makes me think of the relationship I had when I was much too young to know what I was getting into.

It makes me think of Samantha.

I hand the picture back to Emma, and my entire body is swimming with emotions I've been doing my damndest to keep tamped down.

The very last thing in the world I need is this shit coming to a head right as the season is starting.

Then again, it's my fault for avoiding it in a way, isn't it?

Emma stares at the photo for a few moments, and a

visible tear rolls down her cheek. She looks up at me, glossy-eyed, and sets it down.

"What kind of a man are you that you would just fire your assistant for no reason? Don't you have a heart?"

Oh, boy.

"The heart ship sailed a long time ago," I swallow, and I have to resist the urge to wipe away her tear.

She touches two fingers to my torso over my shirt. They start at my abs, right around my solar plexus, and she draws them up slowly toward my breastplate and chest until they land on my neck, close to my collarbone.

What on earth is she doing?

"Sounds really dramatic," she says, and her hand feels so good, I never want it to leave me. It's been a while since I've been touched like that.

"Well, it's true."

"What happened? Was it an ex?" she asks.

"Don't worry about me," I grit out.

"Love isn't always easy. Sometimes, it's a decision and a commitment. And when you've been hurt in the past, it takes courage to love," she says. Another tear rolls down her cheek and she wipes it away. I wonder if she's thinking about her sister's husband. "On the other hand, I don't think it takes much courage at all to push your lowly assistant out of your life just so you can keep your world closed off."

My chest aches, and suddenly I hate this woman. She's onto me and I don't know how the fuck that happened.

She's making me uncomfortable; she's making my conscience come alive... And for the first time, I think about telling someone what I've been hiding all these years.

I'm slow to process her words, but as soon as I do, I clench up.

"Are you calling me a coward?" I ask.

She shrugs slowly. "Have you ever thought that since you seem to enjoy getting hit on the field, you're creating some sort of negative psychological feedback loop?"

My eyes glaze over, and I think back to the very first night I learned the name I would never forget: *Samantha*.

I remember how angry I became.

And how I took it all out during the game, and my opponents were suddenly scared of me.

The average person seeks pleasure...and avoids pain.

I, on the other hand, learned to love the pain of the game.

Her hand slides down onto my chest, and she presses her whole palm into me.

I glance down. "What are you doing?"

"Checking to see if you have a heart. And you're right. No pulse. Are you sure you're not a robot?"

The scent of vanilla and something else floral wafts up into my nostrils from her hair.

Her hand on my chest causes my pulse to quicken.

"I know it was you," I growl.

She freezes up. "You know *what* was me?"

"The fucking necklace." I pull it out of my pocket and toss it on the desk. Her eyes practically bulge out of her head. "You followed me to the park yesterday. Why?"

"I...I..." she stammers, looks away and then at me. "You were acting so cagey at the pool, I thought you were going to just lay around all day. And when you took off suddenly, it made me wonder if you were meeting up with a woman."

My eyes narrow. "You followed me to see if I was having an afternoon delight?"

"Maybe," she says.

"Why would you do that?"

"I don't know. It was a crazy, spur of the moment decision. I shouldn't have. Something came over me. And I had to know. You seem so caviler about women in general, like the ones who are sending you proposals. I just wondered 'why?' And I thought I might get my answer if I followed you." Her hand runs over my neck.

"Why can't I feel your pulse?" Emma asks softly.

"Don't change the subject," I say, my voice gravelly.

If there's no pulse in my heart right now, it's because all of the blood is circulating elsewhere, so to speak.

I don't tell her that, though. She can't know the fantasies I've had about her. I put one hand over hers, then put another on her hip. A soft moan escapes her parted, glossy lips. I lean down and slowly, like opposite magnets on a trajectory for one another, our lips collide.

Her hand slides to my back, and I pull her into me, using her hips as a grip. The heat of our bodies pressing together through our clothes sends intense bolts of pleasure through my whole body.

She moans again, into my mouth, and for some reason that moment of release reminds me that I hate her.

Because ever since she walked into my life as my assistant with her big smile and beautiful curves, I can't stop thinking about her.

Most of all, I hate the way she makes me lose control like this.

No woman makes me lose control.

Except her.

And now, *you, Everett Brewer, are making out with your fucking assistant*, I remind myself.

She pulls away from me for a moment. "Boss," she grins, biting her lower lip. "What are you thinking about?"

I don't answer her. Instead, I fist a knot of her hair at the base of her head, and kiss her harder. My dick hardens, pressing against her skirt. I'm sure she can feel me. Her hands dig into my back and she moans again, louder this time.

As much of a cliché as I am right now—a star making out with his assistant—I can't stop myself. Her vanilla scent, the way her hair feels, the softness of her body pressed up against me causes my body to coil against her. I feel a need to touch her everywhere, to explore, to fulfill the nightly fantasies I've been having about her.

I want to rip the skirt right off her body and see what's underneath, for starters.

Her body caves to mine and she eagerly accepts my assault. I work kisses down her jawline and onto her neck.

I back up into the wall, and her hand is on my chest again, but this time it's through my shirt.

She gets on her tip toes and whispers in my ear. "Definitely not a robot...I think I can feel your pulse beating, finally."

I roll up a knot of her hair, and yank it back slowly, then growl in her ear. "I think you must have breathed life back into me."

"I better go pick up the dry-cleaning," she says. "Since I'm still working for you."

9

EMMA

"How's that new job, Em?" Pam asks. "I really like you as a blonde, by the way."

It's late Sunday afternoon, and one of the *few* Sundays this summer I've been able to get my sister to have a sit-down dinner with me.

I've been meaning to ask her about where she goes late at night when she doesn't tell me where she is, but I realize that's going to result in a whole *thing* that I don't know if I'm ready for. If she gets defensive and denies things, it's going to make for an awkward week.

I guess I'm one to talk. I still haven't told her the facts around my new job.

I have a bad feeling if I tell her how much I'm making, for instance, I'll have to deal with her jealousy. I don't like having to hide things from her, but with the new baby on the verge of being born, I don't think the timing is quite right to jump down that rabbit hole.

So, instead, I've kept things general and told her I'm an assistant for a 'rich family on the north side.'

She doesn't need that sort of stress in her life, especially over Everett the asshole whom I seem to like. Ugh.

"It's been good! I'm just sorry I can't be here more for you and Eve."

"It's alright. Although I am getting to the point in my pregnancy where I'd much prefer to be taking it a little easier, though. So...what are you doing at this new job, exactly?"

"It's a lot of odds and ends stuff. The life of a personal assistant is all over the place."

"So this means you can't take care of Eve this week? I was counting on you for Thursday, since I have a noon class then," my sister says, pausing and not putting a spoonful of the spaghetti squash mixed with sausage into her mouth.

I take a deep breath. "Leave it to me. I'll figure something out."

Maybe I can call in, take the day off or something like that.

"So this new job...you're sure it's going to be a good thing? I mean, not to be selfish or anything, but I liked your flexibility working at the hot dog stand. If I needed you in a pinch, you could get someone to cover your shift. Plus, you didn't have to work weekday mornings. That's when I really needed you. I've had to cut back on my shifts with work."

"As much as I'd love to keep helping you out — I know how stressful things have been — this is a really good position for me."

"For you," she emphasizes.

"Yes, for me. And I should be able to help out a little more once my paychecks start coming in," I say, but keeping the financial details vague.

Hell, I'm in disbelief that my after-tax paycheck will be in the four figures. My first check will be more than I made all last year. "Are you saying it's a bad thing that I do something for *me?* That I'm doing something more rewarding than serving up hot dogs to the general public?"

I know these are combative comments, but I have to know what's going through her mind. I mean, there's only so much that I can do to help her. After talking with Rachel, I've had this nagging thought that I've really started to ignore taking care of myself.

She shakes her head. "Of course not. Just that... The new baby is coming in about a month and...you know, I'm sure it'll be fine."

I clench up. *I'm sure it'll be fine* is Pam's code for *I'm very upset and I'm going to bottle up my feelings until I explode instead of risk a confrontation*.

Clearly we've both learned the same script from our parents.

Pam and I have only had a few fights during the past year, but when they happen, they are ugly.

"Rachel is coming over tomorrow to watch Eve," I say. "She can help out when we need it. In the long run, though, we'll have to figure out something a little more sustainable."

"How much are we paying Rachel?" she asks.

"Nothing. I offered but she refused payment."

"I guess this will work out. For now. How long do you think you'll have this job for?" She doesn't intend to be mean, but all of a sudden I'm feeling queasy. I'm the younger sister, and for most of my life I've been a little behind the curve, always trying to catch up.

Held back for a year in third grade and then graduated college at age twenty-four because I didn't want to go into as much debt as some of my friends, so I took a year off to work.

It hurts to feel like now that I've finally got something

good going, Pam is trying to drag me down. She's been through so much this year, I admittedly have been walking on eggshells around her and trying to let her heal. But I'm getting a little upset myself at how I'm taking her comments.

"When you say things like that, you make me feel like you're expecting me to fail," I finally say.

"Oh, I guess I just assumed this was like a summer thing," she says nonchalantly. "And it's on the north side so...I figured you were sort of a babysitter? Is that not what you're doing?"

My sister rubs her pregnant belly, and a series of disturbing thoughts enter my mind.

"So you're saying you don't think I could get a real job as a personal assistant?" I bite out, noting that she clipped that part of the phrase, and turned it into just 'babysitter.' "*That's* my job. Like I told you. There are no babies involved."

"I'm not saying that at all. Just that you've been pretty vague on the whole arrangement. You're 'working up north' with some 'family' as a 'personal assistant'." Her lips part, and she makes a face.

"You're not...a sugar baby, are you?" Her question throws me, how degrading. I had to ask her again to make sure my anger was warranted.

"A sugar what?"

"You know. Seeking an arrangement. Get a rich older man who needs some company and he gives you money in return."

"No!" I recoil. "Are you kidding me? Of course not. Why would you even think that?"

She shrugs. "I don't know. Is it a mafia family?"

I roll my eyes. "Now you've really lost it, Pam. By the way, what about you? Where have you been sneaking off to these nights?" I raise my voice up from its normally tender tone.

And the question has escaped me. Here we go—confrontation time.

Unfortunately, my sharp pitch wakes the baby. We hear on the monitor that she's stirring and then starts to cry.

"See? Look what you've done." Pam shakes her head. "Eve's crying."

"It's time for her to wake up from her nap anyway," I say.

My sister gets up and shakes her head. "I'm sorry, the nerves are getting to me," she says. "I don't mean to be rude…it's just that I really need you, Em. With Jack gone, I've got no one."

"Well, talk to me. Where did you go the other night?"

"Don't worry about me. I'm fine. I'm not drinking, if that's what you think."

"I didn't say that at all."

"Let's talk about this later. Thank you for getting Rachel to come over. We'll figure out a more sustainable solution." Her eyes drift up to the wall. "God knows where we'll find the money, though, for a childcare facility for two kids."

"We'll figure it out."

She wipes a tear away, plasters a smile on her face, and heads to Eve's room.

I glance out the window of our house, and let my mind wander before I head to my room. There, I glance at my record collection again.

Someday, Ella, I say. *Someday I'll play you again.*

But right now, I've got to go to bed early to be ready to deal with Mr. Everett Brewer again tomorrow.

Wanting a connection and a reason for why I'm doing what I'm doing, I pull the napkin he wrote out from the top drawer and read it over again. Skimming down to the bottom, my eyes land on his closing words:

Love you always,

E

IT MAKES no sense to me that a man who would fire me like he did could also say such soft words.

I wonder what he thinks of our moment of passion in the office.

Does he just think of me as...a mistake?

I admittedly lost control in the office, too. Putting my hand on his chest crossed the threshold. Why do I always have to be attracted to the emotionally distant ones?

Maybe it's not the angry side of him that makes me buzz with heat in his presence. Maybe it's knowing that beneath that muscled frame and stoic, keep-your-distance demeanor, there's a man underneath yearning to love.

Back in the office, I wanted him to do every dirty thing he could think of.

As I fall asleep, he's the only thing on my mind right now. So much so that I can't escape a sexy scenario that appears in my mind.

And it most definitely involves my new boss.

10

EVERETT

The final week before training camp starts.

Two-a-day workouts, game film, and nerves. Since I didn't play last year, it feels almost like I'm a rookie. Well, that's an exaggeration, but still. It's an intense week and I need all of my focus.

I last saw the private investigator I hired, Detective Gates, at the lake when Emma was following me. Since then, he's come back with having no updates on the Samantha situation.

But I've introduced a new variable into the equation this week. And it is, admittedly, all my fault.

Sure, my PA put her hand on my chest first.

But I kissed her.

For the first three days after that kiss, it's like she's been trying to make my life an exercise in self-restraint, especially now that she knows I want her. As attracted as I am to Emma, I don't want to lead her on. Women always want something from me that I can't give them. And with the season starting up, we're going to have to write that kiss off as an outlier.

Even though seeing her every day, it's hard for me to keep my hands off her. Every day, her skirt has gotten progressively shorter, until yesterday when her red plaid school-girl outfit basically gave me a boner the moment I walked into her office.

She chewed on her pen and pointed to the screen, asking me if I preferred the green and red or the green and blue for my special edition "comeback" jersey.

Kind of hard to think about my answers to these questions when I want to rip your clothes off and make out with you up against the wall.

Still, I've got control over my animal urges, as well as my hands and eyes.

I'm her boss, dammit.

Did I mention how good my peripheral vision is, though?

It was like we both agreed without actually saying anything, that we would not acknowledge last Friday's little hookup session. But every time I walk into her office, I get a little turned on when the scent of her vanilla conditioner—at least I think that's what it is—wafts into my nostrils.

And she's been finding more excuses than ever to call me into her office.

Unfortunately for me, she's also been doing one hell of a job as my assistant. She arrives now at seven a.m. — not nine, like before — and stays until six. She's making it impossible for me to fire her.

On her last visit to the grocery store, she even somehow got my favorite childhood candy, Charleston Chew.

How did she know I love those? Is she a mind reader?

Today, she's thankfully still not arrived, even though it's almost 9:30 a.m. Strange. I thought seven would be the new norm.

~

When I get back from my workout in the afternoon, I notice her office door is closed.

Given the nature of this past week and how she's been tempting me like a damn siren, I'm a little surprised she hasn't called me into the office.

As I'm eating a big lunch and checking my Twitter, I hear a noise coming from her office.

Crying.

Is she...? No.

Her cries don't sound like that.

I slowly walk toward the door, the noise getting louder.

I open it.

My jaw drops when I see her in the middle of the room holding a baby over her chest.

"Hey," she says, tipping her head to me.

"Is that...a baby?" I ask.

"No, it's a squirrel." She rolls her eyes sarcastically in my direction. "Yes, it's a baby, what does it look like?"

"Why is there a baby in your office?"

She walks over to me and spins so the baby can see me.

"This is Eve. And she couldn't find a babysitter...no, she couldn't!" She says that last part in a cutesy little sing-song voice.

The baby giggles a little, and I have to admit she's adorable. My heart softens just a little.

"How old is she?"

"She'll be ten months in August," Emma says. "Her birthday is at the end of October, she's a Scorpio. So watch out. She'll bite you. Won't she?" I have to admit, seeing Emma do baby talk with a cute-as-hell infant stirs something inside me on some primal level. I try not to think about it.

"Seriously, though, we're bringing babies to the office, now?"

"Look at this, Eve likes you," Emma says, still holding Eve in her arms. "She can't stop looking at you."

The googly eyes she's giving me remind me of the way that girl — what was her name? Allie.

Ah, yes.

They remind me of the way Allie was looking at Jocko.

"Don't change the subject," I say. "You didn't answer my question."

"Yes, I did. I told you we couldn't find a babysitter for today. Remember? I live with my sister. This is her baby."

"Well, I assumed that part."

"Here, hold her for a moment."

Before I can stop it, I've got a baby in my arms.

She's babbling and looking up at me with big, innocent eyes.

"Geez, your hands are big. She looks like a bowling ball when you hold her," Emma smiles. "Perfect. She seems happy with you. Will you hold her for a bit? I need to answer some quick emails."

"Whoa, whoa, whoa. This isn't daddy daycare."

She spins her chair back around and flips her hair. "Look, Everett. I know we had some weird stuff happen this past week."

"If by weird stuff you mean our little make-out session, sure."

Her eyebrow raises. "Don't talk about that in front of the baby, please."

"Oh, come on. She can't understand us."

"She's soaking everything up."

My eyes flit to hers, and butterflies warm my heart. Damn, she's freaking angelic.

"Fine," I say. "We had a *thing* happen here which we won't repeat."

"Yes. I agree, we need to keep this boss-assistant relationship professional. We'll write off that *thing* as a one-time occurrence. Since I'm sure you don't want to become a walking cliché, some star hooking up with his assistant."

I'm struck by how accurate she is.

"But.." She looks around, then says, "Earmuff her, will you?"

I sigh, and cup my hands over the baby's ears, playing her game. "Yes?"

"Sorry about your blue balls," she says in a hushed tone.

"Oh, you actually feel bad about that?"

"Honestly? Not really. I feel like you deserved them for firing me. But I want you to know that wasn't on purpose."

"Very classy of you."

"How was your workout today?" she says, clearly happy to shift the subject.

"Fine. Why do you care?"

"Just curious. Can you please watch her for a little bit? Play with her, read her a book or something. I know you don't like to read but maybe a kids book would be doable? I just need like...one half hour undisturbed to make it through the task I'm finishing. It won't be daddy daycare, I promise. Just this once. My sister and I are interviewing nannies this week, and we should have one soon to help out.
"

The baby laughs and grips my finger in a baby vise. I look at Eve, and then back to Emma.

"I can't believe I'm doing this for you. This is a *one-time* thing, do you understand?"

"Thank you!" She jumps up. "You're the best."

My heart pounds as Emma moves her face close to mine, and I almost think she's about to kiss me.

She plants her kiss on the baby's cheek, though. Which makes sense, since Eve is a whole lot cuter than me.

My heart stirs.

No, Everett, you're not jealous of a baby.

Why would I be jealous?

Emma sits back down at her desk and logs into her laptop, then swings her chair around for a few moments and just looks at me and Eve.

"What are you staring at?" I ask.

She smiles ever so slightly. "Nothing. Thank you for doing that. I hope it doesn't cut into your day too much."

I swallow a lump in my throat as I bring her out into the living room to play with her for a little while.

It's been forever since I've held a baby.

And I'd be lying if I said it didn't drum up a whole slew of emotions inside me.

While we play, I shoot my PI Detective Gates a text because I haven't heard from him in some time.

Still no word about Samantha.

I crawl around on the carpeted floor with Eve for a while, and we play some version of crawl-and-chase.

When Eve smiles, my heart warms to the depths.

And for the next little while, I completely lose track of time.

We play until she's tired, and she falls asleep on my stomach as I watch game film.

A little while later, Emma comes out of her office.

"Half hour up?" I ask.

Emma laughs. "Half hour? It's been two hours. It's time for me to go home. Awwww. You two are cute right now."

"That was a whole two hours? Seriously?"

"Yep. Guess you lost track of time. What are you watching?"

"Film from two seasons ago when we were in the Super Bowl." I'm not going to lie, there's something fun and surreal about watching a highlight reel of yourself.

I notice Emma is standing off to the side, staring at the TV. I pause it.

"Everything okay?" I ask.

"Fine. Just had a question about the party you want me to plan for the lake house. But it can wait. I don't want to interrupt you."

She squints at the football play paused on the big screen. I'm currently being tackled by three guys but trying not to go down.

"How do you do it?" she asks.

"Do what?"

She shrugs. "Take all those big hits. Doesn't it hurt?"

"Come. Sit." I pat the couch cushion next to mine. She hesitates. "It's fine. You should learn a little about the game anyway."

Eve stirs on my stomach.

Reluctantly, she sits. "You want me to take her? I'm done with most things."

"That's okay. I don't want to jinx her possibly waking up. I think she likes the position she's in right now." I hit 'play' and let the video resume. Emma actually cringes as the next play happens, the one where I'm gang tackled by four guys.

"You asked a question. Does it hurt? Well, it does. But I enjoy playing more than I dislike the pain. That's my secret."

"You enjoy the game? Well, I guess everyone does in a way."

"It's more than that. It goes deeper."

"What do you mean, exactly?"

I think for a moment. "Let me see if I can explain. Do you like taking care of her?"

Her face lights up. "Yes! I've always loved taking care of babies. I definitely have that inherent maternal streak in me."

"Perfect. So you would do it even if you weren't getting paid, right?"

She furrows her brow. "Of course. I mean, I'm not getting paid to take care of Eve, obviously. I just get satisfaction out of taking care of a living thing who can't fend for herself yet. Plus, it's my sister's baby, so that goes without saying."

Emma's scent wafts toward me — it's more on the floral side today — and I think of something else that gives me natural satisfaction: being around her.

Something about the way she sits, the way she talks. It sparks something deep inside me.

I clear my throat and refocus on the point I'm trying to make.

"So me, I don't inherently love taking care of babies like you do. But I love the pain of taking a good hit. Every game, my attitude is, I'm coming *after* the defense. They're not coming for me. I'm coming for *them*. Not many offensive players think like that. It's why I terrify defenses. They know *they're* the ones who are going to go down hard, not me. It feels *natural* to me. Like taking care of a baby feels natural for you."

She shivers. "That's a little masochistic, isn't it?"

"Maybe. It started when I was sixteen, playing high school ball. I wasn't the biggest running back. Or the strongest. But I was the angriest. And the scariest."

It's good timing for my story, because in the next frame of video, I run over a defender, and even though he manages to tackle me, I'm the one who jumps to my feet after we both hit the ground. I jump up and stretch my arms wide in my patented caveman yell.

"Jesus. You *are* scary. That's like..." she stammers, watching the video, then goes on. "That's like the same motion you made in the shower the other day. Arms wide."

I grin. "Good connection. It's all part of my messed-up psychology. I love getting hit like I love freezing cold showers. I just love pain. And that's not normal but it means I'm alive. And it damn well helps me on the field."

Another play on the video. I stiff-arm an opponent and he goes down hard.

"Aren't *they* supposed to be tackling *you?*" she says.

A smirk crosses my face. "Alright, now you're just trying to kiss up to your boss, aren't you?"

"Maybe. But I'm also serious. You're not normal."

"No. I'm very far from whatever normal is."

We sit back and watch the video for a few more minutes.

In my peripheral vision, I notice her face is flushed a little red. Or does she always look like that? My heart starts to pound furiously in my chest, and I realize my attention is no longer on the TV.

My head twists slightly toward Emma. If I didn't catch it before, I do now. She's stunningly gorgeous. Long blonde locks cascade to her shoulders. Pert breasts poke bee stings in her dress.

Can I see the outline of her nipples? Or am I just crazy?

The luscious skin of her thigh tempts me further, though I'm not sure exactly *what* it tempts me to do. She's still technically my employee, and I do *not* want to get into anymore hot water with the organization than I'm already in after my hold-out year.

I'm her boss, I remind myself. It's definitely a no-go situation.

Even though she barged in on me in the shower and got a good look at everything *she* wanted.

That can't happen again.

Eve finally stirs, and Emma takes her from my arms. "Maybe I should bring Eve over again. Seems like you two got along."

"I don't think that's a good idea," I say, shaking my head.

Emma snickers. "I'm no therapist, but it seems like you're avoidant of things that you might actually enjoy. Have you ever seen a therapist?"

"Several, actually. Never helped me. And thanks for the unsolicited advice. Maybe just stick to the emails and the merchandise."

Emma looks at me, then back at the baby. In baby talk, she says, "Did your cuteness crack a hole in Everett's angry armor? Yes, it did!"

I fold my arms. "Stop being so ridiculous. I'm serious. I don't need your opinion on my mental state. That's far, far out of your job description."

"I'm only telling you because I'm worried about you. You're like my sister. She bottles up her emotions, and that only works for so long. Because one day — blam! — they come out all at once."

"Well, unlike your sister, I can take my emotions out on the football field."

"And how's that been working for you?"

"It's been working just fine," I growl.

"So fine you had to take last year off?"

I clench my fists at my sides, and heat radiates from my core. I pull my collar away from my neck, feeling hot. "Like I said, Emma. Job description. Maybe reread that. Doesn't include worrying about your boss' stiffness."

She purses her lips together, then busts out laughing. "You're right. I definitely won't be helping you with that."

Pivoting on her heel, she walks out the front door.

One look at her ass as she leaves, and my dick twitches up.

I really do have a problem here, don't I?

Get me through to training camp.

So I can go back to leaving these issues out where they belong: on the field.

11

EMMA

I sweat as I ride the elevator up to meet with Cal and Rich. They insisted on an in-person meeting for today. Since Everett is playing the featured game on Thursday night football later, he's already at Soldier Field this afternoon getting ready and totally unaware of this appointment.

Really, though, these are my real bosses, right? Cal and Rich hired me and are the only ones who can fire me, so why am I feeling so guilty over all of this?

Probably because I haven't been able to get Everett's kisses, his hands running up and down my side, out of my mind. The way his hips pressed into me is seared into my brain. Not to mention the way he was so tender with Eve. I *knew* the big man had a soft side. I just didn't expect it to be for...babies.

After waiting for a few moments in the lobby, the secretary ushers me into the same big boardroom where I did my interview.

Rich and Cal smile blandly, sitting across from me. Rich gestures to the seat on the other side of the table.

Cal smiles. "So, Emma, how are things going with Everett?"

"Not too bad," I say, unless they directly ask me something I'm playing this cool. "Just getting into the swing of things."

"I hope you have a firm grasp on him by now." Rich raises an eyebrow. "How are his habits?" Cal asks me, so I guess we're going directly to the nitty gritty...hope I'm prepared. I've been thinking over the last few days how to answer their questions without slamming Everett in the process, all while being able to keep my job, too.

"Well, generally, he watches a lot of game film, eats a lot of food, and works out. That's about it."

Cal nods. "You haven't noticed anything, ahh, *irregular* about his habits?"

Oh, boy. "Not particularly, no."

Rich taps a piece of paper in front of him with his pen. Obviously expecting more scoop. Honestly, I can't tell if these guys want Everett to be a success or if they're looking for information to cancel the contract. But that can't be why, since he just signed the darn thing.

"You didn't notice him take off a few times for no particular reason?"

Hmm, now why would they ask that...I shake my head from side to side. "Not especially."

Rich twists his face up, seeming disappointed. "So it's safe to say that you've got nothing at all to report?"

My heart palpitates as I think about the note concerning *Samantha*. Until I know their game plan I'm going to keep my mouth shut.

I shake my head again, "Nothing weird, yet."

They scoff, a little disappointed.

Cal asks another interesting question, which makes me

wonder once again what insight he has on things. "What's this party you're planning?"

"It's after the first exhibition game. He apparently owns a house up on Lake Geneva in Wisconsin. I'm doing the planning for the house all week, sending invites to all of the guests."

Cal smacks his fist down on the table, giving me a startle.

"That's perfect!" he says. "Your golden opportunity."

"Golden opportunity...for *what*?" I ask. Their enthusiasm to find *something* out about Everett is bothering me. Shouldn't they want to see him succeed? If they're concerned, they have a weird way of showing it. Not that this should be a surprise, they did hire me to covertly follow up on Everett in the first place.

Rich nods, and Cal leans in. "This will be a perfect time to get a little closer to him, and his friends."

My morals cringe. How would Everett react if he knew the full truth, that Cal and Rich had *literally* told me to be on the lookout for him?

I know how I would feel if I were in Everett's position: betrayed.

But I figure Cal and Rich don't need to know a thing — of course, if he were endangering himself or others, then that's a different story, but obviously, that's not the case with Everett. All I really know is that he's still got a thing for an old flame named *Samantha*, he can be a little brooding, that he channels his taste for pain into football, and a few weeks ago he got a manila envelope from some man in the park.

And I know he's a fabulous kisser and a sweetheart with children. A smile tugs at my lips.

Maybe Cal and Rich would like to know *that*.

"Is something funny, Miss Foster?"

I snap back to reality. "No, sir. Sirs." I glance over at Rich, trying to be inclusive and not make one of them feel like I respect the other more. It's a little weird how much they work in constant sync, even for a father-son team. "I'm just thinking up ways I could use this trip to my advantage and find out some information that could be useful," I lie, because I've all but made up my mind that I won't be telling them a *damn* thing. But I've got to at least give them some bread crumbs since they are paying my salary. Once I get myself and Pam and Eve back on our feet, I'll look for another line of work, but for now this money is our bridge card to a better future.

"Here's a question. Is that brother of his, ahh, what's his name...is he coming up to the party in Wisconsin?"

"Um, he's got a few brothers. Which one do you mean?"

"Yes, he does, but there's one who's crazier than the rest...Jeremiah...Jordan..."

"Jocko?" I take a wild guess. Jocko definitely seems like he could be a loose cannon.

"Boom! That's it. You get in with Jocko and you ask him what's up with his brother. And if there are any other athlete friends of Everett's who are present, you ask them, as well." Okay, this is getting weirder. Rich is way too enthusiastic about all of this subterfuge.

"Alright," I say, my body stiffening. "Can do."

The closer I get to Everett, the worse I feel about this side of the job. But for now, it's a game I'm going to have to play. I look at it in another way: if they didn't hire me to find out Everett's secrets, wouldn't they hire someone who would *actually* rat him out?

12

EVERETT

Friday.

The day after our first exhibition game and I'm ready to sleep in until at least after ten, maybe the whole day — eh, we'll see how it goes.

Except my thoughts are interrupted around eight a.m. or so when the doorbell rings. I assume it's a package, so I grumble for whoever it is to go away, and turn over in bed.

Where is Emma when you need her to answer the door?

The doorbell doesn't stop, in fact, it rings incessantly, and my nostrils flare. Someone is truly pissing me off.

I grumble as I get out of bed, my pulse racing because yeah, I'm mad.

I don't love many things quite as much as I love my sleep.

What I see when I open the door only serves to make me angrier.

"Heyyyy, brother! What's the matter, doorbell broken?"

My little brother Jocko's smiling face gazes back at me. He's got on pineapple shorts, a tank top, sunglasses, and a backpack.

"What the fuck are you doing here?" I grit out.

"Are you kidding? It's the Lake Geneva Party weekend. Duh." He breezes past me and into the kitchen. "I'll get the coffee started. Great to see you, too, by the way."

I take a deep breath. It's one of the things that has always infuriated me about Jocko. I am a lion who, when active, can crush the strongest men in the world on a football field, but I am not a morning person.

Jocko, on the other hand, never seems to run out of energy, even this early in the morning.

"Did you not bother to call me?"

"Oh, I did. Several times. I also got the invite from your assistant, Emma. Where is she?" He glances toward the foyer as he starts to make coffee.

"Jockster. You've got to slow down, buddy."

"No chance. Did you know there are going to be model-types of girls at this thing? I mean, like real models, from *Vogue* and shit."

"They're not from wherever you said, but yes, of course. Just like every year. It's my damn party, asshat."

He shrugs and presses the button to start the coffee.

"Well, I didn't know if you would see the invitation. Since, you know, you don't get an invite to your own party."

He pulls out the invite and shows it to me. It's a classy postcard, and it's got a picture of myself and some teammates from last year that Emma must have taken from my social media somewhere. I've got my arms around several girls with a big smile on my face.

I shake my head. "You never turn down a good party, do you?"

"Not until I'm forty." He slaps my shoulder lightly. "But I also wanted to see you. You've been so out of it lately."

"I'm not out of it." See, the thing is, my family knows

nothing of Samantha and the hurt I'm in. It's best this way. Guys don't talk about shit like this, and my dad, well, no sympathy there — not that I need it, but why say anything to anyone if nobody knows what to say? And mom wants us all to marry asap, so not going there.

"You're not responding to my texts," Jocko comments. "Too good for that?"

Smartass. "I've been busy."

He raises an eyebrow. "Busy? With what? And I *know* you don't spend that much time choking the chicken."

"Choking the..." I squint, then smile. "Fuck you. I need that coffee so I can get on your level. And I've been busy as hell, man, with training camp and the preseason starting. Did you not see the game yesterday?"

"Of course, I saw the game. I had our entire office over to my apartment to watch it. Sorry, man, you looked a little rusty. On the other hand, it wasn't your fault Peyton O'Rourke tore up your defense. You guys barely had a chance during the first half."

I take a big gulp of my coffee. "It's the fucking preseason — we don't lay it all out there yet."

He shrugs. "Yeah. I guess."

"Everyone knows that. Peyton didn't win a single game during last year's preseason." Truth. Coaches are just seeing how players mesh — even fans know this. How can Jay be so dense?

I hear the noise of a vehicle outside, followed by several car doors slamming, and voices.

Five seconds later, the door flings open.

The first thing I see is Peyton O'Rourke's smiling mug, followed by Emma in a white beach dress, with a bikini underneath. And then there's a pretty brunette with a blue streak in her hair who trails behind them.

Jocko sees what I'm seeing.

"Damn. I don't know how you do it with this assistant, man," he mutters under his breath before they come within earshot. "You two are alone in this house together? Now that's the definition of temptation."

Before I can respond, Peyton yells out to me, "Hey, you running mothertrucker! Can't *wait* for this party. I've had the date marked on my calendar all summer. By the way, your assistant, Emma? The *best.* She picked Maddy and me up from The Drake where we were staying downtown."

Emma shrugs. "It was on the way over. I figured we could all ride up together. Hi, Jocko!"

"Hey, Em," Jocko says, and I'm a little infuriated he's got a nickname for her.

"How rude of me," Peyton says. "This is my fiancée, Maddy. We'll be getting married next April. In Cancún, baby!" He kisses Maddy on the lips before turning back to us.

Maddy smiles and says hello to Jocko and me.

"Well, should we get going?" Emma says. "I packed all of the stuff in Everett's Land Rover yesterday. I didn't know we'd have you, Jocko, but I think we can make it fit. I can drive."

"I'll drive, thank you very much," I interject.

"Whatever. Just trying to be helpful." And it's her smile that kills me…and makes a certain part of my anatomy rise to the day ahead.

Good grief, I'm so screwed.

~

It's an hour-and-a-half drive from my place to my lake

house up at Lake Geneva. Jocko rides up front with me. Peyton, Maddy, and Emma ride in the back.

"I just don't understand why you get a free pass for marriage. Mom rides me so hard to settle down. Why is it *just me* she seems to care about in that regard?"

"Your mom wants you to get married?" Emma pipes up from the back seat.

"Oh, yeah," Jocko says. "She's been on my ass since I've been like, twenty-five. I'm twenty-nine now."

"Ugh. Parentals trying to pressure you is the worst," Maddy comments. "I know all about that."

"What do you mean, Maddy?" I ask.

She responds, "Let's just say, Peyton wasn't exactly their first choice. Or second choice."

"You wouldn't think it, but I'm a total bad boy," Peyton pipes up. "Wasn't exactly popular with the parents in high school. So your mom really wants you to settle down, Jocko?"

"Yeah, and it makes no sense. I've got four brothers and a sister. Why can't she get on them?"

"Well, let's see," I interject. "Maddox just got cheated on by his girl. He's up at Uncle Herb's lake house this summer working on his new album or something crazy like that, so he's not exactly going to settle down soon."

"Maybe, maybe not," Jocko smirks.

I ignore his comment and continue. Maddox isn't exactly the most communicative of the brothers. "Travis is, well, you know what Travis does."

"What does Travis do?" Emma asks.

"He's a...paid *companion*," Jocko says, smoothly. None of us are actually sure what our brother does for a living, though, there are a variety of rumors. "He lives in Vegas."

"Right," I finish for my brother. "She knows to give up on Travis. And then there's Duke."

"Ah, yes, Duke," Jocko comments.

Duke is our older brother, and the richest one.

"Duke is a perfectionist. He'd never settle down unless there was a sign from God. And as for the difference between me and you, I don't know." I sip my coffee. "I think Mom just likes you better. You were always her favorite. And this idea you have about being a bachelor until age thirty-five is totally self-imposed."

"Until age forty," Jocko corrects.

"Why do you want to be single for so long?" Maddy asks.

Jocko's voice takes on a tone of seriousness. "I'm still seeing what's out there. And I happen to enjoy seeing every part of what's out there, if you catch my drift."

"Aww," Emma coos. "Maybe you just need to find *the one*."

Jocko spins around. In the shotgun seat. "No offense to, uh, you two." His eyes float to Peyton and Maddy. "But I just don't believe in *the one*. I think it's a figment of our imagination. We tell ourselves this story about *the one* in order to make ourselves feel good about settling down with one person, when really, we'd be better off if we just kept our options open."

An awkward tension bubbles up in the vehicle. In the rearview mirror, I see Emma's eyes drifting toward me.

Finally, Peyton breaks the silence. "I don't know if everybody finds *the one*. But I certainly did."

More silence. Peyton's hand grips Maddy's bare leg.

Jocko turns his head, and his tone sounds earnest. "When did you know?"

Peyton's mouth turns up in a slight smile. "The very first time I heard her voice."

Jocko and I both scrunch up our foreheads and make eye contact.

"That is some romantic shit right there," I say.

We all laugh, and Peyton says, "I know it sounds crazy. Hell, I've always thought I'm a little crazy."

"You are," Maddy says. "And I love it." They kiss.

Emma and I make eye contact in the rearview mirror again. Basically, I was seeing if she was looking at me and I got my answer. I've got an uncomfortable feeling she knows something about me. Maybe she even figured out my secret. I don't know how she would, but if she's crazy enough to tail me in her car all the way to Chicago, who knows what she's capable of? Plus, she would have kept me in the dark about following me if I hadn't found that necklace as proof and called her out. And that concerns me, because despite that particular deception, Emma continues to grow on me. And right now I get a weird feeling she's the only one who could help me.

If I confessed everything to her…which I would never do.

"Well I, for one, think it's beautiful you two are so inn love," Emma says. "And congratulations, you guys."

"Bachelor for life!" Jocko yells out. We all laugh.

I'm glad Jocko turns up the music so we can stop this silly conversation. It's starting to get to me, making me realize all that I've lost. God, where are all these girly-feels coming from?

A new song comes on as I think about the first time I heard Emma's voice.

Welcome to Wade's Weiner Shack. How can I help you?

A little eerily, the song that Jocko chooses is *Go Loco*, the same gangster rap song that was playing when she said those words.

It strikes me as odd that I remember these details, because I usually don't recall things like this.

It's probably just a coincidence. But now that she's become a part of my life, I'm finding I'm growing accustomed to her presence.

My God, Emma is making me human again.

13

EVERETT

The party. Wine, women, and song. And sunshine. Fuck, yes.

Wisconsin in the summer is an amazing place to be.

I glance over at Emma and Rachel, who arrived separately in her own car. The two of them sit on the dock. I nudge my teammate, Dyson.

"Can you keep that brunette company for a little bit?" I ask, nodding toward Rachel.

Dyson grins. "That hottie? I'd love to."

As we walk the distance to where the ladies are sitting I notice Emma's swimsuit, not the typical barely there style most of the girls are wearing today. The little hot pink suit fits her perfectly, along with the cute Daisy Duke shorts that frame her thighs, leaving little to my imagination. With her blonde hair highlighted by the setting sun, she is stunning.

"Party is going fantastically," I say to both girls and notice how Emma's face scrunches up with suspicion. So I clarify, "I'm *saying*...nice job," I reiterate sincerely. I might be a dick sometimes, but I'll also give kudos when they're truly due.

"Really? You're giving me a compliment?" She straightens instantly. "Well, thanks, Boss."

Her lips curve into a smile. "Jocko said he's going to take me out on a jet ski."

I furrow my brow. Pangs of jealousy flair inside me. That little devil. "Did he now?"

"Yeah. He's went back into the house real quick, and then he's coming back."

I clench my fists at my sides. Jocko *would* pull something like that on me. I wouldn't be surprised if he's just trying to mess with me. But then again, maybe he and Emma have a great connection. Who wouldn't have a great connection with her, though? She's so easy to talk to.

"Yeah, about that..." I say, a troublemaker's smirk pulling on my lips. "I saw him inside, and he actually said he wants me to take you out. He forgot he has to do something."

"Oh, really?"

"Yeah. Let's go."

I wink at Dyson, and he nods to Rachel. "There are two jet skis. Let me take you for a ride, too."

"Sounds fun to me!" Rachel says.

A minute later, we're pulling away, and I see Jocko smiling with his arms crossed at the shoreline.

His smile is an indicator that he's not even mad. Just impressed.

My grin back to him conveys more than words.

Oh, yes, brother, I saw what you were trying to do.

Not this time.

"You ready to fly?" I ask Emma, before I kick us into gear.

"Always."

"Hold on tight."

We head out on the lake and I get our speed up. Emma lets a few "oooh's" fly, and I love the feel of her hands wrapped around me.

"Woooo!" I yell as I get us up to max speed as we cruise by a huge yacht.

Emma holds on tighter, pressing her cheek into my back. I can practically feel her skin prickling against me.

After whizzing around the lake for a little while, I slow us down and pull over for a few minutes so we can take in some sun and enjoy the lake.

"So, question, Boss," Emma says.

"Shoot."

"Why do you hate me?"

Now I scrunch up my face.

"Why would you think that?"

She nervously taps the fingernails of one of her hands against my abs.

"Oh, I don't know. The fact that you scowl whenever I'm in the room. But maybe you just scowl like that all the time, I guess? It's the pain thing you talked about."

We see Rachel and Dyson fly by on his jet ski. Rachel is yelling like crazy.

"Why did you just think of that?" I ask.

"Well, I just heard you go 'wooo' and I realized, I think it's the happiest I've seen you since I've started working for you. Well, now, and when you played with the baby."

My grip on the handles gets so tight that I can see the whites of my knuckles. My stomach quivers a little, and I feel on edge. She's getting too close to home, to my pain, and that's got to stop.

I turn back around on the jet ski. "I don't understand why you care. This is a job, right? I'm an ornery guy. It's just who I am. That'll never change, unfortunately. I've come to terms with it."

"So it's not me you hate, you're just a hateful person? Oops. Not hateful...just, angry. You're an angry person."

I grit my teeth. "I need this anger, don't you understand? It's how I win on the field. It's just the man I am."

"I sort of get that." She shrugs. "But it makes me wonder..."

Our eyes linger on each other, and an overwhelming urge comes over me to lean forward six more inches and kiss her. That's all it would take, more or less. A six-inch lean.

If we kiss once—that's excusable as accident. Twice? That's a habit.

My cock twitches, sending an assault order to my brain. Her eyes run over my body just the same as mine runs over hers. Her hair blows in the wind. We're a mile from my house, and no one would see us out here if we did it.

Did...what exactly?

All the things I've been thinking about doing with her since she started working for me. I'm not really going to be *that athlete*, am I? Hooking up with his personal assistant like she's a little side toy?

No, I won't do that. Getting my head back to reality I know I've got enough on my mind this season already than to add a relationship to it all.

"Everett. You alright? What are you thinking about?"

Her hand rubs across my cheek. "We all go through tough times. It's not good to keep things bottled up. If there's something you want to talk about, you can tell me, you know. I won't tell anyone."

"Fine. I'll tell you what I'm thinking about." I lean my forehead against hers. "Are you good or bad?"

She pulls back. "Is that...dirty talk?"

"No, I didn't mean it like that. I'm going somewhere with this. Do you consider yourself a good person or a bad person?"

She pauses and sees that this isn't just some throwaway question.

"I don't believe anyone is one-hundred percent good or bad. What about you? Are you a good or bad guy?"

"Bad," I say. "Very bad."

She frowns. "I took the question seriously, and now you're making a game out of it?"

"I'm not. I'm being dead serious."

"And how are you bad, exactly? What did you do that's so bad?"

I shake my head. "I'll never talk about it. With anyone. I just can't."

She tilts her head to the side and purses her lips. "I understand. But if you ever want to talk about it, I'm here. I'm not just anyone and I've already told you that I'd never do anything to jeopardize this job."

She licks her lips and parts them, and they couldn't look more like a target with a neon-glowing bullseye on them right now. Her hand squeezes my abdomen a little, and I lunge forward a little. She tries to kiss me, but I turn my head and give her my cheek at the last second.

"I'm sorry, Emma. You work for me..."

"I'm just curious about you Everett. You make me feel things I haven't felt in a long, long time. And we already... you know. Kissed."

Something hardens in my heart. "So curious you tailed me into the city without my knowledge?"

Her face goes pale.

"Did you think I was going to forget about that? Just push it under the rug like it never happened?"

She avoids my eyes, looking down and away. "Sorry. That was a strange thing, I know. I just worry about you, Everett. You've got so much pent up emotion, I wonder if you might explode some time if you're not careful."

"Stop worrying about me."

And with that, I rev the engine, and turn us toward a stretch of open lake where we can fully open the throttle. The white noise of the wind whipping against our ears is a graceful buffer so we don't have to speak.

14

EMMA

"How was your ride with Dyson?" I ask Rachel as I pull a big bottle of tequila out of the refrigerator, along with ginger beer.

"Ride was fun...are you alright?" Her question is hesitant, knowing more than I'm going to say because that's how besties are. She can probably tell by the look on my face.

"Never better. Why wouldn't I be?" I say as I pour a drink.

"Um, because you're not normally a tequila drinker, and you just poured practically half that fifth of tequila into a very tall glass."

I look down at the glass guiltily. "Caught in the act. Alright, no, I'm not okay, actually." In my peripheral vision, I notice some of the party-goers getting rowdy in the living room. I yell at one of the guys who is slouching nearby like a drunken slob, "Hey, buddy, feet off the damn table! Are you serious right now?"

A man looks at me, seeing the seriousness in my eyes as I glare at him for emphasis.

"Uh, sorry, Emma. My bad," he says.

"You just yelled at the Super Bowl Champion, Peyton O'Rourke!" Rachel whisper-yells to me, then smiles at him. "Hi! Great game last year." Oh, shit, the way he was turned, I didn't recognize him from his profile.

"Thanks," he says, and walks over to us. "Sorry about the whole feet up thing. Silly old habit I can't seem to break."

"Well, just don't, err, let it happen again." I bite back. Ugh. Why am I being a bitch?

Peyton raises an eyebrow. "Are you okay?"

"Oh, please, why does everyone keep asking me that?!"

Rachel wraps her arm around me. "We were just going for a walk. Sorry!"

My body tenses as we leave and head out with Rachel down a small path that leads away from the main house and the crowds of people who are outside.

"Seriously, are you okay? Did something happen on the jet ski?" she asks when we are safely out of earshot of everyone.

"No, I'm not okay." I take a good, long sip of my drink. Ack, it's horrible.

All of a sudden, my throat constricts, and I have to fight to hold back tears.

"Talk to me," Rachel says. "What's going on?"

I take a deep breath, then start.

"Well, for starters, my sister is going to have another kid next month, but she keeps going on these adventures whenever I'm home and not telling me where. Meanwhile, I followed Everett the other day to the city to see where he was going — by the way, you can't tell anyone these things."

She raises her drink. "Best friend vow of secrecy. Obviously."

I nod and continue. "So he's being handed a manila folder with some shady, detective-looking guy."

"Wait, wait. You *snooped* on him?"

"Oh, yeah. Big time. It's what I'm being paid to do by the owners of the Grizzlies, if you want to know the God's honest truth, and I'm not proud of it."

Her eyes widen. "Dear God. I mean, wow."

"I know. It's some under-the-radar-type gig they have me doing in tandem with working as his assistant." I wipe my face with the back of my palm, and take another sip of my drink. The buzz is starting to hit me already, and it's already making me feel better. "I never agreed with the spying thing, but the money they offered warmed me to it — financially, even for a little while, this could pay for a lot of things Pam and I have needed for so long." Ugh, there I go again trying to justify not only to myself, but to someone else, my actions — lame. I continue with confiding in Rachel, "Anyway, that's only part of it. I'm really worked up about my sister, too. So both my boss, and my sister, are keeping secrets from me." And I might as well add in the last part, probably the most embarrassing. "Everett is clearly hiding something big, and then, I just tried to kiss him and he turned his fucking cheek!"

Rachel does a double-take. "You tried to...kiss him? On the jet ski!?"

"Out of all that I've said, that's what you're most concerned with?"

"No! We'll get to the rest, but I need to know this first — so you wanted to kiss him?"

"Of course! Didn't you make out with Dyson? I thought that's what we were doing? Like a ride on the jet skis and do a little hanky panky?"

She laughs. "I mean, it felt good to ride, but no, there was no making out happening. Maybe later tonight or some other time — but wait, so he turned you down?"

"It was super awkward, but I thought we were having a moment. And you know, since he's my boss, I thought maybe he'd feel bad about making the first move. Although, he didn't feel bad the first time we kissed."

Rachel's jaw practically drops to the floor. "Did you just say...the *first* time? Meaning there is a time I don't know about?"

"Sorry," I shrug guiltily, the alcohol taking hold and making me bolder. "I meant to tell you about that."

"Well, I'm all ears now." Rachel's eagerness makes me giggle. Actually, sharing all this with her lightens a load off my shoulders.

"After he fake-fired me — I *did* tell you about that — we had a heated argument, and well, it led to kissing. And a little more."

Rachel throws her arms open. "How far did you go with him?"

"We kissed. There were sparks for me and I'm pretty damn sure on his side, too. I swear I wasn't imagining that. And then he turned me down out on the lake just now."

"How far...were you hoping you'd go with him?"

"I'm trying not to have any preconceived notions about anything with him. But I do know I haven't gotten laid, in, Christ, too long. God knows I need some. It's been such a long winter, what with Jack's death, and I've only been focused on being there for Pam. I haven't thought about dating or relationships all year. But..." I swallow. "Something about him just drives me wild. I keep having these daydreams of what it would feel like to be with him."

Rachel's eyes bulge. "Uh-oh. You don't usually talk like this. You're really fired up, aren't you?"

I mean, hormones are definitely a part of it, but it's that it is Everett, too — he makes me want things I shouldn't. "Yes! I mean, I saw Everett naked, and he walks around the house shirtless constantly. And I swear, he was giving me the *I want to have sex with you* eye yesterday. So I figured, if not on a jet ski, when would I get the chance again?"

We arrive at the dock, sit down, and dangle our feet in the water while continuing to sip our drinks. Oddly, mine is starting to taste better. I think my taste buds are officially numb, or maybe the tequila killed them completely.

"You're very stressed right now, and it makes sense why. You planned this whole party, your sister and all that's going on there, and Everett. You're putting a lot in, but not getting a lot back from the important people in your world right now."

"Thank you! You're right, that's exactly how I feel. I'm not getting anything back from the important relationships in my life right now. Except for you. And I'm grateful for that." I hug her shoulder and she pats my knee — we've been best friends for a long while and we've always, from day one, been able to share our innermost thoughts.

"You're welcome."

As we separate and kick our feet about the water, I say, "It's not that I need something back, but, shoot..."

I see another couple out on jet skis, speeding around and having a good time. Except this couple, when they stop, has a serious make-out session.

I touch my fingertips to my lips. "I told Everett I'm worried about him exploding, because he bottles up his emotions. But now that I think about it, I wonder if I might be the one on the brink of exploding. Maybe I'm projecting that onto him."

Rachel smiles and looks at me, "From an outsider's perspective, I do think it was a little strange how Everett seemed more interested in you when Jocko offered to take you out on the lake."

"Yeah! All I wanted was a little jet ski make-out. That shouldn't be such a big deal, right?"

My drink is done, and the straw makes a sucking sound now. I think I'm hammered.

"Making out with your boss is a big deal," Rachel says. "So I don't know, maybe Everett wants to, but he also wants a clear conscience and is conflicted?"

My heart sinks. "Yeah, I guess...but do you ever just wish a guy would want you more than he cares about his guilty conscience?"

"You're saying that it's the taboo-ness about the situation that makes it more fun." I close my eyes and lean back. "It's not that, exactly. I don't even know what I'm saying anymore. I'm drunk, after all."

Rachel puts her hand on my knee again. "You're just fatigued from being there for everyone. Everett, little Eve, your sister. And it would be nice to have a romantic situation where the guy is there for you. I get it. But look, that might happen tomorrow, or it might not happen for a good long while. Until that time, we've got each other, right? You can lean on me."

My chest hitches, and a warmth of emotion comes over me.

"You're the best. Besides, I'm drunk so I'm going to need someone to lean on to keep from falling over," I say, leaning over to give her a hug.

"No, you're the best, drunk or not! Thanks for inviting me up here. I've never partied with superstars, so this is quite the treat."

I set my glass down then roll over onto all fours to stand.

"Speaking of that, what do you say we get back to the action? Mama needs another drink."

"Yeah, sure," she says giggling at my clumsy attempt to pick up my glass. "Just go easy, okay? You know what happens when you drink tequila."

"It makes my clothes fall off?"

"While I do think the Piper dorm of St. Francis greatly enjoyed you showing off to them, I think maybe since this is technically a work thing for you, you should keep the goodies under wraps."

"You're right. Maybe I'll just curb the drinking for a little while and see how it goes."

Once we get back to the lake house, though, what I see makes my blood boil hotter than the seas during the apocalypse.

Everett, riding along with several other football players, is captaining a big green speedboat as it takes off.

A blonde in a bikini leans over and kisses Everett on the cheek. I recognize her as Sarah, one of the Instagram models who was on the invite list.

I don't even have to explain to Rachel what's going through my head.

"It's only a cheek kiss," she says. "Maybe he's the only one who knows how to drive the boat or something?"

My chest caves in, and I've told her everything else so I figure I might as well express what I'm feeling.

"Everett let that other girl kiss him, but not me."

I turn and head into the living room where the fridge is.

"Careful," Rachel says. "I know you're stressed and you've been drinking."

I shrug. "I think you're right about one thing. I need to let loose. I think tonight's the night."

I walk over to a very handsome tall drink of water with a smile on my face. "Hi. What's your name?"

"Adam Cronin," he says, grinning.

"Well, nice to meet you, Adam. I'm Everett Brewer's assistant."

"Terrific. I play wide receiver for the Grizzlies." Cocky and handsome. Perfect.

I reach out and squeeze his bicep. "Do you now?"

Rachel whispers in my ear. "I'm going outside to hang out with Dyson. Call me if you need me."

I wink at her as she walks out, and I continue making football chat with Adam, my new friend.

He's a smiler, which is a huge relief after being around Everett the Grouch so much lately.

Maybe it's not the healthiest way to deal with things, I get that.

But after being Saint Emma for such a long time, I'm finally reaching my breaking point.

And I might have to let Bad Emma out tonight, compliments of some liquid courage.

15

EVERETT

A feeling of stress crops up inside me when I get back to the house.

I didn't like how unsettled Emma and I left things when I turned her down when she tried to kiss me on the jet ski.

And for what? Because I'm her...boss?

But I'm not *really* her boss. She just works for me. The Grizzlies are her boss.

Who gives a flying fuck?

Plus, we had already crossed this line together.

So what did it really matter? It matters because there's more to it than a kiss.

But whatever — boss or no boss, I wanted her so badly in that moment.

It was just like a movie. The sun glistening off the crystal-clear water. Her blonde hair blowing in the wind.

And I gave her the cheek.

Maybe Emma's right, and I *am* emotionally unavailable to a fault. But I can't get over the fact that she *followed* me all the way to the city.

I run a hand through my hair as I make my way through the house, looking for her. The band is cranking out music in the backyard, playing all of the best 80's cover songs, along with some from the 90s.

Great. I'm glad everyone's having fun.

I look high and low for Emma, but she's nowhere to be found.

I walk around the room with urgency, my head on a constant swivel. She's here somewhere. She didn't just get up and walk away...

Right?

In spite of the awkwardness I felt at dropping her off at the docks and her getting up and running straight into the house, I sensed a connection with Emma that I hadn't felt in a good long time. Somehow, she intuitively sensed something was going on with me. It's been going on since we've met, but it's only intensified.

I haven't told her a thing about Samantha. She has no idea that something's been gnawing at my conscience, gnawing away at my life force for years now, with no end in sight. Unless she has an inkling from following me to the city that day, I remind myself. But she couldn't know the actual information, right? All she saw was Gates handing me the manila folder. It could have been anything.

"Hey, O'Rourke," I say, slapping my arch nemesis on the back. He's the heart and soul of his team, same as I am for my team. "Have you seen my assistant?"

"Not in a little while. She was canoodling with, ah, who's that new wide receiver you guys brought in last year?"

He smirks. Peyton knows damn well the name of our new wide receiver Adam Cronin, he just wants to hear me say it.

"You're a funny guy," I say instead. "Where did they go?"

"I think they went skinny dipping out back." He thumbs toward the lake.

My face flushes red, I'm sure of it because I can feel my blood pressure surging.

"Chill, dude. Holy shit! Do you have a crush on your assistant, Everett?"

"I just needed her for something related to the party," I grit out.

"Sure, you did, old sport. I'd know that look anywhere. That is the look of a man with a crush. Maybe not in love, oh no. But you definitely have a crush on this broad."

"Are they seriously out skinny dipping?" He likes to egg me on, so I gotta be sure he's not trying to pull one over on me.

"No idea. But I'm sure as hell about to be!"

With that, Peyton yells and gathers a group of guys to follow him. Girls follow, as well, and before we know it, a whole crowd of people are sprinting outside, shedding their clothes left and right.

I head upstairs to check in all of the rooms to see if there is any funny business going on with any of the players.

My stomach clenches when I picture the possibility of Emma with someone else. God forbid it be a football player from another team.

Or even worse, a player from *my* team.

I open the door to the first two guest bedrooms, and no one is there. Then I hear noises just as I approach the third.

I open it, and my eyes go wide when I see Dyson and Rachel going at it.

"Sorry, guys!" I say, before I shut the door. Shit. That's a visual that'll be stuck with me for a while.

I walk toward my room, a little relieved. All of the guys

know the deal. Hook up in any room you want, except for my room. That would be a severe break of the bro code.

When I open the door, however, what I see blows my mind wide open.

She's there.

Emma stands, swaying back and forth to the music drifting into the room and sipping on a drink.

She doesn't hear me as I watch her from the hallway. She wanders over to the small wooden desk in the room, sits down, and pulls the drawer open.

I step into the room and pull the door shut with a thud.

"Find anything interesting?" I boom.

She spins around and stands up, a look of fright on her face. "Oh, I was just looking for a...pen. To take some...notes."

I cross my arms. "You're a horrible liar when you're sober. And worse when you're drunk."

"I'm surprised you made it up here. Thought you might be sucking face with...what's her name again?"

I furrow my brow. "What are you even talking about?"

She saunters toward me, and she's got some extra swagger in her step, even though she's clearly a little drunk. She looks hot as hell, now wearing ripped denim jean short shorts. Her pink one piece is still on.

I smirk, thinking how I'd like to rip them a little more.

"Why don't we just cut the crap between us, Everett? I made a move, you turned your cheek. But Sarah fake-tits, the Instagram model, kisses you in front of everyone and that's fine. Makes total sense. You're not into girls like me."

"Don't redirect this conversation," I say sternly. "What the fuck are you doing in my room?"

"I was enjoying the concert and having a moment of peace to myself."

"And going through my shit?" I steam.

"I told you, I wanted to make a note. Why are you so paranoid?"

"Bullshit, you have a phone," I point out. "Why not write a note on an app like the rest of the world does?"

"I should ask you the same thing. You love working out your thoughts with a pen and..."

Her words trail off, and her body stiffens.

I freeze. A chill runs over my body to end all chills, and my lips part.

Her face turns pallid, and the room is dark except for the light coming in from the outside twilight, but I swear she's trembling.

I pace around the room, my heart palpitating like a tribal drum. I run my hand through my tousled hair as I consider how well I've covered my tracks over these past weeks.

The day after she got to the office, I installed cameras inside my house to make sure she didn't go into my office.

How could she know?

What does she know?

She looks like a deer in headlights, unable to speak.

"Are you insinuating," I say, "that I like to write things down on paper?"

I figure I'll bring this back to the basics like a lawyer would, and make sure I'm not missing anything.

"Uh, yeah," she shrugs. "I think so. You know, I'm a little drunk, so I'm probably not making the most sense right now."

"Bullshit. You meant exactly what you said," I growl.

I step toward her, and she backs up into a wall. Her feminine scent wafts into my nostrils, and the same urge I felt on the boat seeps back into my bones.

Raising my arm, then placing my hand on the wall, I keep her where I want her and lick my lips again.

"Why didn't you want to kiss me before?" she asks.

"We're not talking about me," I counter. "We're talking about why you were snooping in my room like you're Richard fucking Nixon and this is 1975. How did you know I like to write on paper?"

"Everett, please," she whispers. "It was just a silly comment. If you want to know the truth, I came up here looking for you. I wanted to talk. I feel awkward after everything that happened on the jet ski. It's my fault for prying too far into your personal life, which is none of my business. I just worry about you sometimes. So I found this notepad and pen to write you a note."

Slipping out from under my arm, she walks over to my desk and taps on it.

She did just pull out a blank paper and pen. "The better question is, why are you acting so strange? Is there something in here I'm not supposed to see?"

I sit down on the bed and shake my head.

I open my mouth to speak to her, but nothing comes out.

"Sit," I say, patting the bed next to me.

She hesitates, but sits.

"How drunk are you, on a scale of one to shit-faced?"

"I would say I'm about one under a 'let's go skinny dipping' scale," she admits, nodding to the craziness we can hear happening outside.

"Okay. Well, that's fine, because I can't tell you what's going on with me."

"You had me sit down so you could announce that you can't tell me what's going on with you. At the same time, you're not denying that there's something up with you?"

I scrub a thumb across my jaw, then turn toward her.

"You ever have a secret you can't tell anyone? Like something you can't tell a soul."

She swallows and nods. "I do."

"Okay. Well, that's where I'm at. I can't tell anyone. If the people knew about this, it wouldn't be good for anyone involved."

She finishes the rest of her drink, gets up to set it on the desk, then comes back and lies down on the bed.

Lies down.

Not sits.

She makes herself comfortable, leaning back against the pillows and closing her eyes. She's beautiful the way she spreads out on the bed.

"So you can't tell me your secret," she says.

"You're better off *not* knowing. Trust me."

"It hurts to hold onto a secret for so long."

She opens her eyes, and I notice she's crying. "I'll tell you my secret."

"That doesn't mean I'll tell you mine."

She waves a hand in the air. "That's okay. If you promise not to tell anyone."

"I promise."

"Okay." She takes a deep breath. "Before my sister's husband died, I caught him cheating on her."

My eyes widen. "Holy shit."

"She wasn't supposed to be home, but I just popped in to drop off her Christmas present. And, well, I saw him with her. It happened three weeks before he died. I confronted him about it, and he said he was going to tell her." She puts a hand on her stomach. "God, I just feel so bad for her, you know? And after he died, I decided she was better off not knowing. And I wanted the kids to be able to have a good memory alive of their dad, you know?"

I slide myself more fully onto the mattress. "Wow. That's so much blame to shoulder."

"That's not the worst part. I know where he was going on the day of the accident. He was either coming from her place or going there, I'm not sure. Sometimes, I do wonder if he just wasn't able to handle the guilt and decided, 'to hell with it all.'"

I take hold of her hand. Her palm is clammy.

"You've never told anyone that?"

She shakes her head no.

"Well, thanks for sharing."

Her eyes run over me from head to toe, and land back on my lips. She scoots ever so slightly closer to me, and her leg grazes mine.

"Oh. Sorry," she says. "This is just a little awkward right now. We're holding hands but we can't kiss."

"I know it's awkward. It's not you, it's me."

She giggles just a little. "Seriously? We haven't even kissed — well, kissed *again* — and you're already telling me 'it's not you, it's me'? You've got more commitment issues than your brother Jocko."

"Oh, boy. You talked to Jocko?"

"We had a good, long talk about his issues." She laughs. "And then you took me out on the jet ski before he could."

I've got board shorts on, and the most awkward thing that could possibly happen right now, happens.

I get a boner. And she notices.

"We should probably head back downstairs," I say, swallowing. I pull my hand out from hers, but I make no move to go anywhere.

"Definitely. We should get back to where the people are. They're probably all waiting for us."

"Absolutely," I say, but my hand has a mind of its own. It touches Emma's thigh gently, just above her knee.

Our words and our bodies could not be in stronger conflict than they are currently.

"Totally. Or you can just keep your hand there and we can hang out for a little bit longer."

"One more minute."

She puts her hand on my thigh. "You know, this isn't actually happening right now."

I arch an eyebrow. "It's not?"

"No." Her gaze flits between my eyes and my cock, which is now rock hard, thanks to the way she's touching me.

God, it's her sweet vanilla scent, it's her little hands, it's the way her eyes look in this darkened room. It's that vivaciousness and mystery behind them that make me want to know everything about her, not just this secret.

I swallow, staring at her. Pushing her hair behind her ear, I lean closer to her.

She closes her eyes and slides her hand farther up my leg, landing it firmly on my dick, over my board shorts.

But before I can kiss her, the door swings open. We both jump up to our feet at once, and see Peyton O'Rourke standing in the doorframe, holding hands with Maddy, clad in only a bikini.

"Oh, shit," he says. "Did we interrupt something?"

"This is my room," I say.

"You didn't interrupt anything. Maddy, so good to see you again." Emma says and does an awkward little wave.

"Aw, Everett," Peyton says. "We didn't know this was your room."

"We were just heading downstairs," I say. "All yours, buddy. Have at it."

Emma and I head back downstairs to the party, separately, and mingle with different groups.

After about a half hour, we both look up from our respective conversations and make eye contact.

Sometimes, a look says a hundred words.

And this look between us, says that we were one second away from a high-school-style, on-top-of-the-bedsheets make-out.

And it also says she knows how hard my cock is for her.

I'm sure this won't be awkward when we're back at my house this Monday.

As if it wasn't already.

16

EMMA

Thanks to a ride home from Rachel the next day, I get to avoid what would have been an extremely awkward drive with Everett back from the lake house.

On Monday, I sip my coffee, sift through my emails and do my weekly check-in call with Everett's agent but I get a queasy feeling in my stomach.

I truly wonder how far we would have gone if it weren't for Peyton and his fiancée interrupting us.

It's not exactly nervousness. But I *am* thankful that Everett is going to be down at Bourbonnais at training camp this week, and I'll be staying up here, tending to his house plants and doing generally easy assistant-y things.

It's going to be a relief not to see him today because I've got a lot to sort out.

I still can't believe I shared my secret with him. Did I need to, no. Did I want to, yes. I felt, no I feel, connected to him and the timing was right. I've thought about it and it was because I wanted to tell him. I wanted him to know. And I wanted that because I want him, that's it.

No other reason for his confidence. I didn't tell him to try to get him to tell me his secret — that should have been the reason, that's my job...ugh. But no, it was because I want more from him than he's giving right now and there's too much standing in the way between us.

Yesterday, I went on a little shopping therapy with Rachel at Nordstrom, and picked up a few new summer dresses, skirts, and shoes. I didn't go too crazy after throwing down a hefty chunk of change for Eve's new nanny, but it was nice to at least spruce up my wardrobe with some end-of-summer-sale gear.

I'm deep in my own world when I hear a grumble at the door that gives me a jolt.

"Morning," Everett says.

He's got jeans on and a white t-shirt today, which is basically formal attire for him.

I spin around, and my heart thumps.

"Hey...Boss," I blurt out. "What are you doing here?"

"What am I doing in my own house?"

"No. I mean, aren't you guys supposed to be at training camp this week?"

"Coach called us all this morning and said since it's a record heat wave downstate this week, we're going to stay in the Chicago area. We have better indoor facilities here."

"Oh."

He shrugs. "Global warming. What can you do?"

As he walks into my office, his masculine scent takes over the room, and my arousal is palpable.

Well, for me it's palpable, at least. Everett crosses his muscular arms and stares out the window with a pensive look on his face.

Or he could just be mad. I'm still figuring out the difference between Everett's pissed and pensive states.

"Sleep okay?" I ask, trying to make innocuous conversation.

"Pretty well. You?"

"Slept okay. The baby only woke up once."

Everett stares at me like he's got something on his mind. And not just the normal 'giving his assistant a hard time' B.S.

"You look pensive. Everything okay?" I say.

"Actually, I wanted to chat about something important. It's just, Emma, you told me your secret. And I thought I would tell you one, too."

"Oh?" I try to keep calm, but there's no denying how my heart lights up at just the thought of Everett opening up with me.

And then it happens.

I bobble my Starbucks latte, completely miss my mouth, and half of it unloads all over my shirt.

"Jesus," Everett says, rushing to my side and grabbing hold of the cup.

Without thinking, I proceed to pull my soaked blouse up and over my head.

"I'm lucky it was iced, I guess," I say, holding onto it and trying not to drip.

That's when I notice Everett staring at my breasts.

I look down, and see my white bra is soaked through to the nipples, which are visible, and hard.

I immediately cover them.

"Shit, sorry," Everett says. "I'll get a towel. Do you have a change of clothes?"

"No, I don't. Ugh, I got some on my pants, too," I frown.

"Take those off and we'll get them in the wash," he says immediately, gesturing for me to hand him...something.

I freeze, my face turning red. "Right now?"

"Oh, I mean...not right *now*. I'll go get the towel first and..." he pauses to examine me. "I mean, I suppose it *would* only be fair. I've shown you mine. Show me yours."

My heart hammers.

Am I really doing this?

"Out," I say instead. "No free shows."

"You got a free show," he points out. Is he teasing? At a time like this.

"That's because you were yelling so loud, I thought you were getting attacked Stephen King-style."

He squints. "What does that mean, exactly? Does Stephen King attack people?"

"No, like his *books*, you dork."

"I don't read."

I pinch my eyebrows together. "Wait. You just don't... read? At all?"

"It's never been my thing. You have any more questions about my habits?"

"Maybe we should not have this conversation while I'm covering my breasts."

He smirks a little, and looks at me. "Your nipples are pretty hard for a normal morning."

I note that since he can't see them right now, he clearly stole a look earlier. But he's not wrong.

"The A/C is cranking in here. And why am I defending myself right now?"

"Wait here. I'll be right back with a towel."

Everett leaves. I make a mental note to always bring a formal pair of extra clothing in the future, but right now I realize I have nothing else to wear.

A minute later, Everett appears at the door.

"Here's a towel and a change of clothes," he says.

He hands me the towel, followed by a giant jersey that says BREWER on it.

"Seriously?"

He grins. "What? You don't like it?"

"Give me a moment, please."

He steps out of the room, and I towel off, take off my bra, and put on the blue and green jersey.

"Okay, come in."

He's got an ear-to-ear grin when he comes back in.

"Now *that* is a solid personal assistant uniform," he says. "I think I'm going to have you wear that every day."

I close the door, which has a full-length mirror on it, and take a look at myself wearing his jersey.

"This is longer than most of the dresses I own."

He smirks. "I'm not sure what that says about you."

"It says this jersey is ridiculously big. Seriously? I need to work in this? How do *you* even fit in this thing?"

"Well, I'm *big* all over. Besides, I think you look great in it, personally."

He motions for me to do a twirl, and for some reason, I oblige him because I'm flushed with the innuendo of him talking of his largeness.

"Wow. Yes, I think it looks great on you. Keep it."

"Um, thanks?"

"You're welcome."

I look at the shorts he brought down. I could put those on, but they'd be so long on me it would only add to the ridiculousness of today's outfit.

"So, did you have anything else you wanted to say today? Other than to distract me and make me spill iced coffee all over myself."

"I'm distracting you? Interesting."

"No, I mean like, anything is a distraction when I'm in the zone."

"In the...zone? Like the email-answering zone?"

"Just because you're my boss doesn't mean you have to be a dick."

He smirks, then walks over to my desk and leans onto the empty part of it right next to my computer.

"I did want to tell you something, actually. I thought a lot about this weekend."

My ears perk up. "Oh?"

"Yes. And I wanted you to know..."

He trails off for a moment.

My body flushes with desire and possibility.

"...to know that I really appreciate you telling me that secret of yours. It took guts, I'm sure. And I'm not going to tell anyone else. I promise."

I nod calmly, pretending like I'm actually reading the email I have pulled up.

"I just thought it was the right time. You seem...troubled by something. I thought you should know other people go through troubling things in life, too."

He puts his hand on my shoulder, and it sends a jolt of electricity through me. "I know. Thanks. You're a good person, Emma. And a friend. I don't trust a lot of people, but I'm getting there with you."

I open my mouth and almost blurt out *Is that because of Samantha?* but I manage to hold my tongue. I want his trust more than I want to know his secret right now.

"But we do need to talk about what you were doing in my room," he adds, and my heart hammers, my nerves chipping away at me.

"Of course," I say.

"Turn toward me," he says.

I minimize my email and spin my chair so I'm facing him. Any trace of amusement on his face from earlier is gone. I feel a little like I want to scurry away and stick my head in the sand.

I didn't feel good about how much I had to lie the other night when he caught me in his room at the lake house.

I was just up here to think. Total lie.

I wanted to write you a note on paper. Another lie. I was very much snooping.

I would never tell anyone what we talk about. Okay, that last one, I'm not sure I would tell Cal and Rich, unless I was worried Everett was engaging in behavior that was harmful to himself or other people.

"What happened on the bed—" I start to say, but he cuts me off.

"I'm not talking about what happened on the bed," he says, and his eyes are so intense they make me feel queasy. "Although we should talk about that at some point, too. I'm talking about the fact that you were in my room and I don't know what you were doing."

"I told you, I wanted to write you a note—"

"You could have 'thought' and 'wrote a note' anywhere in the house. Why were you in *my* room?"

My mouth dries, and all of the sudden the room doesn't feel like it's cranking A/C any more. Is it getting hot in here?

He leans forward. "And lastly, *how* did you know I like to write things out when I'm feeling stressed?"

My chest hitches, and my body heats. Almost subconsciously, I reach out with my hand and put it on his leg.

I have a flashback to the other night on the bed with him.

"I don't understand why you're grilling me like this. We had a moment on the jet ski, I wanted to follow up on that moment. So I went in your room, okay? Yes, I wanted to be in your room! I wanted a chance at seeing you. And maybe a little more. I was tipsy."

"You're still not answering my main question," he says, his voice low.

I realize he's massaging my forearm, and I don't know if he's doing that on purpose or he is just nervous like I am. "You don't fool me, Emma. You're a smart one. I don't know what you're up to, or who put you up to it, but I've got my eye on you."

I feel lightheaded all of a sudden.

"No one put me up to anything," I manage to say. "I'm just...worried about you, Everett. Like I said."

"So you say," he squints.

I sink into my chair. The tension in the air grows thick.

Pulling my hand from his leg, I shake it off, then return his gaze, considering the reality of the situation.

This is my boss.

Another hookup would have complicated things substantially.

It's pure denial to think that I'm not attracted to him, but that doesn't mean we have to act on this.

Again.

In addition, I didn't do anything wrong. I haven't told Cal and Rich a thing. Rachel is the only one who knows even one iota of the secret part of my role as Everett's personal assistant.

I look Everett in the eye, and I say, "Look, if you ever want to talk with me, I'd love to be an ear."

He clenches up.

My phone buzzes, and I go to check it.

"Can you give me a moment? Personal call."

Everett leaves, and I lean back in my chair as I answer the phone.

"Hey, Josh! What's up?"

Josh starts to talk, and as I spin around in my seat, I notice Everett glaring at me from the kitchen.

Something coils inside me as we make eye contact. I'm hot with desire, and it's not for the man I'm talking with on the phone who is offering to take me on a date.

It's for my closed off, ridiculously buff and handsome boss, who refuses to make a full move on me.

I spin back around and sit at my desk facing my computer, then adjust my mirror so I can see his brooding face as he stares at me.

The man clearly has issues.

And the fact that I'm so attracted to him makes me wonder about my own.

What in God's good name is so tragic about your life that you can't share it, Everett?

"Yes, I can make a date tomorrow," I say loudly, and I'm not sure if Everett can hear me. The way he glares at me, I think he can.

And it hits me then…I'd almost forgotten. I'm sure he was about to tell me something heavier before I bobbled my coffee.

Now I guess I'll never know.

17

EVERETT

Sleep is hard to come by when you're hanging onto something, I've decided. The anxiety has gotten worse over the past couple of days. Relaxing in Wisconsin at the lake with fresh air was great, but now that I'm home, the tension invites itself all over again. Ironically, the fact that Emma was able to be so open about her secret with me just made me feel more stifled and foolish about not owning up to mine.

I was about to tell her before the coffee incident, but I've decided she can't know.

No one can.

Well, except for Detective Gates.

I can't deny that I've gotten used to having Emma around the house. Dare I say, I even enjoy her company.

Some days, she'll point out things in my own game film that she sees, that both my coaches and I somehow missed, and I'll wonder if she's secretly been studying film at home to impress me.

But I somehow know that's not the case with her. Emma is all genuine, all the time.

And for the past few nights, I've been replaying in my head the nice glimpse of her gorgeous breasts I got, thanks to that coffee incident earlier this week.

My conscience teeters back and forth with a devil on one side telling me to just go for her, and an angel reminding me that this isn't the time to get involved.

In the end, the part about me being her boss doesn't seem as wrong as the simple fact that I can't be getting distracted as I head into the biggest football season of my life.

On Thursday, we have a five a.m. to noon practice and video session.

It's a grueling session, and for some odd reason I can't put my finger on, I'm looking forward to seeing Emma when I get back to my place. She's been a breath of fresh air to my days this week after practice.

And then I get a text:

Emma: Hey, Bossman! I got ahead yesterday on the workload, and I'm taking the day off. Text me if you need something urgent

Everett: Alright. Big plans for the day?

Emma: Just going on my first date in over a year. Seeing the Jaguars play ball in Wrigleyville. NBD ☺ See you tomorrow!

"No. Big. Deal?" I say out loud. My face burns with anger, and I can't believe how jealous I'm feeling.

Am I imagining things, or did she just throw it in my face that she's going on a date? I bet it's with that Josh character who she talked to the other day.

I can't control the burning sensation in my stomach. Or the fact that picturing her on a date, drinking and laughing with this faceless guy, makes my muscles tighten.

I go over to Dyson's locker, where he's just finished tying his shoes.

"Hey, man, you want to go to a Jaguars day game today?"

He stands up. "Actually, that sounds fun. I've been thinking about going to visit Rachel. She works at one of the bars around there as a cocktail waitress."

My frown flips slowly into a grin. "Perfect. Let's head there now."

WRIGLEYVILLE HAS the most bars per capita of anywhere in the world. Someone once told me that, and I don't know if it's true, but walking down Addison before the game, it certainly feels like it. It's not even noon yet, and the patios are full with rowdy fellas and good-looking Chicago girls ready for some summer fun in the sun.

The game is electric. The crowd and the hot buzz of competition in the air gets the two of us pumped for our upcoming football season. Dyson and I are thankful that we live in a city with such enthusiastic sports fans. The Jaguars win — of course, they do with Jake Napleton on the mound — and the whole city is ecstatic. Afterwards, we head to the place where Rachel works called Big Country Mike's BBQ Barn. It's right across from Wrigley Field. Even though it's packed after the game, she gets us a perfect table on the patio close to the sidewalk, which I like since I can keep an eye out on the crowds passing by and I want to keep an eye out for Emma.

"So, what made you decide to come to a game today?" Rachel asks as she sets a couple of Goose Island beers in front of us.

"Just felt like catching a baseball game before the summer's end," I say.

Dyson is one-hundred percent checking her out. I will

be the first to admit, or maybe the second, after Dyson, that she looks distracting, indeed, in her cute server outfit.

"Damn!" Dyson says, never one for subtlety. "Someone is about to hustle all the money today."

"You know it." She winks and does a little twirl for us. "Does it make you a little jealous knowing how all the guys are going to look at me today?"

Dyson laughs. "Aw, yeah. Very jealous, babe. I'll be tipping you extra, too."

Rachel giggles, gives Dyson a peck on the cheek. "And I'll be giving you extra special service," she winks, then walks off to check on other tables.

"She looks fine in that uniform." He stares as she walks away, then turns to me. "Ah, yes, romance is in the air, my man! Goddamn is it ever in the air!"

I chuckle a little at the irony, what with the girl I can't stop thinking about being on a date with another man. "Totally in the air."

Rachel comes back to our table. "Need anything else before the rush hits?"

"Just this," Dyson says, and kisses her on the lips.

"Honey," she says, blushing. "I'm at work."

"Couldn't resist," Dyson grins.

"So what's Emma up to today?" Rachel asks. "I haven't talked to her since yesterday."

"You should text her and see what she's up to."

"I don't need to text her, I see exactly what she's up to right now." And with that, she gives a head nod toward the crowd of people just outside the bar.

I glance toward the sidewalk, and out the corner of my eye I see her.

My jaw flexes, and I stare at the two of them as they come toward us.

"Hey!" Rachel yells. "What a coincidence. We were just talking about you!"

Emma jerks her head around and looks at us. I think I see her let out a small gasp.

"Wow...well, this is a coincidence," she says over the waist-high rope dividing the bar from the sidewalk.

"Hi...everyone...holy shit. You really do work for Everett Brewer!" Emma's date exclaims.

Emma rolls her eyes. "This is Josh. He didn't believe me that you're my boss. Anyway, we were just about to head to a bar down the road."

"You could stay here," Dyson inserts. "Word has it Rachel is hooking us up with free drinks."

"It's true," Rachel grins.

"Free drinks, really?" Josh smiles. "Let's do it. I'd love to hang out with your boss. This is like...a once-in-a-lifetime opportunity!"

Emma's body language is stiff, but she finally relents. "Alright. Fine," she sighs.

"Yes! Come join us. It'll be fun," I grin, maybe a little maniacally.

She levels me with her gaze and shakes her head almost imperceptibly.

"See you in a minute."

I lean over and watch her walk into the bar. She's got these frayed denim short-shorts on, along with a green and black Jaguars tank top. My arousal is piqued. I roll off into fantasy land for a moment, where I'm ripping those shorts off of her and bending her over that desk in her office where she always works so hard. Then I think how can I change up the office dress code so she wears something like that into work?

"Everett! Do you need another beer, or are you good?"

I look over at my glass and notice I've already whittled it down past the halfway point.

"I'll have another, sure."

Emma and Josh make their way to the patio, and sit down next to us, ordering beers from Rachel, as well.

"So remind me," I say. "How did you two originally meet?"

Emma scowls subtly at me and shakes her head.

"Well, that's a really funny story," Josh says.

"It's not *that* funny," Emma corrects.

"I still want to hear it," I say.

Dyson rubs his hands together. "Let's hear it. Romance is in the air today!"

Josh gives Dyson a funny look and continues. "Well, I was just on my regular shift at this vintage clothing shop, and Emma ducks inside, all out of breath."

Emma's face is a ruddy red hue, and I can't tell if it's because she's sun-kissed after being in the sun today, or this story is truly embarrassing to her.

"I wasn't that out of breath," she shakes her head.

"She totally was. She was running from someone, I think—"

I furrow my brow. "Running? From who?"

"He's exaggerating," Emma says. "It was more of a brisk walk."

The way Emma keeps trying to diffuse Josh's story makes me even more interested. Why is she so opposed to this guy talking? "Where do you work?"

"He works at a vintage clothing shop. I'm sorry, Josh is a bad storyteller. The point is, I came in, bought some clothes, and he gave me his number. Ballsy, right?"

I think back to when I first saw the number. "Where did you say you work at, again, Josh? In the city?"

Before he can answer, Rachel comes back with beers and changes the conversation topic.

I notice Emma is peeling the label on her beer. In some silly psychology periodical I once read that beer label peeling is a sign of sexual frustration. I let my gaze fall to hers, and my lips quirk in a small smile.

"So, Everett, like, how did it feel when you won the first Super Bowl for Chicago since 1986?" Josh asks.

"Oh, man, it wasn't for me that we won it. It was for the city."

"Yeah, but you ran for two-hundred twenty-eight yards that game. It's a record."

I shrug. "Back in my prime. I just hope I can pull off another one this year. Excuse me, I have to use the bathroom."

I get up to use the john, and when I come out, I'm greeted by a frowning Emma with her arms crossed.

"What the hell are you doing?" she seethes.

I shrug. "I'm enjoying the day. How about you?"

"You came all the way to Wrigleyville just to cockblock me on my date? What's wrong with you?"

My jaw hardens. "It's a free country last time I checked. I'm allowed to go where I want. You made the suggestion of a game this morning, and it sounded like a good idea. It's a beautiful day."

She pinches her eyebrows together. "So you're not jealous of Josh at all?"

"Why are we talking about me right now? You're the one who is acting all strange."

"No, I'm not."

"Yes, you are. You won't even let Josh get a word in edgewise."

"Because you're interrogating him."

"Am not. He's obsessed with me."

Her gaze shifts down and away, then she brings it back to me. "You're unbelievable. I was serious about what I said last Monday. I'm not letting you rule over me any more. You want me, you don't. You turn away from my kiss." Stepping forward, she puts her hand on my cheek then pulls it away, as if realizing she's here with another man. "What do you want from me, Everett?"

At this point, we're making a little bit of a scene, and people are staring.

"Excuse me," I say. "I'm going back to the table before we're another viral video online."

Emma comes back from the bathroom a few minutes later with a smile on her face.

"Ah, yes, where were we?"

"Everett was just telling me about the time he went head to head with Aaron Rodgers in 2016," Josh says, and I smirk.

"No," Emma says. "I think we were about to do this."

She leans over, grabs hold of the front of Josh's button polo, and kisses him on the lips.

My entire body flares with the jealousy that had been dormant for some time.

I nod to Dyson. "Alright, man. I think it's time I get out of here."

18

EMMA

I stew in my car as I drive to Everett's place on Friday morning, the day after my date. I'm hungover, and my mind races as I roll down the highway. The hosts of the morning show on the radio sound like muffled Charlie Brown voices with the way I ruminate.

He ruined it.

Everett Brewer *ruined* my date.

We were having a terrific time until we met Everett and Dyson at the bar. Why were they even at the Jaguars game to begin with? I see Everett's schedule, and I know he wasn't planning to go until I told him I was on a date there.

And why didn't I push to go somewhere, *anywhere* else? I should have known what Everett would get up to.

My phone buzzes, and I press the green button to turn on my speakerphone.

"What is it?" I answer, a little annoyed.

"Is that how you usually answer your phone?" It's Cal.

"I'm driving. What do you want?"

"Well, I saw you turned down my calendar invitation to come into the office today."

I clench my fist a little harder on the steering wheel.

"That's right. There are no updates on the situation that we do not speak of over the phone."

"Yes. And that's what we need to talk about."

I don't know if it's the hangover, or the fact that many parts of my life have been building to a boiling point, but I'm feeling extra saucy today.

"Look, Cal. Everett's angry, but he's not in danger of ruining his—or the organization's—reputation like you're worried about. He's got some bottled-up anger, sure. But don't we all! Besides, it'll probably resolve itself once he's hitting people on the field."

I can hear Cal scoffing through the phone. "Are you doing okay?" he asks. "I've never heard you talk like this."

"I'm fine!" I shout into the receiver, and I have to swerve out of the way when a car cuts me off. "Jesus, people! Watch the road!" I yell out.

"Maybe this isn't the best time to talk."

"There's no update, Cal. You will be the first to know if I figure out what Everett is up to. I tried everything you suggested. The only things I've found out is that the guy loves working out, even other professional football players are a little afraid of him, and he's a fan of jet skis. I don't need to come all the way downtown to the office to tell you that."

There's a long pause on the phone. "Fine," Cal relents. "But we'll need you to come in next week."

"Alright," I say through gritted teeth.

I hang up. A few minutes later I pull into Everett's U-shaped driveway, get out and slam the door.

When I walk inside, he's talking to a man who looks like an even more muscular version of himself. Which I thought was almost impossible.

"That's perfect, Jason. Thanks for coming by. We'll be in touch about everything else I need," Everett says, then shakes the man's hand. The man leaves, passing me in the foyer. He looks like a professional bodybuilder, complete with veins popping out of his neck. "Hi," I say.

He flashes a toothy grin, and breezes past me. "Morning."

When the door shuts, I walk to the kitchen island and put my purse down.

"Morning," Everett says, taking a sip of his coffee. "Cup of joe for you today?"

I pinch my eyebrows together.

"What is the matter with you?"

He shrugs. "Not a single therapist I've ever had has been able to answer that question. Can you believe that?"

"No, I mean, yesterday. Calling over Josh. Interviewing him. You destroyed our date."

Anger flares inside me.

"Oh? I didn't notice you guys had anything going on. He seemed like he wasn't really your type, anyway."

My heart pounds furiously. "Why do you care who I date?"

"You're my friend. I think I should look out for you."

"I'm not your friend, I'm your employee as you so often like to remind me. Do you stalk all of your 'friends' when they're on dates? Or just me?"

"Do you tail all of your bosses when they decide to take a day trip to the city?"

Damn. Got me there.

"Besides," he goes on, "I'd been thinking about getting to a Jaguars game all summer. The fact that you were going just reminded me."

"Somehow, I doubt that."

"Fine. You want honesty? Take a seat. I've been doing some thinking and I should probably just level with you. Get some things off my chest."

Something about his tone is unusually serious, so I obey.

He's quiet for a few moments as he stands in front of the panoramic window in my office that looks out on the greenery of his giant backyard. As I sit back, I wonder if I'm dreaming for a moment. A month ago I was working at a hot dog stand arguing with this man about tips, and now, I'm staring at Everett Brewer, AKA sex on wheels with morning messy hair that he makes look incredibly hot. He wears jeans, and the blue ribbed tank top shows all my favorite parts of the man's shoulders and forearms. It's almost unfair what the man can make me feel just by being in the same room.

I chew the inside of my cheek and hope my arousal isn't too obvious.

It's completely unfair how when Josh — a good guy, a nice guy — and I kissed yesterday, I felt nothing.

There was no butterflies-in-my-stomach feeling when his lips touched mine.

I've had more tingles run through my body when the barista calls my name for my iced coffee, as a matter of fact.

Yet, with my boss Everett, who puts me off, turns me down, and erects a giant, emotional wall between us, I can't stop thinking about him.

"Did you have something to say?" I ask. "Or are you just going to stand there, looking all..."

I'm about to say sexy, but I manage to stop myself. "Broody."

He looks down, then fixes his stare on me.

"I'll be honest. I can't stand the thought of you on a date with another man. It drove me wild. Still drives me wild."

"So, let me get this straight. You won't so much as kiss me, boss. But you don't want me to be with someone else? Are you insane?" I ask these questions all affronted, but really, I'm dancing in my shoes because Everett likes *me*.

"I wanted to kiss you, Emma," he says. "But Peyton interrupted us."

"I don't buy that." Nope, not gonna make this easy on him.

"What do you mean? He definitely interrupted us. That's just a fact."

"Yeah, but if you wanted to kiss me, you would have found a way." I chuckle. "Am I supposed to believe that you, a known killer on the football field because you decide what you want and you take it, is going to be deterred by a little setback if you really want something?"

He's silent.

"So, I'm right."

He sets his coffee down. "Stand up," he says in a low and growly voice.

I feel the heat racing through my body at his command. His tone is different than I've heard him in the past. More authoritative.

I stand and my heart pounds furiously.

He crooks his finger, making a come-hither motion.

I walk toward him slowly, my heels clicking on the ground.

His expression is even as I approach him.

When I'm standing next to him, he runs a hand through my hair, pushing it behind my ear.

"You were drunk. Well, the second time you were. If we're going to go again, I need to know you're okay with what we're getting into. And not after you've had a bunch of tequila drinks."

Excitement rushes under my skin. So he was just trying to be...respectful of me? I guess I *did* consume quite a few drinks that night. Maybe I was drunker than I thought.

"Why are you so hesitant around me?" I ask. "It doesn't match up with your personality."

His palm lands on my cheek.

With closed eyes, he leans down, rubbing his scruff lightly against my cheek before he kisses me softly on the lips.

The tips of my fingers tingle as I hold onto his jean belt loops. My whole body, from head to toe, pulsates with desire for him, all the built-up self-denial between us spilling free.

Our lips touching is an electric feeling, and it seems like it lasts forever, even though it's probably only a few seconds.

When he pulls away, he opens his eyes, and so do I.

He then sets his coffee down and backs me up against the glass window, kissing me all the while.

I clutch his hair as our lips duel, my body filled with need for him.

His hard body presses me into the glass, the pressure of him causing my body to burn up. I moan into his open mouth and his tongue slides between my teeth.

Writhing against him, I hold on to his belt loops as he drags his hand down the length of my back.

His hand reaches the end of my dress and his fingers rub my thigh. My body twists at the touch of his fingertips on my flesh.

He pulls back. "You ticklish or something?"

"Are you?" I say, because once I admit that I *am* ticklish, I have a bad feeling Everett will turn that into a game of torture.

"No," Everett shakes his head.

"You sure about that?" I whisper the words in his ear before I slide my tongue down his neck. I yank up on his tank top, and he obliges me by putting his arms up so I can take it off.

"Jesus," I mutter, as I trail my hand down his six-pack. His torso is so hard, I almost don't believe it's a man's flesh.

"See?" he growls. "Not ticklish."

My hand doesn't stop at the bottom of his abs, though. It keeps going as I nibble on his ear.

I rub the outline of his cock over the fabric of his jeans, and his breath thickens. Then, he kisses me as I undo his top button and unzip his jeans.

I'm surprised when I feel his flesh already. Not even a briefs man, apparently.

His groans are low as I run my hand over the length of his cock, and we continue to make out.

His hand reaches toward my inner thigh, but I stop him.

"It pains me to say this," I whisper. "But it's that time of the month for me."

He nods. "I see."

"But that doesn't mean we can't do something else."

I drop to my knees, wrap my hand around his hard length, and lick the sides of his shaft.

Slowly at first, I take his tip in my mouth. Holding my free hand on his abs, I can feel his stomach contracting with pleasure and feel his moans vibrate through my arm and into my body.

I look up for a moment, and seeing the way his eyes are hooded over with pleasure is a giant turn-on.

After a breath of air, I take him deeper into my mouth, while pumping his cock at the same time. He fists my hair and rubs the back of my neck ever so slightly with his fingertips, driving me insane.

When I take him as deep as I can, he moans loudly, which triggers something inside of me, too.

"Emma," he mutters, his voice gravelly. "Jesus, that feels so damn good."

His hand on my shoulder. My own arousal building, driving me insane. When he puts his hands down my dress, rubbing his hands on my breasts, the pulse in my clit throbs and I wish like hell for release.

Finally, his groans get louder and I can feel his dick pulsing.

"Christ, Emma, you've got me on the brink."

I pull my mouth away from him for a moment.

"I want it, Boss," I moan, pumping him with both hands and my mouth.

A low guttural noise escapes him.

"I'm gonna..." his words trail off and he unloads his hot cum down my throat as he orgasms.

When we're done, he stands there a few moments, looking down at me, and blinks a few times.

"Where the hell did that come from?"

I shrug, and wipe my mouth.

"Emma...fuck you look hot right now. I mean, you always do."

"Do I?"

He pulls his pants up, sits in my chair and motions for me to sit on his lap, which I do.

"Yes, you do. God, I think about doing things with you... naughty things...every day I see you. And even when I don't."

"I haven't done that in a long time," I comment.

He raises an eyebrow. "Well, it sure didn't show."

He wraps his arms around me and kisses my neck.

We sit like that for a few minutes in my rolling work chair. I rest my head on his chest.

I'm about to ask him about the secret he mentioned the other day, maybe he'll be loosened up in his post-orgasmic state. But just then, his phone buzzes in his pocket.

He shifts his weight to pull it out. I hear a man's voice on the other line, that says, "Are you alone? It's about Samantha."

A chill comes over me when I hear the name. Everett motions for me to get up off his lap, and I do. He stands up, looks back over his shoulder at me, and walks out of the room.

He comes back a few minutes later with a flustered expression.

"I need to go," he says, then looks at his watch. "Shit. Practice is starting soon, too."

"Who was that? Is everything okay?" I ask.

He shakes his head. "It's nothing to worry about. I've just gotta go."

"Everett, please tell me what's going on with you..."

He pauses as he grabs his shirt. "Honestly?"

I nod. "Yes, I'd prefer honesty."

"That's just it...I don't know," he says.

He kisses me goodbye.

"Talk soon," he says. "Oh, and make sure I get my suit clean for that charity thing next Friday."

"Talk soon," I say back to him, like we'd just wrapped up a lunch meeting or something as ubiquitous as that instead of me just going down on him. In my office, no less. "Sorry I wasn't able to reciprocate. Rain check?"

"Sure."

And as he leaves out the door, I feel a little deflated.

I consider tailing him again to see where he's going, all secretive.

But our recent sexual encounter seems to have knocked the wind out of me.

One step forward with this man...two steps back.

19

EMMA

Everett doesn't come back later on Friday. I assume he's staying late after today's practice. I'm still mulling over the call he received, wondering who called him and what they told him about Samantha, that much I could hear. I think that guy from the park that day was a private investigator, maybe he hired him to find out why she left him or could it be something more — a child, maybe? Okay, I'm letting my imagination run wild. Why won't he confide in me? We have a connection, physical and more. I'd like to be more than just his personal assistant, maybe his confidante, his lover...more.

The following Monday, he finally heads down at Bourbonnais for training camp all week. I'm invited to head down, but with my sister close to having her baby, and I work it out to stay up in the Chicago area.

Plus, Everett's plants aren't going to water themselves.

Tuesday comes, and Wednesday passes as well. Cal and Rich want an update, I lie to them and tell them *everything's great here!* And no updates, so no point in doing a face to face.

Not a total lie, considering, the messages and calls I've made to Everett don't even have read receipts, and I don't see or hear from him at all this week.

If there's any week I actually *have* been worried about him, it's this week.

My heart has been fluttering thinking about what a silly idiot I have been in this whole situation.

Going down on your boss? Really, Foster?

It's been a rough time. Plus, Rachel is out of town on a family vacation, so I don't get to see her for a little friend therapy.

So in order to cope, on Thursday after work, after I put Eve down for the night, I have myself a bubble bath. I need to try and take a load off. But to say that I'm annoyed that I haven't heard from Everett for almost an entire week after I gave him the blowjob of his life is more than an understatement.

So I settle in with a nice big glass of wine and a summer book I've been meaning to get to, wondering why the hell I put up with shit like this from men like Everett. He did at least say the thing about reciprocating when he gets a chance. But six days and *nothing?* Really?

My own thoughts are distracting me from reading when Josh texts me.

Josh: What's up? Sad we didn't get a chance to hang out this week. What are you up to this weekend?

My heart flutters, and not because of Josh.

It flutters because him asking me what I'm up to this weekend makes me realize that although it's Thursday and I'd like to do something fun this weekend, the man whom I would *like* to see hasn't been returning my texts all week.

After I gave him the blowjob of his life.

I sink down into the water, and my phone buzzes again,

but this time with a text from Rachel, asking me what I'm up to tonight.

I snap a picture of my bubble bath situation for her, and two seconds later she's calling me.

"Hey there! I just got back from Hawaii with the fam! Looks like a sexy little time you're having tonight," she says.

"Yeah, sexy time, right. I have a question. And answer honestly."

"Sure."

"Does something about me attract emotionally distant men?"

She clears her throat. "Why is that on your mind?"

"Everett hasn't texted me all week! He's the only man I've gone past third base with all year. I'm asking you as someone who knows me well — what's the matter with me?"

Rachel sighs on the other end of the phone.

"There's nothing wrong with you, Em. You took a risk and put yourself out there, you should be proud of yourself."

"So what do I do now? Just wait for Everett, who has gone totally dark, mind you, to text me back? Like some princess in an ivory tower waiting to be saved? It's not right. And now Josh is texting me and it's making me doubt my choice to be with Everett. Sure, maybe he doesn't have ridges in his abs that I want to lick, but at least Josh knows how to answer a freaking text."

I clench up, a hard knot in my gut.

"You should do what you feel is best. You're not inclined to be loyal to either guy. You're dating around. Enjoy it while it lasts."

I scrunch up my face. "What do you mean, 'while it lasts'?"

"Oh," she hesitates. "Because one day, you'll meet someone, and he'll be the one, and you won't want to be with anyone else."

I hear a man's voice chuckling in the background and saying something that I can't quite make out.

"Dyson!? Is he there right now?"

"Hey, Emma!" he yells into the phone. "Yes, I'm here with your girl. I drove up for the night. Don't worry, I'm treating her right."

So the players *are* alive. In my mind, I was sort of excusing Everett with the rationale that he was deep into a week of practice.

Now I know that that's bullshit, if Dyson was able to drive the two or so hours up from Bourbonnais to be with Rachel just for the night, then Everett could've at least texted me back.

"Two questions. One, do you guys have practice tomorrow?" I ask Dyson.

"Just a morning film session. Then drills Saturday, home game Sunday. I'm surprised they don't give you the schedule."

"Me, too. They've just shifted the schedule so many times this season."

"And the second question?"

"Are you two officially dating?" I ask.

"Yes!" Rachel jumps in. "We officially started dating yesterday when Dyson took me out to dinner."

"Well, we officially started when we got back from dinner last week. I took you to bed and—"

"Babe!" Rachel interrupts. "That's TMI. Anyway, yes. Just have faith that everything will work out, Emma."

When I hang up the phone, I don't have a great feeling

in my stomach. I pull up and scan my latest text threads, which are to my sister, Rachel, and then Everett and Josh.

As much as I would love a guy like Josh — whom I *know* for a fact is very into me — I can't deny the lack of a spark when we kissed and that's a no-go for me.

And as much as I wish I had feelings for a guy who didn't seem like he was playing a constant game of cat-and-mouse with me, I can't deny what I'm feeling for Everett.

Why is that always how love seems to go for me? I want what I can't have, but have little-to-no interest in someone like Josh, who just doesn't do it for me romantically.

The cat chases the mouse. The dog chases the cat. But who chases the dog?

Maybe the wine that's buzzing through me gives me a little courage, but I know what I have to do.

I send a message to one of the two men: "I'm sorry, but we can't do this anymore."

And then I pull up the picture I took and sent to Rachel...the one with my thighs suggestively poking out of the bubbles and send it to the other.

Josh gets the turn down.

Everett gets the suggestive photo.

At the end of the day, I can't deny my heart is in Everett's court. And if that picture doesn't get him to return my texts and calls, I don't know what will. If it's still a radio silence after that, I'll know exactly where we stand.

I sink farther into the tub, enjoying soaking in the warm water and taking in the relaxing scent of my Japanese cherry blossom candle.

I hear my phone buzz, but I'm deep into my book and finally feeling relaxed for the first time all week, so I just ignore it.

It buzzes a second and a third time.

Okay, now that has me intrigued so I look and see Everett's name flashing on the caller ID and I pick it up.

"So that's it?" he says. "You're shutting me out?"

I frown. "Um, you're the one who's shutting *me* out," I correct. "And nice to know you're alive. Where have you been all week?"

"I just saw your text. *'I'm sorry, we can't do this anymore.'* How is that not shutting me out?"

My relaxation immediately converts to nausea.

"Hang on."

I put Everett on hold for a moment, and check out the messages I've sent.

Jesus. I sent the sexy bathtub picture to Josh, and the 'not doing this anymore' text to Everett.

Uh-oh.

Josh has already sent me a string of texts, including smiley faces, asking all sorts of naughty questions, and asking if I'd like him to come over right now.

Whoopsies. That's a matter to be rectified after I talk with Everett.

I take Everett off of hold and decide that if my accidental message got his attention, I might as well play like it was on purpose. He deserves that after ghosting me all week.

"Well, I'm glad you at least are getting this message since you've ignored my others. I go down on you and then I get radio silence — what's the deal with that?"

He clears his throat. "I didn't notice any messages that were urgent. And I had to attend to some things."

"What kind of 'things'?"

"You don't need to know the details. I just had to get out of town for a little while and clear my head."

"Are you even at training camp?"

"Yes. But I took the last couple of days off. It's fine—I spoke with Coach about it."

"What's going on?"

"I'll tell you tomorrow. For now, I need you to look something up for me. Public schools in Chicago don't start up until after labor day in September, and there's a summer reading program for kids on the near north side of Chicago. I think the church is called St. Ambrose. Can you sign me up to be a volunteer there tomorrow? I'll be back in the city tomorrow afternoon. You can come to the church, too."

I pinch my eyebrows together. "I haven't heard from you in a week, and the first thing you need me to do is...sign you up to be a volunteer? May I ask why?"

"I've recently had a come-to-Jesus moment, and I realize volunteering is very important. That's all."

"Somehow, I doubt that. You don't even *like* reading. What's the real reason?"

"Just make it happen, Emma."

"You got it, Boss. Anything else?"

He doesn't say anything for a moment, and the tension thickens, even over the phone.

"Yeah," he says. "Don't scare me like that and say 'we're done,' or whatever. I know I've been unavailable this week but I've had my reasons."

My throat clenches up. "I've got a lot to say about that. But I think I'll save it for when we meet in person."

"I'll meet you at the reading buddies program. It's around one. See you then."

"Okay."

"Oh, and Em?"

I feel my insides flip. Might Mr. Emotional Wall actually be feeling a tinge of something for me?

"Yeah?"

"Nothing," he says. "Sorry, see you tomorrow."

I hang up, and I my body swims with a mix of anger and excitement. Even just Everett's voice has the ability to make my stomach twist.

A mischievous grin lifts my lips, and I shake my head, wondering if I'm totally insane for thinking I might have something with this man. Everett's a superstar who could have just about any woman he wants.

My train of thought is interrupted when my phone flashes with another text.

It's a question mark from Josh, who is wondering why I haven't responded to any of his suggestive texts.

Guilt racks through me that I'm leading him on. I ponder what to send him, and settle on a short and sweet text, since I can't handle responding to all the over-the-top, sweet nothings he just sent me just from his reaction to a single partial selfie that wasn't intended for him in the first place. Although, I will say I am looking pretty hot in that picture, even if it's just the thighs down.

Emma: Hey! Sorry, it's getting late and Eve needs me... talk later ☺

Part of me wants to just tell him it's not going to happen. But I figure letting him down easy can't hurt.

I get out of the tub, towel off, and head to my laptop for some evening emailing to the head of summer activities at St. Ambrose church to see about reading buddies.

Luckily, the director is a huge fan of the Grizzlies, and when I namedrop Everett Brewer, he has no problem getting back to me, late as it is on a weeknight.

So we make arrangements for Everett and I to both be reading buddies for students at their daily summer camp tomorrow on Friday afternoon.

And still, I'm having trouble imagining how Everett's week of no communication resulted in a newfound, genuine-seeming interest in community service because I know this has something to do with that phone call he got, I just know it.

20

EVERETT

To tell her, or not to tell her, that is the question I try and wrap my mind around as I drive back to Chicago.

I should be running over play formations in my head, but football is the furthest thing from my mind.

Luckily, this week I got the chance to talk about what I'm going through with two men who have been on the other side of the coin from where I'm standing: Chandler Spiros and Carter Flynn. Chandler even came down to Bourbonnais to chat with me in person.

Both of them have made themselves into something great, in spite of their upbringings. And their counsel was very much needed this week.

They're the only souls — well, aside from Detective Gates — who know my secret. I can't even tell my own brothers. And when you hold onto something this big, it slowly eats away at you, little by little, like a caterpillar eating slowly through a leaf, stealing energy from your heart.

The more people who know, the more of a liability I become. Gates was very clear on that point.

As I cross the Indiana border into Chicagoland, I ponder whether or not Emma could become a liability...if I told her.

Christ, I'm an asshole. She's the nicest assistant I could ever have.

We took things...probably way too far on Friday, cementing another out-of-the-blue encounter. But there's no doubt in my mind we have something. This connection I'm fighting is not going to lay dormant, and now I know I don't want it to.

I hated running out on her like that, but when Gates called me with that update, I freaked out.

I needed to get away somewhere and think to myself, and I didn't want Emma to see me possibly breaking down.

When I arrive to St. Ambrose church, Emma is leaning against the doors of the parish community building. She's got on sunglasses and a white and red floral summer dress, which makes her look hot as usual.

"The students are in the community center section of the church. Obviously when they found out you were coming, they freaked. I told the community engagement director you didn't like to announce your appearance too far in advance, because when you do it turns less into being about the kids and more about press time and the parents, and that's not your intent."

"Good move. You want a medal?" I'm teasing but it comes out, instead, like an asshole remark.

She folds her arms, raising an eyebrow.

"So," she says.

"So...?"

"So are you going to tell me what the hell has been going on with you?"

"Just training. The regular season is starting soon. So I don't have much time for anything but football right now."

She sighs.

A man pops through the doors, interrupting us.

"Holy...shnikes! You're really here, in the flesh! I'm the director, Waldo Howes. Mr. Brewer, thanks so much for coming. We greatly appreciate it."

We shake hands. "It's no big deal, really."

Emma puts a plastic smile on her face, even though beneath it she is clearly pissed. Honestly, I think I shut out others to protect myself — Emma's making me see this, and it is really shitty.

"I just have to ask, what piqued your interest for volunteering at this parish?" he says with a smile.

"You know, I'm probably going to try and canvas more places around the city. It's an idea my new assistant came up with. Reading's an important thing, and these kids should know that."

I swear I can see Emma rolling her eyes.

"Well, come on in. I assume you'll do a quick Q&A with the kids before you start?"

"Of course. But just a quick one, okay? We want to make sure they know reading is serious business."

"Alright. I'll get the stage ready. See you shortly."

Emma folds her arms. "I can't believe you. Promoting reading...and you don't even like to read."

"Just because I don't like to read, doesn't mean I can't encourage them."

"It's a little hypocritical, don't you think?"

The director pokes his head out of the parish doors. "Mr. Brewer. We're ready for you."

I smile, nod, and walk into the community center part of the church. Cheers erupt and I let them know I want to say something, so they quiet down a bit.

After the Q&A, I do a little PSA. "Kids, one more thing I want to note. reading is important. Let me tell you why."

I wink at Emma.

She folds her arms, and her expression is even off-stage, but I can see the hint of a smile tugging at her lips.

"READ IT AGAIN!" Naomi says, leaning into my shoulder. Well, more like *demands*. "Do the voices again!"

"You already know what happens, though," I tell her. "Why don't I read another book?"

"No, this one. I just like the sound of your voice when you read this."

I shrug and go with it. There's nothing like a ten-year-old girl getting her way.

After I read again, I smile and head outside for some air.

Emma has been reading, too, and she sees and follows me.

There's a sports camp also going on, and when I walk over to watch, they all stare at me. I wave, and they wave back.

It's a sort of day camp for the area, for all ages. Some of the games are even run by teenagers.

While I'm getting a drink of water, a few boys walk up to me and ask me for my autograph on a playbook, which I oblige.

My palms sweat, and I hope I'm not making too much of

a scene, exactly like Gates, Carter, and Chandler said *not* to do if I planned on going through with this.

A woman in her twenties or so blows a whistle, and the kids all run to line up. Apparently, this is the big, end-of-the-day game of Red Rover. I chuckle because I remember that game fondly, and all the clotheslining of kids over the years as the opposing side sent them 'right over.'

The kids beg the woman in charge to let me play with them, and after agreeing, I oblige, under the condition that Emma gets to play, too.

Somehow, I end up on the all-boys' side.

A ten-year-old boy calls to me. "Hey, Mister Everett. Start the game!"

My stomach twists as I run my eyes down the line of girls lined up across the field, including Emma and the organizer on the other team. The director has joined up with our game.

I take a deep breath.

This is it.

If Gates was right, I'll know within a second who I'm looking for. How crazy to find out during a game of Red Rover.

I confront the pit in my stomach and call out, "Red Rover Red Rover, send Samantha right over!"

One millisecond feels like four eternities.

Nothing happens, it seems, for a minute.

And then, the camp organizer in her twenties, the one who blew the whistle, takes off running.

I narrow my eyes as I watch her run.

My stomach flutters.

No. It can't be her.

It truly can't.

Laughing, she runs and breaks the line, then selects me to go over to the girls' side.

"Looks like we're going to win, now," she says, then leans in as she walks me back to her side, hand on my shoulder.

The girls all giggle and cheer, and the boys boo.

"How did you know my name was Samantha?" she asks.

"Lucky guess," I blurt out, and as I'm put on the girls' team, I see Emma glaring at me. "It's a common name."

Samantha grins. "True. Normally we'd have another Samantha here. But she didn't come today."

My adrenaline shoots through the roof. I take a deep breath and keep calm.

"Oh, really?"

She nods, but our conversation is cut short when she runs to the other end of the line, then calls out for who the boys should send over.

21

EMMA

When I get out of my car in front of Everett's place, I'm met with oppressive heat.

My mind has been going crazy on the ride back from Chicago today.

Could she be *the* Samantha? And, if so, now what?

There are too many facts adding up for him calling out 'Samantha' during Red Rover to only be a coincidence.

Why did he even want to be there?

How did he know that woman's name?

I look to the sky in the west, and it's black.

Maybe some rain will help this ridiculous heat go away. But that's Chicago in late summer for you.

Everett pulls up a few minutes later.

When he opens the door, I'm in the kitchen getting a glass of water.

He comes toward me and he's got a disheveled look on his face.

"You okay?" I ask.

He shakes his head. I notice there are bags under his eyes. "No."

“Probably wasted effort for me to ask, but do you want to talk about it?”

He shakes his head and takes the glass of water I’m offering him. His usual dickish smirk is nowhere to be found, and he even seems a little defeated. “I’ve got to get a workout in today. I’m meeting up with Dyson at Midtown gym and we’re gonna knock it out. I’ll be back around six. Will you still be here?”

I shrug. “I don’t know. Is there a reason I should be?”

“Depends if you’ve got something to do tonight, or not.”

I twist up my face. I’d sort of planned for having the night off. Not that I thought anything was going to happen with Everett, but I was hoping something *would* happen between the two of us.

Everett leaves and heads out for the workout, and it’s then that I decide I’m done.

Not done with Everett.

But I’m done playing by his rules.

I need to know more.

I need to know everything about this Samantha girl.

Who is she?

And why did Everett stay talking to her for a half-hour after summer camp, while she didn’t even seem like she had met Everett before?

Something doesn’t add up.

So I creep up the stairs.

I open the door to the office Everett has forbid me from entering.

I even have myself a little glass of whisky while I’m in there, pouring from the old ten-year bottle he has in the office.

First, I pull out the Samantha napkin that I’ve been carrying in my purse ever since Everett left it behind.

I reread it, and have a sip of whisky. It coats my throat nice and easy.

Looking outside, I notice that the skies are gray and a trickle of rain has begun.

I look through a few of the drawers, wondering where he might have more letters to Samantha. I need to get to the bottom of this mystery, and my patience is wearing thin. Looking in the bottom drawer, I find a little key. I pull it out, then notice it seems the same size as the keyhole to the top, locked drawer.

"You're in a lot of trouble. I hope you know that."

When I hear my boss's voice, I practically melt into the chair in shock.

He closes the door behind him, and my heart pounds furiously.

"W-What are you doing here?" I swallow.

He chuckles, and the next words that come out of his mouth sound positively menacing.

"Oh, I think we both know that's not the question we're going to answer right now."

My throat tightens.

He walks toward me slowly, and I don't say anything.

Sitting on his desk, he tips my chin up toward him.

"I'm very disappointed in you, Emma. Very disappointed."

I stand up, whisky in hand, and try to slink out of the way.

The thunder claps outside, and the rain starts to come down in buckets.

"So what are we going to do to make this right?" he asks.

"I don't understand," I say, playing dumb.

He takes the whisky out of my hand and has a nice swig of it.

"Please. What do you know about me that you haven't been telling me?" he growls, handing me back the glass.

"Nothing," I blurt out, which is stupid, but I can't stop myself.

"No more lies," he growls. He takes the key out of my hand and tosses it on the desk.

Then, walking back to me, he pushes me up against the shelf, holding me a hair's breadth from his face. I can feel the warmth of his breath. My hand rests on his chest and I can sense his beating heart.

"So, what," he pauses, looking me dead in the eye, "are you doing here?"

My heart pounds like mad. I draw my mouth open as I cycle through any possible explanation.

His hands hold mine against the wall, trapping me.

"You're drinking my whisky," he growls. "And going through my things. You better have a good fucking explanation."

I try to wiggle away, but he uses his body and holds me in place against the wall.

I can see every detail in his face, every little piece of stubble. His cheeks are hot red, and as much as I want to run away, I'm also very turned on right now. It's this weird dichotomy of emotions and I'm so flustered that I don't even know which way is up.

He breathes close to my cheek, and runs his lips against mine, not kissing me, barely touching me, and sending a chill throughout my entire body.

Finally, he presses his lips to mine vigorously, then pulls back.

"No more lies," he repeats.

I break. At this point, the truth might be the only thing

that will set me free. I mutter, "I just want to know who Samantha is."

I nod toward the napkin note that's still set out on his desk.

His hand runs up my thigh, caressing my lower back.

"If you're in love with someone else, some unrequited love for a woman you never got over, just tell me. I'd rather know that instead of finding out a year from now that I'm just the girl you're using to try to forget a lost love. And honestly—your behavior would finally make sense if that were the case." He pinches his eyebrows slightly, the strangest look coming over his face.

"That's what you think? That I've got another romantic interest on my mind, and that's why I've been acting strange?"

I nod. "What would you infer from your note to Samantha?"

He pulls his hand away from me, and his expression softens. The rain hammers hard on the windows.

"Let's go downstairs. This is going to take a while," he says as he leads me down the steps.

EVERETT POURS ME A NICE, tall gin and tonic with a lime, and a whisky neat for himself.

We sit down on the couch, and there's a noted hint of vulnerability in the air.

"That's funny you think I had my heart broken by some ex named Samantha."

I sip my drink and sink farther into the couch. "I mean, what would you assume after reading that note, considering that I didn't know you?"

"I see what you mean. But why would I write it on a napkin?"

"I asked myself that same question and came to the conclusion that you just did it for therapeutic purposes. I did think it was odd for a man who claims not to read, to write so eloquently."

"When you write from the heart, you don't have to be a professional writer to say deep things. And, by the way, we're still not done discussing the fact that you broke into my office after I specifically told you, on multiple occasions, not to. We're going to deal with that."

"Sorry," I say, and I think about adding something like 'I didn't mean to pry' just because it seems like the right thing to say. But the fact is, I *did* mean to pry. Adding anything else would just be a lie.

"So I suppose I should just get into it."

I return his gaze. "By all means."

"Once I tell you, you're in the circle of trust with me, a circle that only a few people are in. What I'm about to tell you, no one knows. Not even my own family."

I nod subtly, and have another sip of my drink.

Something tells me a little buzz might be helpful tonight.

Everett takes a deep breath. "Here goes. When I was a sophomore in high school, I made a little mistake. Well, not little."

My heart hammers as I wonder. His hand is shaking as he speaks. I scoot closer toward him, and put my hand on top of his. It's cold.

"You made a little mistake," I reiterate.

"Except that it wasn't a mistake," he continues, nodding. "It happened about fifteen years ago now. Back in high school, I slept with someone I met from out of town. It was a one-night thing, and she got pregnant."

My heart clenches and I squeeze his hand. He squeezes back. I shift my body so I'm sitting yoga-style on the couch, looking at him.

"Wow. Talk about bad luck."

A twisted, slight grin pulls on his lips. "Isn't it ironic how that happens? I know couples who've been trying to have children for years. But when you're not trying, it can happen just like that." He snaps his fingers.

"Who was this girl?"

"She was the older sister of someone from our high school team, and somehow, one thing led to another at a house party . We found ourselves alone and drunk. I'd never had sex before that, and I guess I was still young and naïve and I didn't quite understand everything as it was happening. Out in Nebraska, if you were good at football you were damn near a celebrity in my small town. And I'd just played one hell of a football game."

"So you had unprotected sex with her? And I'm not judging you, by the way...it's just that that's so young."

"Yes, we did," he nods, then laughs. "Probably lasted all of two minutes because I was like fifteen."

His expression becomes more serious. Thunder claps outside, the grey light of the storm reflecting into his eyes. "She was older than me at the time, a freshman in college, and I knew through her younger brother that she told absolutely no one about the pregnancy. When she started to show later in the year, she dropped out of school for a semester. She moved to a town out west and lived by herself and had the baby."

"Oh. My. Gosh. And how old were you while this was happening? Sixteen?"

"Fifteen when we did it. Sixteen when I found out about the baby."

Chills rock through me. My heart feels like someone is grabbing it and twisting it as I put myself in Everett's place "Sixteen. What could you have done, though, even if you knew about the baby?"

"I might have moved to be with her, if I'd had any idea she was pregnant," he says. His voice is strained. "She got pregnant in September, had the baby the following year in June, then put her up for adoption."

My mouth is agape.

His eyes gloss over. I lean forward and interlock his fingers with mine. I can practically see his heart pounding so hard, it's making his shirt vibrate.

"So did she ever tell you about it?"

He nods. "She did. The following season, she happened to be back in town for our first game. I was a pretty good athlete, but she called me over before our first game of the season, and told me everything. I was so angry, Emma."

His grip on my hand tightens.

"At her?"

He shrugs. "How mad could I really be at her? It takes two to tango. Even though she was years older than me, I was no idiot. I knew the risks of unprotected sex. I tried to process what she was saying. I remember the moment like it was yesterday. We stood under the Friday night lights in our first game of my junior year, in late August. She said, 'I thought you should know. We have a child. It couldn't be anyone else's. Yes, I'm sure. I made sure she got adopted by a good family. Nice family from Chicago. Her name? It's Samantha.'"

My heart flutters, and breaks a little as I see the pain in

his eyes. I can't think of anything I could say that could comfort him, so I run my hand across his cheek.

"I was sixteen at the time, and obviously teenage boys aren't great at expressing emotions. I couldn't handle the stew of anger, disappointment, self-loathing, love for this Samantha, hate for myself for my recklessness. So I expressed my emotions the only way I knew how at the time. I snapped that night and ran for two-hundred-and-eighty-nine yards. A school record. I was growling at the opposing team members. Trying to run them down even when I had the ball. I wanted their blood. I wanted them to feel my pain. They were supposed to be trying to tackle *me*, but I was going after them on defense. Some of the footage from that game went viral, and I became known as the scariest running back in the state. Teams would have entire practices centered around how to stop me. But they didn't know my secret: I *wanted* the pain. I *wanted* them to hurt me."

My chest aches. "All because...you had just found out about Samantha."

He nods, and his hand rubs back and forth on the top of my thigh, over my jeans. "For the longest time, I suppressed, or maybe, channeled my emotions, into the game, and that worked. But in the end, I was avoiding the hard fact that I had a child out there whom I didn't get to see. I just laughed it off as one of the things that happens to some kids. But a couple of years ago, I went to a teammate's place for dinner, and he had a seven-year-old daughter named Samantha. I couldn't keep it together. I had to lie and say I had food poisoning, but really I went home, hung my head, and cried for everything that I never knew that I wanted."

My stomach knots. "Jesus."

"You probably think I'm weak or a coward."

"I think that it's not good to keep something like this bottled up for so long." Which is true, I've had my own secrets that I've shared, but nothing that could amount to this.

"After that encounter with the little girl named Samantha, I couldn't stop thinking about my role in all of this. But I couldn't very well tell anyone, either. I just *have* to know she's okay, Em. I have to see her."

He squeezes my thigh, and I grip his hand harder. A tear rolls down his cheek.

"So...where is she today?" I whisper.

"Well, the thing is, I can't legally look into where she's at. I had to hire an off-the-books detective, if you know what I mean. He costs big bucks, but he doesn't mind getting his hands dirty. He's also an expert at keeping things off the cops' radar. It's illegal for me to just jump back into my daughter's life. I can't just appear on her porch where she lives with her adopted parents and say, 'surprise! I'm your biological dad!' With me being a superstar, that only complicates matters. The press would *love* to get ahold of this story. They love airing out the dirty laundry of sports celebrities. And I don't give a shit about my reputation, but I can't stand thinking about the stress it would cause Samantha. She's just a teenage girl living her life. Who even knows if her family has told her she's adopted. Not to mention, if her family decided to sue, I have substantial assets they could obtain. So they'd be highly incentivized to do so."

"I see how that could get complicated — and ugly — very quickly."

"But, I couldn't resist. I needed to just *see her,* at the very least, you know? I was talking with some other athletes who have experience with adoption, and they told me it would be a fine idea to just get involved with the community at large, first, to dip my toes in the water. First, Gates only knew that Samantha was living with a family on the north side of the city. He had it narrowed down to a few, but he wasn't sure which it was. So, I would go to the area, get a hot dog, and write her a letter, never to send. The letters were just for me."

"The napkin letter." Everett's story is making me an emotional mess. I want to take care of him, heal his anxiety. I want to help fix it. Thinking about Pam and her loss oddly creeps into my mind, although totally different scenarios because someone in each case has lost something. And just like I wanted for Pam, too, I want to make Everett's pain all better. It's just my nature as a person. But something tells me when it comes to Everett, there's no simple fix for what he's going through.

"Exactly. But then a break-through. Detective Gates found out which summer camp Samantha was at, so I had to try it. And then as luck would have it, she was sick today. I guess it just wasn't meant to be."

He lets out a long exhale.

Strange relief pours through me that I know his secret.

Leaning forward, I kiss him on the cheek, and rub his shoulder. "Thanks for telling me. My lips are sealed. I hope you know that."

I feel my insides flip as I think about the next time I'm going to be interrogated by Cal and Rich. Now, I do know what they wanted me to investigate.

Obviously, though, I can't tell them this.

"I know that," he says. "I don't know why, Em, but I trust you totally. And another thing."

"What's that?"

"Thank you."

"For...?" I ask, perplexed.

"Well, for being you. I wasn't exactly nice to you from the outset. And thank you for making me realize that I've been holding on to this secret for so long that it's been eating me from the inside. I told a few other guys — local athlete friends of mine — who were adopted to ask for their advice on the matter, but you're the first person I'm telling simply to tell. And it feels like such a weight has been lifted."

Outside, the rain is really coming down now. He wraps his arm around me and I lean my head on his chest.

"Do you know why you feel better?"

"I guess it just feels good to not be so alone with a secret."

"Mind if I get a little geeky on you? I studied a little about this in psychology."

"By all means. Use that degree, Em."

He squeezes my shoulder, and I feel like his teddy bear.

"It's like this. The degree of your unhappiness is relative to the alignment of your subconscious and conscious mind. If you hold on to something at the subconscious level — like having a secret — you'll feel constantly stressed. But when you tell someone, you bring it up to the level of conscious thought."

Everett nods and takes a pull of his drink.

"You're a nerd, all right. But that does make sense."

"Guilty as charged."

"It's sexy when you talk that way."

I arch an eyebrow playfully. "Yeah? But does it make you want to read a psychology book?"

He grabs hold of my neck and leans in, his lips brushing against my ear. "No. But it makes me want to tell you some of the other thoughts I've been having about you at the subconscious level, so I can bring them up to the conscious level."

My body goes limp with desire. "Wait," I say, pulling back. "Everett, if you were having these thoughts..." The pained look he gives me completely stops me in my tracks.

"I was a complete mess this week. With the new information from Gates about Samantha, and the fact that it was a grueling week of practice. And I didn't know what to say to you."

"'Been a weird week, see you Friday,' would have been nice," I say.

"I screwed up. You're right. But I've done a lot of thinking, and I know what I want now."

I swallow a lump in my throat. "What do you want?"

"I want you, Emma," he growls, and kisses my lips softly.

22

EMMA

My body caves to him, and a surprising amount of relief pours through me as we make out on the couch. I run my hands all over Everett's body, and eventually they find their way under his shirt. A whiff of his musk causes the wetness to build inside me.

"Wait one second, though," he says, pulling back. I feel the weight of his stare on me. "I'm still not over you snooping in my office after I told you not to go in there. That was unacceptable."

"I was just curious about the Samantha note," I say, nerves kicking in again. He just poured his heart out to me, and I can't tell if he's being serious or not right now. "I hung onto that napkin, and I couldn't believe it was a coincidence that you called the name 'Samantha' during Red Rover."

He balls up my hair in a fist, and pulls my head back a little, exposing my neck. He likes that move. My eyes hood over as we make eye contact.

"I'm just disappointed you didn't talk to me first and tell me what you knew."

"Talk to you? I tried, Everett. It was like trying to get through to a rock."

His body presses against me, and he runs a hand up my body. Today I've got on a simple blue t-shirt with jeans.

When his hand finds its way under my clothes, onto my stomach, and eases under my bra.

"Speaking of rocks," he mutters, running his fingers roughly across my breasts. "Are your nipples always this hard?"

I force deep breaths in and out, need flaring inside me. "Don't change the subject, Everett."

He rocks my body onto the couch so he's on top of me, and kisses me while he fondles my breasts. I feel his thick hardness pressing into my leg, adding to the heat growing inside of me.

Dipping two fingers under my panties and on my flesh, he fixes his eyes on me.

"This subject's much better, don't you think? You sure you want to do this?" he says.

My face burns with desire, and, a little anger. "Yes, of course. Don't you realize that by now?"

"At the end of the day, Emma, I'm still your boss."

I wrap my hands around his back. The edges of my world blur, my fingers trembling.

"Is that a problem for you?" I ask him.

He drops his eyes to my nipples for a moment, then brings them back to me. "Honestly, Emma. I don't give a fuck who you are. I wanted you when you were the damn hot dog stand girl."

I almost come then and there.

He doesn't leave room for a response, instead kissing me again. I wrap my legs around him, my body shaking from the core.

His hand, which had teased me by dipping a few inches lower and arousing my sex even more than it already is, pulls back up and lands behind my neck.

After who knows how long of making out and dry-humping on the couch, we find ourselves up in his bedroom.

He drops me on the bed, I'm only in a bra and jeans at this point.

After pulling my jeans off, he stands at the side of the bed looking down on me.

"You know you're gorgeous. Right?" he says in a low, husky voice, then hovers over me on the bed and kisses me. "You know what an impossible task it's been to keep my hands off of you from day one as my assistant."

The ache between my legs begs for release.

Settling to my side, he runs a hand along my stomach, then wraps it around my bra to unhook it.

"Have you ever touched yourself while thinking of me?" he asks as he tosses my bra to the ground. His eyes stay locked on me as he drops his shorts, leaving only his boxer briefs, and *sweet Lord, I forgot how big that thing was.*

Getting back on the bed, he straddles my torso, licking and cupping my breasts, swirling his tongue around my nipples.

I arch my back, waves of pleasure racking through me.

He looks up. "That wasn't a rhetorical question."

"Two times this week," I manage to eek out.

His smirk turns more cocky and evil. "That's it. Tell me more."

"Once, I thought about us in the office," I admit.

His need for me only increases my desire for him. Repositioning himself between my legs, he pulls my panties off, and licks his lips like a hungry animal. He thumbs my clit and says, “I can’t wait to taste you.”

“Then do it, Everett, please,” I say.

“Oh? Who’s the boss now?”

When I say nothing, he arches an eyebrow. “Nothing to say?” he adds.

He tongues my clit ever so lightly, teasing me with the light pressure.

“I thought about you bending me over the — oh, God — desk.”

“Mmm,” he says, his voice low and husky. He’s finished teasing me, and now he presses his tongue fully into my opening, sucking on my clit.

I reach my hands behind me and hold onto the bars of the bed for balance. Then he adds his fingers — I can’t tell if it’s one or two, and honestly, what does it matter because I’m a slave to the sensation — and now I grip his head for fear that I might just float away.

He laps me up with his tongue, fucks me with his fingers, and I’m clawing his hair. The man seems insatiable, and it turns me on all the more. My body heats like a wild fire as he licks and sucks my clit.

“Yes,” he looks up at me and says, his face wet with my juices. “You taste fucking good, Em’.”

When his tongue touches me again, it’s too damn much. I come, my body trembling in his grasp.

Finally, after what seems like an eternity, he moves his face slightly up my body, kissing me on the stomach, then gets up.

Going to his dresser, he pulls out a pack of condoms, and lets his briefs down, then gets back into bed with me.

Opening the pack with his teeth, he holds a condom in one hand, kneeling at my side.

"Do you want to do the honors? Or should I?"

"I will," I say.

He's as hard as an oak tree, so it's not difficult to put on. I roll it down his length, as he almost groans in response to my touch, and he wastes no time in positioning himself between my legs.

He pauses for a moment, and my eyes dip to look at his cock as I lie on my back.

"What?" I say when he doesn't move for a few more seconds.

"I'm always going to remember this," he says, and without a second thought, he eases into me.

Before I can ask him *why* — not that this wouldn't be memorable — my eyes roll up in the back of my head.

Oh, yes.

Wow.

He lets out a low, guttural moan as he thrusts in and out, slowly at first, and then faster.

Putting his arms on either side of me, I grab hold of his biceps, everything in my body pulsating as he pushes in and out of me.

Interlocking his hands in mine, he presses them down behind my head.

His eyes stare into mine, and through my orgasmic haze, I mutter, "I'm so wet, Everett."

"Fuck, I know, Emma."

Gradually ratcheting up the intensity, he moves in and out of me deeper and faster. I wrap my legs around him, anchoring him inside me.

Our eyes lock together, and I swear he sees into the depths of my soul. When another orgasm comes crashing through me, he swallows up my moans with a deep kiss.

"Oh, God, Emma," he groans. "Fuck, you feel so damn good."

I clench around him as my orgasm reverberates, and the tightness of his hands intensifies as he buries himself inside me as he comes.

When he pulls out, takes off the condom and ties it off, then uses a towel to wipe a layer of sweat off of my body. It's a tender gesture.

He lays down next to me so I can cuddle on his chest.

"You worried?" I ask.

"Worried? Why would I be?"

"I don't know, you've fought so hard not to do that."

"I've decided that whatever happens between us, Em', happens. I like you a lot. It's not easy for me to let go, but with you, I feel like someone new."

I smile and hug him tighter. "I like you a lot, too."

"Tired?" he asks.

"No. You?"

The rain is still coming down outside, the sound very cathartic, almost hypnotic.

"Hey," I say, putting my hand on his naked leg. "That was amazing."

"I know."

I roll my eyes. "Oh, Everett the Grouch is gone and now we meet his alter-ego, Everett the Stud, right?"

"Can't help it. I mean, look at that thing." He glances at his dick.

I pull the sheet over us to get rid of the distractions. As much for him as for me.

"I know we just had sex, but I had something slightly serious I wanted to say."

His body stiffens, and he seems to brace himself. "Yeah?"

I thread my fingers through his hair. "Yeah. All that stuff

you told me...you've got to forgive yourself. It was over a decade ago. You're a new person now. I'm not saying to forget about Samantha, far from it. But it's out of your control at this point. You're right, you can't just randomly approach her in public or whatever.

His Adam's apple bobs in his throat. "I know. I have to let it go."

I tip his chin toward me. "Yes, you do. For your own sake, for her sake. Start living your life."

"I'm going to try," he says in a husky voice. "Damn, you know what? I care about you, Emma. A lot. I like what we're doing right now. Suffice it to say, I haven't been this intimate with someone in, well, it's been a while."

I swallow and nod. The words aren't much, but coming from a man like Everett — who barely issues compliments, let alone, heartfelt confessions — they mean a lot.

"When she's eighteen, she'll be able to contact you," I say, wanting to comfort him. I need to be careful with my words, because the truth is, we don't know if she'll contact him or not. But no matter the case, Everett needs to find a way to forgive himself for his past deeds about Samantha that he had no decision in making. "I know those four more years must seem like a lifetime. But you *will* be able to explain to her. You'll show her the letters you wrote. She might forgive you or she might not. You've beat yourself up so much already. You've got to let it go, Everett."

He grabs my forearm so lightly, and knowing how powerful he is on the field, I feel like I've tamed the beast, in a way.

"Let it go," he echoes. "I'll try. It's not easy, though."

"I know it's not."

He actually sniffles a bit, and wipes a tear away.

Leaning into me, his kiss feels so much more tender than any of the previous kisses.

"You're an amazing woman, Emma. How many men have told you that?"

My stomach knots, and now I'm the one with my eyes glossing over.

"Zero," I say, our foreheads knocking together.

He shakes his head. "No. Not zero. You're wrong."

"I'm wrong?"

He laughs. "Yes. You can't count very well. Because the answer is *one*. Me."

23

EMMA

"How do you like your eggs?" Everett asks me in his bathroom as he finishes toweling off and pulls on a pair of shorts.

We're both extra awake today, thanks to the hot and cold contrast shower he insisted we take to start off the day. And I may or may not hate him right now. That temperature change is not for me, even on my best days. But I will admit I feel more awake than usual after that jump start.

"So many options," I say, leaning over the sink and giving him a kiss. "I wasn't expecting you to cook this morning."

"Well. I am," he wiggles his eyebrows. "And you've got two options. Scrambled or sunny-side up. I can't do the over-easy flip. Too dangerous and my culinary skills end with the first two options."

As he starts to pull a white t-shirt over his head, I stop him "How about shirtless eggs?"

"Huh." He squints curiously at me. "I've not heard of those."

"Me neither. But that sounds perfect to me."

He brings me in for one more kiss. I throw on one of his obscenely large jerseys, reminding me of the coffee incident all over again.

Downstairs, Everett cooks some scrambled eggs and bacon, while I start the coffee.

"Want to eat on the deck outside?" I say. "The rainstorm last night really brought the temperature down, so it's nice out now."

Right as we've got our plates ready and we're about to eat, the doorbell rings incessantly, and we give it a good stare, not really sure who would be here this early.

"Who the hell...?" Everett squints toward the door, then sets his plate and coffee down.

When he opens the door, we're met with Jocko's smiling face.

"Brother! You didn't think I was going to miss the game this weekend, did you?"

Everett gives him a death stare, and then looks out at his car.

"How'd you get here so early?"

"I'm on Eastern time, bro," Jocko says, as if that explains everything about how he made a five-hour drive from Detroit to arrive here at nine a.m. "You know how much I hate wasting time in day-time traffic. I wanted to get some quality time with you if I could before practice today. Smells delicious in here, by the way."

Jocko steps in, and sees me.

"Uh-oh. Well, hello there, Miss Assistant Emma. I bet I know what you've been *assisting* with this morning."

Choosing to ignore his innuendo and opting for professional — well, as professional as I can be standing here in Everett's jersey, I reply, "Hi, Jocko. How are you?"

"Not as good as my big brother is, apparently." He glances between us. "Are you two...?"

"We'll be out on the deck, enjoying breakfast. Feel free to cook something up. And please, give me a heads up next time you're going to drop in like this. At least the night before."

"Oh, I texted you, bro. You must have been too busy to look at your phone." Jocko winks. "No big deal. I like my eggs over-easy anyway, and I know you can't do the flip."

I have to laugh as we head out to the patio to eat.

"As annoying as he kind of is, I sort of love how Jocko drops in to check on you," I say.

Everett nods. "There's a reason he's my mom's favorite. He's kind of the glue guy of the family."

"Glue guy?"

"Yeah. He keeps us together and connected."

"CLOSED a one-point-two-million-dollar deal for some desktop computers with the North Shore district last week," Jocko says. "High five, bro. And you, too, Emma."

We both high five Jocko, and Everett laughs a little.

"Shit, man, I haven't seen you with a smile on your face like that in *too* long. What's got you going? Is it the new season or the new girl?" His eyes drift over to me, and my stomach knots. "Are you two officially a thing yet, or just messing around at the fifty-yard line? Can I Snapchat this early morning hang? Or would that be too intimate?"

"Dude, slow down," Everett says. "I know you woke up at the crack of dawn and drove like five hours to get here, but we're still waking up. You're too intense, man."

"Sorry," Jocko says. "I shouldn't have had them put those extra shots of espresso in my Starbucks today."

"Or you could just give up coffee altogether," Everett adds.

"Like that's going to happen. So, Emma. All kidding aside," Jocko says. "How has working for my big bro been?"

"It was a rocky start, to be honest, but I'd say we're getting along now."

"Clearly," Jocko smirks, then clears his throat. "Sorry. That was low-hanging fruit, but fruit, nonetheless."

"It's okay. I kind of walked into that one."

"It's great to have her as my assistant," Everett chimes in. "I've got my hands full re-learning the playbook after taking last year off. I don't want to pull a Michael Jordan and *not* win it all in my comeback year."

"Oh, really? You think you can win it all this year?" Jocko asks.

"As long as our defense doesn't play too shitty, absolutely."

I chime in. "Yeah, well, you better watch out for Peyton O'Rourke. I have a feeling he's going to be on his game like never before this year."

Jocko puts his coffee down on the clear glass table in front of us. "Really, Emma, why do you say that?"

"He's got zero distractions. Maddy is obviously his dream girl. They're getting married next year. Make no mistake: behind every championship, there's a good woman keeping her man focused and stress-free."

"Damn," Jocko says. "I've never heard it put quite like that. You're almost making me want to settle down before age forty."

"Oh, yeah? Do you have any candidates in mind?" I ask.

Jocko puts one finger up. “Like I said, *almost*. But not quite.”

I bite into a delicious piece of bacon. Not too crispy, just the way I like it. I glance over at Everett, and his eyes are on me. I raise my eyebrows and lick my lips.

There’s a lull in the conversation — unusual with Jocko — and a cardinal flies in front of us and lands on a post.

Everett looks at his watch, then stands up.

“Well, I’ve got to get going. Practice starts soon.”

He gets up and heads into the house, closing the sliding door. One second later, I hear it open.

“Hey, Emma, would you come here for a sec? I have a quick question about some of that merchandise I forgot to ask you about.”

“Sure thing,” I say, standing up. “See you around at the game, Jocko.”

“Absolutely. I’ve got tickets to the VIP box if you want to come with me on Sunday.”

I shrug. “Maybe.”

Inside, I follow Everett to my office.

Seeing his bare back from the ‘shirtless eggs’ makes the ache between my legs return. So if I were looking down on us from the ceiling, that’s what he’d look like when he’s on top of me.

Once we’re in my office, he closes the door. I look at the boxes of jerseys in the corner of the room.

“What question did you have?” I ask.

“Did I sign all of these yet? I forget.” I squint at the jerseys. “Yes, you got all those. Unless you forgot some on the bottom.”

He examines them. “Hmm. Okay. Good.”

Turning around, he grabs hold of the jersey of his that I’m wearing. “What about this one?”

"Why would you sign this one? Are you planning on selling it?"

Knotting up the bottom of the jersey, he brings me in closer to him. "No. But I still think I should sign it."

"How do you want to sign it?" I breathe, staring at his lips.

"Oh, I don't know."

Before I can process what's happening, we're tearing off each other's clothing. He presses my body against the wall once we're disrobed and begins fingering me. I can't even breathe from the glorious invasion.

"You're already wet again," he observes.

"I don't think I've stopped being wet since yesterday."

Growling a kiss into me, he bunches up the blue and green jersey that says BREWER 29 on the back, spins me around, and bends me over my desk.

"Remind me again if this is how your fantasy went."

Before I know it, he buries himself inside me and I come so many times I lose count.

24

EVERETT

My coach pulls me aside after the next game. We don't win, but hey, it's still the preseason. I break off a few big runs before they take me out in the second half to give the backup a shot, just as our coach likes to do in the preseason.

"Everett, my boy," Coach Fontana says, calling me as I pass his office. "Come on in. Have a seat."

I do as he says. "Coach. How's everything going?"

"Perfect. Great. You looked fantastic out there. Even stronger than I thought you would after taking the year off."

"Well, I didn't miss a workout."

"Your running style is different now, though."

"Is it? I didn't notice." I answer carefully, not sure what his meaning is.

"Just last night I noticed it. Instead of going for the bulrush ahead, every time you injected just a little more finesse into your game. That's exactly what I want to see out of you. That's what I've been *trying* to get you to do for your entire career."

"Thanks, Coach. So I can expect a performance raise, then." I'm smiling so big, trying not to crack up laughing.

He laughs heartily. "Good one. Just whatever you're doing...keep it up."

When I get up, I can't help but connect the dots to mine and Emma's conversation on Friday.

As I walk through the locker room on the way out, I'm smiling, high fiving guys on the defense — which I never do — and just generally joking around with everyone.

"What's gotten into you?" Dyson asks me as we walk out together.

"What? I'm just having a good time. It was a good game."

"Dude, you *never* joke around with the defense. All you do is tell them how much they suck. What gives?"

"I'm trying out something new."

Plus, I feel like the weight I've been walking around with for fourteen years has been lifted.

Okay, Not fully lifted — I still haven't seen her. But after talking it out with Emma this weekend, I wonder if I need to focus on that anymore, and instead wait until she's an adult.

As I get in my car, I'm whistling to pop music. I call all four of my brothers, just to check in and see how they're doing, and they're all a little mystified at my initiating contact with them.

I feel a little like Scrooge at the end of *A Christmas Carol.*

I send Emma a text before I hit the road.

Everett: Can you stay over tonight?

Emma: Have to keep an eye on the baby tonight. My sister is due to pop any day so I sort of need to stay close.

Everett: Gotcha. Tomorrow?

Emma: Negative. I have to hurry home. My sister has night school.

Everett: Worst assistant, ever.

Emma: I'll make up for it the next time I can stay over, promise.

Everett: On another note, I'd like you to look into more charity appearances for me this coming year. Specifically, for foster care promotion and cancer patients who are kids.

Emma: Someone is having a moment! I can absolutely do that! People are going to be surprised, though!

Don't I know it, hell, I'm even surprising myself.

PRACTICE IS GRUELING THIS WEEK.

With opening day coming up next week, it's really crunch time now. No more messing around.

It had totally slipped my mind that I would be two hours away at the central Illinois training facility, so it's actually fine that Emma can't stay over.

I get back on Friday afternoon, and she helps me unload my car with the gear I've been keeping downstate.

"Feel good to be back home?" she asks.

"Definitely. I understand why they want to get the team out of the city for summer training camp, but I always feel like a little bit of a vagabond until I get back here."

There is a flicker of sadness in her eyes as she carries one of my bags into the living room.

We set them down, and I notice there's a heaviness about her.

"You okay?" I ask.

"What you said back there, about being a vagabond? Well, that sort of describes my life right now. My sister resents the fact that I'm invading her space, but she needs me to help with Eve at night, not to mention the baby who's on the way. A lot of my stuff is still in boxes at my storage facility. I still just feel like I don't have a home."

I wrap my arms around her waist. "That's not a good feeling."

"It's not. And I don't know what to do right now. She's been really passive aggressive around me lately, and I'm just trying to help. The nanny's there now, but she still needs me sometimes." Her eyes turn down. "Sorry for unloading on you."

She leans her head on my chest, and I can feel her beating heart against my stomach.

"You've got a lot on your plate right now. What do you think you're going to do? Move out?"

She shakes her head. "I just can't. As much as she keeps mentioning how she doesn't know where the baby is going to live when he's born, I know as soon as the baby is born, she's going to be in dire straits. Even with the part-time nanny I hired."

I furrow my brow.

"You hired a nanny?"

She shrugs. "I mean, I'm not doing this job for the company," she baits.

"Oh, how dare you," I say. She laughs wildly as I swing her around to the wall, and press my hips into her.

"One more thing before I forget," she coos.

"When you keep talking, you make it harder for me to kiss you."

"I know, but after I get this out I'll be able to concentrate more on your kisses."

"What is it?"

"She's been doing this thing for months now where she sneaks off at night, and I have no idea where she goes."

"How do you not know? I don't understand."

"She's just really shady about it, and I'm worried about her."

I kiss her neck, then an idea pops into my head. "What are you doing for dinner tonight?"

"Eating here?" she says.

I shake my head. "How about we eat at your sister's house today. I can break the ice a little. Maybe I'll ask her what she's into."

"Oh, so you're a private detective now? You're not the most charming man to be around. No offense. I mean, I like you, but you're a little broody."

"I can channel my inner Jocko charm. It just takes a little more work. Plus, I'm just curious to check out your place. If you'd want me to, that is."

She pauses, linking her hands behind my neck.

Hoping to sweeten the deal, I tell her, "I'll pick up some delicious food on the way. Do you like fried chicken?"

"Love it. She does, too."

"Perfect. There's this hole-in-the-wall chicken place on the south side of the city that I love." Emma's face still seems perplexed. "You're still thinking, though. What's on your mind?"

"Yes. I've been thinking about something this week. Can we keep things quiet? Between me and you, I mean. Whatever *this* is."

"I mean, I'm not planning on blabbing about this all over town. The only one who knows is Jocko and he knows I'd knock him out if he told someone about my private life." I pinch my eyebrows together. "You don't want people to know about us?"

The look on her face is all apologetic like, "It's not like, the end of the world, but I just would rather it not come out that I'm dating my boss. I'd like people to base their judgment of me on the work I do. If they know what we're up to..."

"I understand, totally. Got it," I say. "No non-work stuff from nine to five."

"Exactly."

"But you know, in your position, this is more of a twenty-four-hour gig. You're available at all times."

My hand slips slowly down her skirt. "It's a slippery slope, isn't it?"

THE SMELL of delicious fried chicken and biscuits fills the air as I sit down at the dinner table with Emma, Pam, and Evie.

"The first time Emma told me she was working for Everett Brewer, I almost didn't believe her. If I'm being honest."

Pam takes a big bite out of a chicken leg. Even Eve, who I find out hasn't had the greatest week, has a big smile on her face.

"Well, she is," I say. "She's really something else." I wink at Emma for effect. Her cheeks turn a ruddy hue.

Something else, alright. Let me tell you about how she sounds when she's bent over her office desk.

"I'd love to hear what makes her such a good assistant," Pam goes on. "It was quite the jump from her old job selling wieners."

I stifle a laugh. Not because it's funny that Emma *was* a wiener sales associate not more than a couple of months ago, but because of Emma's comments to me about her and Pam's relationship.

Maybe it's not funny, though, that even after just a few lines of dialogue, I've got their dynamic down as sisters. And

I can see why this makes Emma a little perturbed. When my older brother Duke used to make fun of me, we would simply fight it out. But that's not how the girls' world works.

"I actually bought a wiener from her at that old job," I say. "Best wiener I've had all year."

Pam snickers. "Yeah, I think everybody knows about that little sale. And for the record, I agree with you, Everett, about the tips. God knows I ain't got the money to be tipping every time I buy an empanada around the corner."

Pam reaches for a thigh in the fried chicken bucket. "Baby is hungry tonight!"

Emma feeds Eve a little more of her baby food, and gives me a nod that reminds me that we came here to get information.

"So, Pam, what do you like to do when you're not working, or taking care of Eve these days?"

"And going to school for nursing," she reminds me. "Although, I'm taking next semester off with the baby coming."

She puts the chicken on her plate for a moment and looks out the window. "Due date is Jack's birthday, coming up in a couple of weeks."

When she says that, it's like the air gets sucked out of the room. I feel a knot in my stomach. I look over at Eve, who has a big smile on her face, and Emma, who is dutifully feeding her as she sits in her high chair.

My skin prickles with the true realization of what Emma has been going through this past year. She's been playing nanny for her sister, who, while she isn't a bad person, clearly is broken up from her loss and takes it out on Emma from time to time.

A pang of guilt rises up inside me.

Emma's here, doing all this for her family, and meanwhile I'm just firing her for no reason...well, there was a reason, fear of someone getting close enough to find out my secret.

"Here comes the airplane," Emma says, spinning the spoon in the air until it gets to Eve's mouth.

Then, all of the sudden, an image of Samantha pops into my mind. I don't know what she looks like, so I suppose I see her in every baby I meet. Right now, Eve is looking a whole lot like I imagined she would, smiling and babbling and clueless.

Taking a deep breath, I remember what Emma and I settled on. *Let it go.*

And I do. I would have been, what, sixteen or seventeen when Samantha was around Eve's age anyway. I couldn't have been a father to her. Not the good kind, at least.

I clear my throat, redirecting my focus to the task at hand. "Can't believe it's only three more weeks. And you're stuck here. I mean, what do you do for fun?"

"Well, I do like to watch football. Especially when the Grizzlies are good. Are you going to be good this year?" Pam asks.

"We are."

"Well, your preseason didn't go so hot."

"Last year Peyton O'Rourke lost every game inn the preseason and then won the regular season. So that comparison is meaningless. Hey, how about this. I'll make sure you and Emma have VIP tickets to the games this year. Would you like that?"

"I'd love it! Wow, this is my lucky day! First a visit from Everett Brewer, and now free tickets? So lucky..."

The way she emphasizes the word *lucky* makes me wrinkle my forehead. "It's no big deal, really. I'm happy to do it."

She gets up and walks over to my side of the table and hugs me. "Thank you, thank you!"

"Em, do you hear this?"

Emma smiles. "I hear it. That's really cool."

"You have the coolest boss ever. He's so nice."

"He is now. I've tamed him," Emma bites out.

Pam gives me a surprised look.

"It's true," I say. "Totally domesticated. But that's just because Emma puts in so much work behind the scenes that I'm totally and completely relaxed."

"I know," Pam says. "She's been having to work every day. Which I don't like, but now that we've got the new nanny, I suppose it works out."

"You have a nanny? Like full time?" I ask, these questions are part of my plan.

Pam nods. "Just part time for now. Emma hired her."

Emma shrugs. "The late nights were getting to me, of having to come home and watch Eve after working all day." She's too humble to expand on the true rationale, and leaves unsaid the unspoken truth that she could never leave Pam in the lurch. She continues, "The nanny will be full time once I've saved up enough money. I'm kind of waiting until the new baby comes. That's when we'll really need her help."

A warm emotion comes over me as I look at Emma. No, it almost *bowls* me over like a bowling pin.

I thought Emma was gorgeous from the moment I saw her — yes, I even saw those pert little tits and hips through that ridiculous red and yellow Wade's Weiner Shack uniform she was wearing the first time. There was something written on her face that got me all riled up.

But now, my attraction to her has reached a whole new level. Not only is she my ultra-sexy assistant, not to mention great at logistics, but she's got a deep level of love for her family, as dysfunctional as they might be.

Maybe the more dysfunctional a family has, the more love they need.

"Well, this has been so much fun," Pam says, interrupting my train of thought. "But you know what? Since you two are here to watch Eve on this lucky night, I think I'm going to go out for a little drive."

My ears perk up. She's ready to pop at any minute with that baby, and she's just going for a *drive*?

"It's a lovely night," I say, playing dumb. "Where are you heading?"

"Oh, just out," she says as she takes a set of keys from the key rack. "So amazing to meet you, Everett. I look forward to going to your games." She comes over and gives Eve a smooch on the cheek. "Is Aunt Emma and Everett going to take care of you tonight? Yes, they are! Bye, Em! Thanks again."

With that, she walks out the door.

"See?" Emma says. "That was weird, right?"

I shake my head, baffled. "So weird." I look at Eve, who is starting to fall asleep, then glance at Emma. "Let's follow her."

"*Follow* her?"

"Yeah. Wouldn't be the first time."

She shifts guiltily in her seat. "What about Eve?"

"Can you put her car seat in my car?"

"I'll do it quickly."

"Alright. And let's roll. We're getting to the bottom of this mystery once and for all."

I carry Eve out to the car, and she sets Eve in it, in the backseat.

“That’s her car pulling out right now,” Emma says, pointing ahead.

Luckily she’s not making the fastest getaway, so when we pull onto the highway, we’ve got her in our sights.

“Do you think it was strange how she kept emphasizing the word ‘lucky’?” I ask.

“You noticed that, too?”

“Oh, yes. Makes me wonder...”

“Wonder what?”

“Nothing. I don’t want to say it out loud, and we’ll know soon enough. What do you think she’s up to?”

“I don’t think it’s drugs,” Emma responds. “She’s got her head screwed on enough not to do those when she’s pregnant.”

“Good.”

A few minutes later, she’s pulling off the expressway and heading toward Lake Michigan on the south side.

She pulls into the entrance of the parking lot of a big building, and Emma and I both nod together in recognition.

“The casino,” Emma says.

25

EVERETT

We walk into Southside Casino. It's a shady place. They have the only gambling license within the Chicago city limits, which they got through an underhanded deal with crooked politicians decades ago. Now, they attract a fair number of characters from the area.

It feels good to have solved this mystery, although the look on Emma's face doesn't seem relieved at all.

"She's *gambling?*" Emma says, seething. "Here I am, working my tail off, trying to make money, and she's frittering her money away!"

I'm about to respond when my phone rings. I reposition Eve — who is wearing baby earmuffs to lessen the noise inside the casino — in my arms and pull it out.

Jocko.

I answer.

"Where are you, you stinky S.O.B.?" he says. "I swung by the house at night this time, so you wouldn't get your panties all in a bunch."

"You're at my house right now?"

"Yes. I brought my key. Where are you? Are you out partying? Can I come?"

"It's a long story, but I'm at the Southside Casino."

"Bro, you're playing some games tonight? What are you playing?"

"Not playing anything. It's a long story."

"I'll drive down right now. See you soon."

"No, Jocko, seriously, we're—"

He hangs up, and I shake my head.

"Everything okay?" Emma asks.

Just like her to be asking if everything is okay with *me* when we just discovered her very pregnant sister has a secret penchant for casinos.

"Everything is fine. My brother Jocko is just crazy, that's all."

"He's something, alright. Maybe it's better if he stays single. Until he, you know, calms down."

I remember the night we went out together and his attractive coworker kept glancing furtively at him. Jocko, who is one of the biggest flirts I know, went out of his way *not* to flirt with her. A lightbulb goes off in my brain.

Is that a tell? Maybe he could be into this coworker of his...what's her name...Allie?

Eve makes a little stir still sleeping against my chest, and I notice Emma is smiling at me. "Jesus, you look cute with a baby," she says. "It's almost unfair."

I wiggle my eyebrows. "You looking to make some babies sometime soon? Because we'd have hot ones."

She rolls her eyes as we walk inside. "Oh, there she is!" she points.

I'm brought back to the task at hand when I see Emma's sister Pam sitting at the slot machine.

Emma blows out a loud exhale. "How should we do this?"

"I think we should just be straightforward."

"Good idea."

I don't know if Emma's heart is pounding, but my heart is, as we walk up to Pam. I'm not usually an amateur sleuth, and I have a bad feeling about this sister-to-sister confrontation.

"Hello, Pam," Emma says. Her voice sounds stern, like a teacher's.

Pam turns around, and her eyes practically bulge out of the side of her head.

"What are you *doing* here?"

"I think the better question is, what are *you* doing here?" Emma responds.

"You brought the *baby* here? How could you?"

"Eve is obviously in fine hands," Emma kicks in.

The two sisters stare each other down for a few moments. "So now would be a good time to fill me in on what's going on," Emma says. "A slot machine, really? We're trying to *save* money, not *lose* it!"

Pam pulls the slot, and her money shows as having gone down to zero.

She stands up slowly, hand on her belly, teary eyed.

"It was supposed to be my lucky night though," she cries.

"What? Lucky...night?" Emma asks.

"Yes! First, Everett Brewer shows up to my house with fried chicken, then he gives me free season tickets! Lucky things happen in threes, right? So, I figured tonight would be my lucky night."

Emma's expression softens. "Is this where you've been sneaking off to all this time?"

Pam nods, sniffles, and wipes a tear away from her cheek. "Yes. I…I didn't know how to tell you. At first it was just once. I won a little money here and I felt good. So I kept coming back. I haven't won too often lately, but I swear, the universe *has* to even things out for me. It has to! Because it's been pretty shitty to me so far."

Emma and I give each other a couple's look, that knowing look that says more than words ever could.

"Pam, why would the universe *have to* make up your losses to you? You know the house always wins, right? That's just math. It's how casinos stay in business."

As soon as I say the words I regret it.

"Jack *died*! Jack's dead, and I've got no one now. I've got to make it on my own. It's not *fair!*" Pam shrieks, and I realize we are making a bit of a scene. Eve stirs a little in my arms.

Emma takes hold of Pam's hands. "I know it's not fair. Life isn't fair sometimes. Well, a lot of times. But we're going to make it through the next few years, I swear. Okay? Look at me, Pam."

Pam is full-out bawling now. Emma hugs her as she cries into her arms.

Most of the people in the casino, if they haven't already stolen a look at us, is staring now. A casino manager walks over.

"Everything alright, here?" he says.

"It's fine," I say. "Just some sisterly love happening right now."

"Holy shit, you're Everett Brewer," he says.

"Dude, not in front of the baby," I say, pointing to Eve.

"Oh. Sh…I mean, *shoot*. My bad."

"Like I said, we're fine. We were just heading out, anyway. Pam, Emma, let's head out. We can talk more back at your place."

Pam is saying something in a whisper to Emma, whose face has changed to one of utter concern.

"Everything okay?" I ask.

They both turn their heads toward me.

"I think my water just broke," Pam says, clutching her belly.

Oh, baby.

"DRIVE FASTER, Everett, seriously! How far is the hospital?"

"We're getting there safely. We've got two babies on board now, people! Two!"

My phone rings. It's Jocko again.

"What?!" I yell into the speakerphone as soon as I pick it up.

"Uh, geez, man, you okay?" Jocko says.

"No! Not okay. Emma's sister is having a baby."

"Oh, yeah? Where is she?"

"She's in my car."

"She's having the baby in your car?"

"No, we're driving to the hospital. Look, I can't talk now."

"Which hospital are you going to?"

"Mount of Mary."

"I'm almost to the casino. I'll reroute. See you soon."

Some nights, Jocko's behavior drives me absolutely insane.

But on a night like tonight? I'm happy to have some backup with all the craziness going on.

We pull into the hospital a few minutes later, and Emma helps Pam out of the car while I go park with Eve. She's still asleep, and I bring her into the hospital on my chest.

In the lobby, I run into a huffing Jocko.

"What did I miss? Was the baby born yet?"

"Since when are you into births?"

"Are you serious? Births are the most beautiful thing in the world. I'm here to support you, Emma, and, what's her sister's name again?"

"Pam."

I've filled Jocko in on the backstory for Emma, and how she's been dealing with a lot behind the scenes of her personal life this past year. Somewhat ironically, for a lifelong bachelor, Jocko tell me again that he loves when babies are born. Go figure.

I wonder to myself if maybe that whole bachelor-until-forty thing could change, if he met the right woman.

"Pam," Jocko says. "Sounds like a beautiful name. Does she need help?"

I furrow my brow. "Like what kind of help?"

He shrugs. "I don't know. A shot of whisky, a Pop-Tart, a hand to hold?"

"Do you know anything about how babies are born?"

"Do you?" he fires back.

I choose not to tell Jocko that, *yes,* when I was sixteen and found out I was a father, I obsessively raked through the depths of YouTube and found out more than most young men know about how a baby is born.

My phone buzzes. "Emma just texted me. We've got the room number. Come on."

We head into the room, and we're met with the doctor.

"The baby is crowning. Do you know what that means, sir?"

Emma and I stand off to the side in the room, comforting Eve, who has finally woken up amidst all the commotion. The midwife looks at Jocko.

"Uh, me?"

"Yes, you. With the face. Come on, hold her hand, will you?"

"No problem."

"What's your name?" Pam asks looking at Jocko.

Emma and I sit on the chairs in the delivery room, watching a wide-eyed Jocko interact with Pam. For an avowed bachelor, he actually seems more interested by what is happening in a delivery room than shocked.

"Jocko," Jocko says.

"Jocko..." Pam repeats, and grabs Jocko's hand and squeezes. "It's an odd name."

"Yep. I'm pretty sure my parents were angry when they named me."

"And...a beautiful...oh, wow. Here we go!" Pam says.

I wrap my arm around Emma, and we look on at the scene happening between Jocko and Pam.

"You know, I'm actually glad he's here. Does he know what he's getting into?"

We look over at Jocko, who is cheering like he's at a sports event. "Push! Do it! You got this, Pam!"

"Sir, please," the doctor says. "Just hold her hand and maybe her leg when she starts to push."

"My bad, Doc."

"I don't know about you, but I think this is a Snapchat moment, don't you, Jocko?" I say to him with a shit-eating grin on my face.

"Not a chance, bro, not a fucking chance."

MANY HOURS, and much hand-holding later, the baby is born.

"What are you going to name him?" Emma asks.

She looks over at my brother. "You know, I didn't like the name 'Jocko' at first, but it really grew on me."

Emma's eyes practically pop out of her head. "You're naming him *Jocko?* Are you *sure?*"

Even Jocko, who has a high threshold for being shocked, is speechless.

Pam smiles and cradles the baby. "I'm just kidding. Jackson. After his father, of course."

A wave of relief rolls through all of us, even Jocko.

Emma and I make impromptu eye contact, and I lean in and kiss her.

Pam's jaw drops.

"Wait. Are you two..."

Fuck.

I totally forgot Emma didn't want anyone to know we were a *thing*.

I just looked at her parted lips and it felt so natural to kiss her in this moment, as she held Eve.

With all the eyes on me, my phone buzzes.

Detective Gates.

Why is he calling me at five in the morning?

"I've got to take this," I say. "Give me one second."

I head out into the hallway and pick up my phone.

"Do you ever sleep?"

"Sleep is for sissies," Gates says.

"Seriously. Why are you calling me at this hour?"

"Are you sitting down?"

"No."

"Well, you should be."

"You know, I've been thinking. I've kind of come to terms with the fact that I'm not going to see Samantha unless *she* wants to see me. I don't know what you've dug up, but I'd like to call off the investigation."

Gates blows out a deep sigh. "What if I told you that you might not get that chance?"

"Go on."

He tells me the news that warranted a phone call at 5 a.m.

My veins turn to ice.

26

EMMA

The week after the baby is born, I'm basically my *sister's* personal assistant.

Which I don't mind. After having a baby, I'll give her a grace period.

And on the bright side, we called our little spat of secrets even, her hiding her gambling secret and me dating my boss.

But a new problem arises this week, and I'm so distracted with texts and calls that I don't notice it until Thursday.

I'm having déjà vu feeling of that week Everett couldn't pick up his phone.

No calls.

No texts.

No communication.

Which all makes no sense, considering the tender moments we shared the day Jackson was born.

But after a week of no communicado from my boss, I'm walking around with a lump in my stomach. Of course, he's also extremely busy this week, so that's probably the reason.

And we haven't had the talk as a couple to determine how often we will call each other, or something like that.

But something eats away at me, and I'm not quite sure why.

Football Sunday, week two, for the Grizzlies is a home game in Chicago. The next couple of weeks will be away. But I decide to take advantage of the VIP booth tickets I have. Jocko is going to today's game as well. My sister feels like staying at home. I feel bad for leaving her, but it's only a three-hour game — well, four with commute — and it's not like she's a first-time mom. She knows what she needs to do for the kids.

Plus, I haven't seen Cal and Rich in a few weeks, and they've been sending me a litany of texts to come meet with them and discuss Everett.

I've been putting them off the scent for two reasons. One, I really *have* been busy. There's not much more distracting than your only sister having a baby.

And two, I don't know what I'll tell them. I know they have suspicions of Everett's off-the-wall, other times depression-like behavior after his year of not playing, but the fact is, he's been worrying about his *daughter*. That explains the psychological symptoms he's been exuding this past year and long before.

And now that his game has changed, he has changed, why would they need to know any of this anyway. I'm not going to tell them. Not that I ever intended to in the first place. But now, my mind is made up more than ever. I'd rather lose my job than narc on Everett. If he decides to go public with his child, it's his decision, not mine.

~

I REMEMBER the very first sporting event of any kind my mom took my sister and me to, when I was a freshman in high school and we just moved to Chicago. We sat in the "nosebleed" section of a White Sox game, and Pam and I remarked we were so high up, the players almost looked like little ants below.

"We're so high up so the rich people can have their luxury boxes," she said, pointing to the thirty-or-so-feet high, tinted-glass windows that separated our upper deck seats and the regular box seats on the field level.

That stuck in my mind, and I always felt a little angry whenever I would go to a sporting event and note the VIP suites.

And today, that is my life.

Jocko and I file in to the owner's suite so we can watch the noon Grizzlies game, and I'm absolutely stunned at the luxury of the place. There is a full bar, restaurant, and hors d'oeuvres servers walking around like it's a wedding. Not to mention the fact that the game, which is right in front of us, is being broadcast from a solid hundred or so large-screen televisions throughout the place.

Jocko and I each get a drink and find a spot where we can see the game. At least the windows are open on this fine September afternoon. I note that there are a lot of people who are simply watching the game, on TV, at the bar, any of the countless places that they can see the plays except for watching the field.

Why even come to the game in the first place? I think.

The Grizzlies start with the ball, and it's evident from the start their main game plan: hand the ball to Everett. See Everett run.

And run he does.

He seems especially fired up today, and he's definitely

using his technique of 'run straight into the defensive line and try to kill them.'

It seems to be working well, because by halftime, the Grizzlies are up 21-14 and Everett's broken two long touchdown runs.

At halftime, Cal and Rich approach us, along with another man in glasses and a suit.

"Miss Foster. Good to see you. And you, Jocko," Cal says.

"My good sirs," Jocko says, shaking all of their hands.

Somehow, I'm not surprised Jocko has already met the owners. It's just the type of person he is.

"Miss Foster, we had some business to discuss with you," Rich says, and I follow his lead into a sort of personal, private suite. They close the windows so we're shielded from anyone who might eavesdrop.

"What's going on?" Rich asks.

I shrug. "Nothing much. Sister had a baby last week. How about you?"

They still don't introduce the man in the suit.

"We don't mean to be rude, Miss Foster," Rich goes on, "but we're not here to exchange pleasantries. We mean with our updates. You've obviously been avoiding us."

I try not to show my nervousness at the fact that they're exactly right.

"Honestly, there hasn't been any updates."

Cal crosses his arms and leans in. He's always seemed like a nice guy since we met, and the scowl on his face is foreign.

"Miss Foster, when we *hired* you for this job, we made clear our expectations of *weekly updates* about the person in question. This is non-negotiable."

"I'm sorry about that. What do you want to know?"

Cal and Rich both look to the man in the suit.

"Hi, by the way," I say, waving at him.

"Hi," he says, in as unfriendly a tone as possible. I reach a hand out to shake and he doesn't take it.

"So you've noticed nothing strange about Everett's behind-the-scenes behavior?"

I shrug. "What would be strange?"

"Is he ever unreasonable? Go into rages?"

I hesitate. "He's not exactly a happy-go-lucky guy, but I wouldn't call him a rageful person, no."

The man in the suit nods. "Have you ever seen this man at Everett's house?"

He pulls up a picture of a muscular man who appears to be in his forties or so.

I do recognize him as the body-builder, very muscular man who was at Everett's house one morning.

"Ah. Yes," I say. "He came by the house one time, and I saw him as I was leaving. Really built, muscular guy."

My answer makes the man in the suit's eyebrow tick up. "Really? Interesting."

"What's so interesting about that? By the way, what's your name?"

"His name is not important," Rich says. "But, good work. Wow, we weren't expecting him."

"Who *is* that man?"

"Why don't you ask Everett?" Cal frowns. "Alright. You can take off. Enjoy the game."

As I leave, I hear the three men having a conversation in hushed voices.

"What was that about?" Jocko asks when I'm back.

"Just had to take care of some PA stuff."

"I see they brought in the league investigator. There's not anything wrong, is there?"

"League investigator?"

"Yeah. The guy in the suit. I saw him in the news last year. Some players were gambling on the games, and he got them banned for life from ever playing in the NFL again."

"Oh. wow."

My stomach twists up in a knot.

"You *sure* everything's okay?"

"More than okay," I say. "Tip top."

THE GRIZZLIES WIN the game 42-37, and it's another superhuman performance by Everett that seals it. Jocko heads home — five-hour drive back to Detroit and all.

I show my PA pass and then wait in the players' tunnel for them to leave the locker room, my heart pounding.

Something is definitely up with the league investigator and that muscled guy they wanted me to identify, and since Everett is not returning any of my texts, I need to get the word to him in person and make sure he understands the magnitude of the situation.

After waiting for some time, Dyson walks by and says hello.

"Everett in there?" I ask.

"Yes. He's inside. Man, something's up with him, though."

"Why do you say that?"

"He took the longest shower I've ever seen a man take in my entire career. Now he's just sitting in his towel, staring at his locker."

"Any idea what's the matter?"

"No idea, but that performance he just made on the field was MVP caliber, so I don't know what he's got to be sad about. We *never* beat Green Bay. And we actually won today, so most of the team is happy as hell. I'm going to see Rachel right now. Gonna celebrate," he winks. "Congratulations to your sister on the baby, by the way. Rachel told me."

"Thanks. And, hey, do you think it's okay if I go in the locker room?"

Dyson furrows his brow. "I guess so. I can let you in. I've got my key card. Just be prepared to see players' junk, you've been warned."

Dyson flashes his card and I head inside as I chuckle.

The lights are dimmer than I thought they'd be, maybe because it's more than two hours past the conclusion of the game and most of the players have gone home. In fact, I don't hear a peep of movement.

Everett is in the corner, sitting on a bench with a white towel wrapped around his waist. Just like Dyson said, he's staring straight ahead at his locker.

I approach him slowly, almost feeling like I'm interrupting him from what, I don't know.

Finally, I put my hand on his shoulder.

"Hi, Boss."

He jumps up, spins around, and grabs hold of my hand, then exhales loudly.

"Oh. It's you."

"Who did you think it was?"

"I didn't think anything. I can't think right now."

"What's going on with you?"

He looks away from me for a moment, then levels me with his gaze.

"How's the new baby?"

"Are we going to play the 'avoid Emma's questions' game today? Because I'm not in the mood for that. I asked you something first."

Stepping toward me, he caresses my cheek with the back of his hand.

"You look beautiful. Thanks for coming today."

"Of course. That was quite a game. Where have you been all week, though? Phone broken?"

He looks away again. "Sorry about that."

"What is going on with you, Everett? One day you're spilling out the secrets of your soul, and the next you can't even answer a simple text?"

The words sputter out of me clumsily, and I'm a little embarrassed at their neediness. I try to refocus, remembering the purpose I came down here with: to come clean.

To let him know, once and for all, that Cal and Rich hired me because they thought I could report back to them.

And I don't know what they've got on him, or why they would try to get their own player in trouble, but after my encounter with the league investigator, I have a feeling time is not on my side when it comes to this confession.

"I've had a lot on my mind this week," he grits out. "And I knew you had the baby to deal with. I didn't want to burden you."

His hand runs down the side of my summer dress.

"You're not *burdening* me, Everett. I'm happy to take care of you. You should know that by now."

A silent tension envelops both of us. His face moves inches from mine, hovering over my lips.

"What's on your mind?" I ask, seeing a clear sadness in his eyes.

He responds by kissing me, gently at first, then ravenously.

Soon, my body makes a thud as it presses into the locker behind me.

"Someone could come," I say. "We can't do this here."

He shakes his head. “Everyone’s gone.”

“Are you sure?”

My hand runs down his abs, settling on the base of his cock. His towel drops to the ground.

We make out like that against the lockers, him naked, and when I look in the mirror behind us, I see our reflection. My cheeks glow red as he kisses my neck, and his ass looks magnificently impressive as he grinds against me.

“I need you now,” Everett growls. “I fucking need you, Emma.”

There’s an urgency in his voice I’ve never heard before, and it shoots me over the edge. Heat pools between my legs, begging for release.

“I need you, too,” I whisper.

My dress comes up over my shoulders, and my panties come down. His hard tip rubs against my opening, causing my entire body to shudder from tip to toe.

His raw skin feels so deliciously pleasureful against me, and I ache to know what he’d feel like all the way inside me like that.

Luckily, Everett has enough sense to reach inside his locker and grab a condom out of his wallet.

He lifts my body up by my hips, and I guide his sheathed cock inside me. God, the man is strong, holding me up like I weigh nothing but a feather.

I’ve seen this position in movie love scenes, and I never thought it would be doable in real life. But here I am, feet wrapped around Everett’s waist, arms around his neck, biting his shoulder as he buries himself inside me. The lockers make a loud noise that reverberates with every one of his thrusts — and fortunately, it sounds much louder, but doesn’t hurt.

I clench around him and I moan and shudder as I come

the first time. Everett growls as I grip him, surely feeling the pressure. His thrusts turn more intense, and the pleasure I'm feeling rachets up again.

"Yes, Everett, yes. Like that."

He slows his thrusts, and I wonder if he came as he gently lets me down onto the ground.

But he kisses me intensely and growls, "Turn around."

I do, pressing my forearm into the locker, and he slides into me slowly from behind.

"Oh...Everett," I moan.

"Fuck, Emma. You feel so damn good."

He kisses me on the throat, then the lips. "All mine," he whispers, his voice husky in my ear.

"Yes. Yours."

His thrusts intensify, and I'm whisked away to a land far away.

Heaven on Earth?

He feels so powerful taking me from behind, my toes curl and my torso trembles with pleasure. I have to get in rhythm with him and press my upper body hard into the locker so he doesn't push me forward with each thrust.

He slaps my ass lightly, then runs his hands over my hair, tugging a little.

I've been trying to be quiet since we're in the locker room, but I can't help the next, very loud moan that escapes my mouth.

"Coming. Again," I mutter, and I think that sends Everett over the edge, too. He holds deep inside me and mutters some unintelligible nothings into my ear as I squeeze him, feeling the sensations.

When we're done, he caresses my body from the hips up, pressing his back into mine. We're almost cuddling in a standing position. With him still inside me.

He pulls out, ties off the condom and tosses it out, then wraps me up in his arms and makes out with me.

"I needed that," he says. "I needed you."

"I'm here for you, Everett." I brush his now-sweaty hair back on his head. "But there's something I need to tell you. I've been holding it for a while."

He brushes my hair back in the same way.

"No. I think I'd better tell you why I've been acting so off this week first."

My stomach clenches. I really want to get this whole thing off my chest about the circumstances under which Rich and Cal hired me.

As a spy, essentially.

But his eyes are so full of deep pain, I let him go first.

He pulls on his boxers, and then a pair of athletic shorts. I follow suit and put on my dress and panties.

"What is it?"

"It's about Samantha. I got a call from Gates last week, the morning after Pam's baby was born, actually."

"Okay. There's an update? Everything okay?"

Everett shakes his head, and his eyes gloss over.

"It's not okay at all. Samantha..." A tear rolls down his cheek. "She has cancer."

27

EVERETT

Emma blinks several times in succession. She doesn't believe it. Kind of like I didn't, at first.

"Samantha is fourteen, and she has...cancer," she repeats.

I swallow and nod grimly. "Leukemia. She's been recently diagnosed."

"Oh, my God, Everett. I'm so sorry."

I wrap Emma up in a tight hug, and never has it felt so good to have her warm body pressed against mine.

"After the past month or so, I've finally started to calm down and accept that she's probably happy. After Gates told me this news, I've been so angry all week. Worst of all, I was back to square one of not knowing how to direct my anger."

Emma stares directly into my eyes, and squeezes me a little harder.

"That's why I've been so out of it this last week," I continue. "I knew you were dealing with the baby. I typed out — and deleted — several texts to you. But I didn't want to bug you with what you were already dealing with."

"You're not *bugging* me," Emma emphasizes. "I want to be there for you. Let me be there."

"I'll try. I'm just used to dealing with this shit in my own way for so long."

A heavy tension hangs in the air as she processes what I'm saying. Finally, she says "What can I do to help?"

"Well, here's the thing. I just want to make sure she's getting the attention she deserves. I can make an appearance at the children's hospital this week, and I'll just go around to all of the different rooms. If the parents happen to be there, we'll play it off like a total coincidence. But I need to see her, Emma. I can't go on like this."

She cups my cheek, and squints at me. "Is this why you played so crazy today?"

"What do you mean?"

"You're back to your old ways of channeling your anger into the game. I thought you had added some finesse to your game like you did in the preseason, but you're back to your mow-them-all-down way of playing."

"You didn't really think I was going to stop that, did you?"

A door thuds shut in the locker room, and Emma and I stare at each other wide-eyed, mouths agape.

"Oh, hey, Coach," I say nonchalantly to Coach Fontana, who is whistling as he walks out the door with a clipboard.

I give him a *we definitely didn't just bang in the locker room* look.

He smiles, then takes an earbud out of his ear. "You say something, Brewer?"

"Yeah, I was just saying hello. Didn't know you were still here. Didn't know anyone was still here, matter of fact."

Also, I really hope those earbuds make it hard for him to hear other sounds, but I don't say that out loud.

Coach Fontana shrugs. "Oh, yeah. Of course, I'm still here. Good game today. See you at practice tomorrow. Hey there, Emma."

She offers a wave. "Hey, Coach Fontana."

He looks between us for a few moments, then winks. "Have a nice night, you two. Stay out of trouble."

When we hear the door shut, she turns to me. "Do you think he...heard us?"

I shrug. "If he did, I bet he liked it."

THURSDAY EVENING, I take Emma out to a nice dinner, and afterward we head to the children's hospital on the north side of the city. She planned the entire visit from start to finish.

We're met with surprise by the people in charge at the hospital.

"Mr. Brewer, we're so grateful that you chose our hospital to be involved with for community service."

"I'm so glad I could help in any way."

One lady at the desk says something under her breath, and the others laugh. When I insist she tells me what's so funny, she says, "I just had this image of you in my head as the 'no tips' guy."

I look at Emma, whom they apparently don't recognize from the video. "I probably deserve that, but this leopard has changed his spots," I say, and we pass through into the first wing of the hospital.

It's as depressing as it is uplifting. Seeing children who have the ability to laugh in spite of terminal illness, coming to terms with their fates without fear, provokes a mix of emotions from deep within me.

I'm a superstar to these kids; there's no denying that. Jaws drop and eyes pop out of their sockets as I roll through the cancer ward. We also visit some children who are permanently crippled. I shake hands and try to keep a smile on my face as we talk to the little ones. A few kids crack me up, asking me why I run so crazy.

It's especially moving when we're talking to some of the kids in wheelchairs who look at my ability, not only to play football, but simply to walk, as a superhero power of some kind.

On the one hand, it makes all of the problems I've had seem so insignificant. Here I am, held back by this secret I've been holding onto forever.

On the other hand, I can't help but feel partially responsible for shaping the fate of my daughter.

Do I even have the right to call her that?

I don't.

Before we head up to the third floor where Samantha is, Emma and I go outside to the park next door to get some air.

"Jesus," I say. "This is nerve-wracking. Also makes me so damn grateful for every day."

I look around, and there's no one watching, so I steal a kiss from her, then pull back.

"Checking for something?"

"You never know when the paparazzi could pop up."

"Fortunately, it's one of the good things about you being such a curmudgeon through the beginning of your career. People would never expect you to visit someplace like this."

I take Emma's hand and hold it. "I have to thank you. Because I don't know if I would have been able to come here alone."

"Stop," she says, waving her hand in the air. "You would have made it here."

"Em, I can run a football all day without physical fear of being hurt. When it comes to stuff like this, I'm scared shitless. I've got to walk in there right now, see my daughter for the first time while she has cancer, and pretend like I don't know her."

She puts a hand on my shoulder and massages it a little. "It's going to be fine. We couldn't control this. This isn't your fault. It's just...the randomness of nature."

I clench my fists. "Sometimes, I wonder if it *could be* my fault."

She pinches her eyebrows. "How could it be your fault?"

"I've been doing a lot of research this past week. Obsessive, obscene amounts of research. I read this academic paper—"

Her eyebrows raise. "You did some reading? I thought you didn't read."

I shoot her a death glare.

"Sorry," she says. "Bad timing. Go on."

"Point is, have you ever heard of psychosomatic cancer?"

"I studied all about psychosomatic illnesses in college. That's when a physical disease is brought on, or made worse, by psychological stress and anxiety. Kind of like how you were so stressed over your secret, you found it hard to sleep."

"Right. So, what if Samantha found out she was adopted and it caused her a great deal of psychological stress? That's *my fault*. It's all my fault. I should have figured out a way to keep her. I should have been more communicative with that girl and we could have been a family to her."

She puts her hand on my knee. "I suppose it's within the realm of possibility, but it's incredibly unlikely. No one really knows how some people get leukemia. You can't go on blaming yourself like this, Everett. Especially for something that you don't even know is true. We'll never know how much psychological factors played into her cancer. For all you know, her mom's side of the family could have leukemia in their medical history. Plus, she might still have no idea she's adopted."

I breath a heavy sigh. "Maybe. Fuck, I don't know."

"Come on. Let's go see her," she says, standing up.

I stay frozen to the bench for a few moments, my heart pounding. Finally, I get up.

"Let's do it."

"Can't be worse than your contrast showers," she says, trying to lighten the mood.

"I beg to differ."

My heart is a steel drum as we head up to the third floor, to the room where we know Samantha is located. Part of me wants to turn back. Part of me wishes my first time meeting her wasn't like this.

But it has to be.

I take a deep breath and enter the room with a smile on my face, hand on the small of Emma's back.

She's lying in her bed, watching sports.

"Hi, there! This is my friend, Emma."

"Hi!" Emma says, waving to Samantha.

"And I'm Everett—"

"I know who you are," she says.

Oh, boy.

This is one permutation I was not expecting: her parents already told her I'm her father?

I gulp and take a moment to look her over. She's pale,

her skin lacking the typical hue of a bright young teen. Still, her smile is broad and her brown eyes sparkle.

"Do you?" I gulp, then clear my throat.

I'm at a loss for words as I realize she's got *my* brown eyes.

Houston, we may be in over my head.

"Yeah," she grins. "I love to watch football, and you're my favorite. My dad says I shouldn't watch you because you're mean, though. But I still watch you."

"Oh, well, thanks. Your dad sounds like a very smart man."

"So you *are* mean?"

"Well, sometimes I am."

"Some of my girlfriends say I shouldn't watch football because it's not for girls. But I still like to watch it."

I walk around to the side of her bed and take a seat.

Yes, a seat is good.

I'm so wracked with a mix of strong emotions right now, I'm worried that if I'm standing, I might just fall over.

Plus, I don't even know what to say to her. It's like all of the basic conversation skills I've learned throughout my whole life have been thrown out the window.

"So, what do you like to do?" I ask.

"I like to play flag football. I used to play at camp, but since I got sick, I can't go. I heard you came to my camp a few weeks ago. That was the first day I got sick. I was so sad I missed it. They told me you played Red Rover with the kids." She giggles. "And you called my name. Samantha. That's the leader's name, too."

It's her laugh that sends me over the edge. I've got to turn away. I gesture for Emma to toss me a jersey so I can sign it on the table closest to the window. I don't want Samantha to see her favorite superstar wiping away tears.

Not to mention her biological father.

"So, Samantha, what kind of music do you like?" Emma asks, noticing that I'm a little preoccupied.

"I like Katy Perry and Ed Sheeran and Justin Bieber," she says. "I also like this new country-rap song."

Emma laughs. "I've heard that one, too."

After signing two jerseys, I turn around and hand them to her.

"Samantha, here's two jerseys. One for you and one for a friend."

I hold them out so she can see.

"You know what's funny? Twenty-nine has always been my favorite number. Even when I was little."

"Funny how that works. So what are you doing about school while you're here?"

She shakes her head. "I'll be taking some time off to do chemotherapy. They don't know how long it will last. I'll be doing my homework here, though. I think my parents are going to drop it off."

"That's good. Everyone's taking care of you, then?"

She nods. "Yes. My mom and dad are coming tonight with some more books for me, I think."

My heart skips a beat. I really do not want to have to run into her parents, impromptu. It's enough that they're going to see her signed jersey and will know I was here. And they know I'm the father.

"What's your favorite book, Samantha?" Emma asks.

"Mmm...probably *Harry Potter,* or this new witch series." She says the name of the series and it's something funny that I don't remember. Emma shoots me a look.

"I haven't heard of that one," I say. "But I'll have to read it soon."

"You should! It's amazing."

Emma taps her watch.

"Well, they kick everyone out of here who isn't family at eight, so we should go."

"If you want, you can stay and watch Thursday night football with me. It's just starting. It's okay. I won't tell if you don't."

"That sounds like a fantastic idea. I'm going to head down to the cafeteria and get some water. Do you two need anything?"

I shake my head, and so does Samantha.

She puts the game on, and of course it's Peyton O'Rourke playing tonight. He is looking sharp this season. It's only week three, and the announcers are talking about his MVP-worthy performance.

Not if I have anything to say about it, though.

We watch the game in silence for ten minutes or so, until she says, "Hey, Everett, would you hold my hand?"

My palms begin to sweat more than any first date, more than any big game I've played in my life.

"Sure," I croak out.

"I sometimes get a little lonely here," she says. "My parents stayed for the first week, but I also have a little sister, and she sleeps at home."

I slip my hand into hers, and we watch the game for an hour. I ask her questions about the players and she tells me so many things about the game, it makes me wonder if I could have passed down my interest in the game genetically.

"I want to be a football player someday," she says, gauging my reaction.

I'm surprised, and I don't say anything.

It's not that I want to limit her.

But hell, I had to fight my own mother every step of the way to play football. Even as a rowdy young man, it was dangerous. And what with all the drama coming out about concussions...

"It's a dangerous sport," I say. "Do you like dangerous things?"

She laughs. "Just kidding! I don't want to play."

A whoosh of relief surges through me.

"But I would love to be a football news anchor," she says. "George at school says girls can't be football anchors, though, because they don't know how to play."

A feral anger rises up in me, and I squeeze her hand a little.

"Ow," she says.

"Oh, sorry," I say, loosening my grip. All of a sudden, I picture some fourteen-year-old playground kid who I will teach a thing or two.

"Well, you tell George he doesn't know what the..." I stumble, not used to filtering my vocabulary. "...what the *heck* he's talking about. If he gives you any more trouble, you let me know and I'll take care of him."

She smiles. "Really? Will you respond if I tweet to you?"

"Yes, of course, I'll respond. And seriously — you can do anything you want to do, Samantha. Remember that."

It's almost halftime for the Thursday night game, and I realize I've been in the room almost an hour and a half.

"Look, Samantha, I've got to go. I've really loved hanging out with you."

"Me, too."

I want to give her a kiss on the cheek goodbye, but I settle for a squeeze of her hand, it being the first time and all.

My heart is both heavy and light as I leave the room. I'm happy and sad at once. Samantha is both a jewel, and the reason my heart has been so weighted down all of these years. I go in search of Emma so I can process everything that I'm feeling and thinking.

"She's a happy kid, good parents obviously," I say, sitting across from Emma, who is sipping a coffee in the cafeteria. "And thanks for giving me some time with her."

"I thought you needed that."

We hear a couple squabbling behind us in the cafeteria that distracts us. We both turn our ears and listen in.

"Twenty-thousand a month, Ben! What are we going to do?! Put it on our credit card? Dear God."

"Be reasonable, Stacy. We can't just *not* get the treatment. What happens if we don't get the treatment?"

"We leave it up to God. I was researching this homeopathic remedy—"

"Absolutely not."

"It's twenty-thousand a month! And we don't have it!"

Around and around their circular argument goes.

"Christ, that's so sad," I say. "Can we just give them some money?"

"You can. You would have to start a foundation, though."

"I can't just cut them a check?"

"Crazy as it is, people get suspicious when you just *give* money away."

"That's some bullshit."

"I know. The world is messed up."

She looks around the room, seeming a little nervous. "So you doing okay after that?"

I nod. "Feeling a lot better, actually. I just hope there are no repercussions."

"Like what?"

"I don't know, she's going to tell her parents, they know I'm the father since it was an open adoption."

"We'll play it off like we had no idea."

"Plausible deniability works since we visited just about everyone here, I suppose. But I spent an hour and a half in her room."

Emma takes my hands across the table, warm from being wrapped around her coffee cup. "Just relax."

"What if they sue me?"

"What's more important, seeing your daughter, or losing your money?"

I reach across the table and take a sip of her coffee. "Right."

I put the coffee back down, and reflect on the huge changes in my life over the past couple of months. It's been the most tumultuous time in my life, but there's been one constant through it all: Emma.

I lean forward. "Hey, so I was thinking—"

"I wanted to tell you something," she blurts out.

"Something important?"

She nods.

"Can it wait?" I say. "I'm a little bit emotionally drained at the moment and not sure I can process anything heavy right now."

"Alright," she says, somewhat reluctantly.

"I was thinking we can get together next Monday night. We've got a game in Seattle this Sunday, so we're flying out early Saturday and we have Monday off. How does that sound?"

"I think I could do that." We stand up. "Oh, and we're going somewhere nice. So wear a dress."

She cocks her head and smiles a little. "Are you *ordering* me around, Boss?"

I smirk. "Yes, I am."

I lean in and take in her scent, which never fails to arouse me. "And you look good in red."

"Duly noted," she smiles.

We get up and head out together.

As we're leaving, I notice we're right behind the couple who was arguing about money for treatment.

"I just hope Samantha can hang in there while we find the money," the dad says.

Emma notices, too, and we make eye contact.

What was a pleasant feeling after the visit, changes into a sick-to-my-stomach feeling.

And it lasts all weekend.

28

EMMA

Rachel and I get together at my place on Sunday and watch the Grizzlies play Seattle on TV. She wears her DYSON 88 jersey and I wear my BREWER 29.

We watch Eve while she plays on the carpet in the living room. Pam sits, relaxing on an easy chair and cradling Jackson.

At halftime Pam goes out to sit on the back porch as she takes a phone call.

"You've been quiet," Rachel says. "Everything okay?"

"How are you and Dyson doing?"

She raises her eyebrows, a little hesitant to answer because she sees I'm dodging her question. "Well, besides the best sex of all time...he's actually a pretty decent guy. A little eccentric in some respects."

"How so?"

"Like, he can only cook bacon."

I grin. "Well, if you're only going to cook one thing, that's a good one to know how to cook."

"True. Why do you ask? And why didn't you answer my question?"

I take a drink of my sparkling water, and watch Eve crawling across the floor. A lump solidifies at the bottom of my stomach.

"Well, you know that thing I told you about...why the owners of the Grizzlies hired me?"

"To spy on Everett?"

"To keep an *eye* on him," I correct, but then realize I'm using the same sleight of language that Cal and Rich used when they first explained to me my job. "For the past week or so, I've been trying to tell him."

"Why didn't you?"

"Well, I wanted to tell him in person. And then..." I shut my mouth and look around. "It ended up being a really busy week. We even went to the children's hospital and Everett signed jerseys for some kids. It just wasn't the right time."

As good of friends as we are, I just can't tell Rachel the whole story. Everett's child who was put up for adoption is no one's business but his and the family's.

"You've got to tell him, Em. If he finds out...that's not going to be a good situation. If you tell him, you can manage the angle of the news. Tell him how you didn't know what you were getting into exactly. And much less didn't know you would strike up a relationship."

"This sounds easier said than done, though."

MONDAY EVENING CAN'T COME SOON ENOUGH. I spend the day running around the city, doing errands, and then I land back at home and get ready for our date. I put on my makeup and a red dress, and it's not too long before Everett shows up at my house.

He's wearing jeans and a black button down with several buttons opened, and looks positively sexy.

He smiles broadly as he saunters up to me.

"Stunning," he says, giving me an up-and-down from head to toe that sends shivers down my spine. He runs a hand along my dress from my thigh up to the small of my back, then pulls me into his hips and kisses me senseless. "I've been thinking about this date all weekend."

"Me, too," I choke out.

"You have your overnight bag?" he asks. "Because we've got some things we need to make up for tonight."

"Oh? What kind of things?"

He kisses me again, and lets his mouth suck on my neck close to my jawline for a few moments, then looks back at me. "I think you know exactly the kinds of *things* I'm talking about."

I head back inside and grab the bag, while Everett says hello to Pam, Eve, and Jack. The new overnight nanny is here, too, helping with watching the two of them. We wave goodbye and head out.

The ride to where we go seems to happen in slow motion.

"This place is in River North, and it's got *the* best seafood in town. You're going to love it."

I nod, smiling. I'll wait until we order our food and then I'll tell him.

"You okay?" he says. "You seem a little off tonight."

"Not off." I shake my head. "Just been a long day of driving around for my boss." I rub my hand on his knee, and he smiles. "He's a real whip-cracker and I don't want to disappoint him."

"Oh, baby, you could never disappoint me in any way."

God, I hope he really means that when he finds out what I need to tell him.

29

EVERETT

When we arrive at the restaurant, Emma seems like he's got something on his mind.

"So, there's something we need to talk about," I say, right after Emma and I order our food.

"Oh?" she asks. "I actually have something to tell you, too."

I take her hand. "Let me go first. I did a lot of thinking this weekend while we were in Seattle. About Samantha... and life...and you."

Her eyes soften when she looks at me now, and my palms sweat because I'm not used to having these sorts of conversations.

"You're beautiful, Emma. I don't think I tell you that enough. And I don't just mean in a sexy, want to rip your skirt off and bend you over your desk on the regular kind of hot."

Her cheeks flush hot at my mention of taking her like that.

I continue. "I mean, you're the kind of beautiful where I

don't understand how you're single, or how lucky I am that you started working for me as my assistant. You've got this contagious joy that has spread to me and changed me forever. Last year, I walked around feeling awful most of the time, carrying around this anxious guilt about Samantha. And now that it's out there, I feel totally different. Even though last week I got the worst news of my life — about Samantha's cancer — I'm not worried. We're all going to get through this together."

She takes hold of my hand and pumps it. "Everett, wait," she chokes out. "I need to tell you something."

"Let me finish. All I want to say is, well, do you want to make this official?"

She stammers. "Make this official, and...? What do you mean by 'official', exactly?"

"I've been thinking a lot about exclusivity, and trying to put things out on the table. I can't imagine being with anyone else," I say. "So I'm asking if you want to be my girlfriend. And be officially exclusive."

To my surprise, she clams up a little bit. I was expecting her to be excited that I was taking initiative and having *the talk*. Maybe I'm not the only one with commitment issues?

"I don't mean to be overly suspenseful," I add, "but hold the thought. I've got to use the restroom."

After I use the bathroom, I come out and smirk as I walk toward her, and I even mouth the word 'damn' because she looks so hot tonight.

"Everett," she says when I sit down. "There's something I need to tell you first. If I explain, we can get it out of the way."

Just then, my phone buzzes, and I pull it out of my pocket.

"Strange," I say, looking at my phone. "This is the emergency line from Rich. My phone is on silent except for a few filtered numbers. Hang on."

"Hello," I say, a little perplexed at why they would call me at this time. "What's so important?"

"Everett, we need you to come into the office."

I pinch my eyebrows "What? Not a chance. Not at this hour."

"Your call..." Rich goes on. "I'll just tell you what's going on. We have evidence that leads us to believe you've been using banned substances."

"That's a crock of shit," I yell, maybe a little too loudly. "Where did you get that information?"

"Don't try to argue with us," Rich says. "We *know* for a *fact* that Jason Brennan was at your place. And he's the ring leader of the whole thing. We can't have the Grizzlies being associated with him. And you're named in Foley's report that's dropping in the media any day now."

Something squeezes my heart. "Brennan came to my place, yes, and gave me some *legal* supplements. Wait a second, how did you know he was even there? He came by *once* all summer."

There's a long pause, and over a minute or two, Rich elaborates on how he knows Brennan was there. What he says makes my veins turn cold.

"Rich...alright...bye."

I hang up the phone with a scowl.

Emma's face looks worried. As it should.

"That was so disturbing. I don't even know what to make of it," I say.

"What did Rich say?" she asks. I can practically see her heart pounding through her dress.

I have to fight to look Emma in the eye. "He said...that you were hired to keep *tabs* on me? Is this fucking true, Emma?"

Emma sinks into my chair, a guilty look on her face.

"Only partly," she says, putting her hand on mine. "It's sort of a complicated story."

I remove my hand. "It's not complicated. It's a yes or no answer. When you interviewed with Cal and Rich, did you, or did you not, take the position with a stipulation being that you would fucking *spy* on me, as he just told me."

"More like keep an eye on you," she says weakly.

"So, it's true."

She nods. "But, Everett, that's what I was trying to tell you! They said stuff about your mental health was off...they made it sound like I would be *helping* you. Plus, I had no idea we would end up having the connection we do. I really care about you, too. And my answer is yes, I want to be your girlfriend. Of course, I do. You've helped me in so many ways, too, as gruff and stoic as you can be. I care about you a lot, too."

She looks as though she's fighting back tears now. Still, I can't believe she'd break my trust like this and not come clean to me as soon as we realized the attraction we had between one another.

"This is my fault, though," she continues. "I should have told you all about this sooner. I tried to on a few occasions. But I couldn't bring myself to tell you with everything that was going on with Samantha."

She lets the words settle in the air, probably hoping they don't fall on deaf ears.

The way I'm looking at her is different now, like she's a stranger I've never seen before.

"What did he tell you anyway?" I ask. "I never told him about Samantha or, basically anything worth knowing."

"You told him *nothing?*"

She squints. "Well, they *did* ask me if I had seen this muscle-bound guy in your house, and I said yes."

I clench my jaw and type something in my phone. "Was it this guy?" I show her the picture. The man's look is unmistakable, like a middle-aged Arnold Schwarzenegger. "That's Jason Brennan."

She nods. "That's him."

"And who did you tell?"

"There was some guy with Cal in the VIP box at your last home game. The league…investigator?"

"Fuck me," I slam my hand on the table. "That's Dan Foley. He's in the middle of a big steroid and doping investigation of the league, and Jason Brennan was just identified as the number-one supplier for players. Obviously, I don't touch the stuff, but now I'm guilty by association." I pause, and look at her for emphasis. "Because of you, and your spying."

"I didn't mean to tell them anything, Everett. I didn't even know who Jason was, or who Dan was at the time." She starts to tear up. "I'm really sorry."

My eyes go distant, my gaze unfocused. "Fuck, Emma. This hurts." Standing, I toss my napkin on the table.

"After how much I trusted you, this is what happens? I told you all about Samantha, and you swore I could trust you."

"I would never tell anyone about her! I still won't."

"I don't think I can finish this dinner. I need to take some time to think."

I pull out some money and put it on the table. "Here's for dinner and for a cab home."

I take one more glance at her.

"I thought we really had something. I guess not. I guess it was all in my head."

Before she can say another word, I walk out.

30

EVERETT

During game day on Sunday, my mind is a scattered mess, and it shows. I play so badly the coach has to take me out by the third quarter. Not that it matters, because we're getting crushed anyway, but still.

In the locker room after the game, I hang my head and think to myself.

I thought about going to visit Samantha again this week, but it seemed like a selfish thing to do. I got the one visit, I met her and enjoyed it, but a repeat visit would raise some flags, it seems to me.

Then there's Emma.

Still my assistant, even though I'm so conflicted and very much wish that I could go on having nothing to do with her, all the while I can't stop thinking about her. The way she tastes, the sound of her voice, the way her ass looks in a skirt...

And then I remind myself that she lied by omission. She gained my trust in order to find things out about me.

My head throbs when I recall the first night we slept

together and I told her all about Samantha and the ghosts of my past.

She could go blabbing those secrets, too, any time now.

Still, I don't feel great about not talking to her. We'd slowly built up such a strong connection, But who *can* I talk to if I can't talk to Emma? She slowly became my rock, my confidante.

You confided in her and she informed your bosses, you fool.

I curse myself for being weak and giving into her. She seemed so beautiful and pure-intentioned.

Even beautiful things have sharp edges, though. She made me forget that fact for a while.

Now, I'm regretting it.

I'm also fuming at the ownership of the team. Spying on your own players — what kind of fucked-up shit is that?

I glance toward the coaches' locker room, where Coach Fontana is speaking firmly with someone right now in raised voices. Something changed with Coach's attitude toward me this past week. Or maybe I just noticed it after Emma came clean. But Coach has been distant.

If he thinks that I'm illegally doping, that could most definitely explain the change and that has me very worried. I also don't want that accusation getting out to my fellow teammates.

A couple of players ask me if I'm doing okay on their way out, and I wave them off. They probably think I'm pissed about my shitty performance tonight.

But their logic is reversed. I've been pissed all week, and that's what resulted in my shitty performance.

"Brewer," Coach says, startling me with a hand on my shoulder. "Need to talk to you."

I raise an eyebrow. "Okay."

"Let's do it in my office."

When he closes the door, he's got a somber look on his face.

"Now don't shoot the messenger on this," he says. "But I've got some unfortunate news. You're being suspended...indefinitely."

My blood curdled. "Indefinitely? On what grounds?"

Coach folds his hands. "I think you know what this is about...Illegal substance usage."

I inhale a deep breath to keep my calm. The worst thing I can do is act like some 'roid-rage freak with no ability to control my temper.

"With due respect, Coach, you know that's not true."

"Do I? You know the league is really cracking down this year. And your friend was busted running a major supply chain. And the league confirmed he was at your house just before he got busted with all the needles."

"How does him being at my house prove a thing?"

"Well, the league is convinced that you've been up to something this past year. I mean, come on, Everett. You're not a twenty-three-year-old running back any more. You're thirty, and it makes sense that maybe you want drugs to be what you were in your prime."

"I'm running faster this year than I did two years ago," I point out. "What's that got to do with anything?"

"That's exactly it. No one runs faster when they're older."

"What about Tom Brady? He's like forty and still winning champsionships."

Coach scoffs. "The point is, you've acted erratic for the past year. You know, holding out and not signing a contract all year. And that poor hot dog stand girl you lectured about tips. Among other things."

I clench my fists at my sides. "For fuck's sake, Coach, I bought a pack of gum in a pharmacy the other day and they asked me for a tip. We all know this is getting out of hand."

Awkward tension hangs in the air.

"Kidding aside, though, you can't prove a thing," I continue. "I haven't taken a piss test all year. I'm going to call a players' lawyer, and we'll take care of everything."

Coach looks a little somber. "Look, Everett. I'm not saying I don't believe you. But the road ahead is going to be very tough for you, even with false accusations. The league's steroid and substance problem has gotten worse over the past few years, and they need someone they can make an example out of. And that someone is you, unfortunately."

"So they're taking me down just to make an example of me? You know that's bullshit, Coach!"

"I don't disagree. But I will ask you this: what's gotten into you these past few years? I've been your coach for six of the years you've been playing, and you *have* been acting very strange. Something's on your mind, and I want to know what it is. If you're innocent here, tell me, so I can help you."

I clench my jaw and cock my head to the side. "Wish I could, Coach, but it's not something that I can talk about."

"Well, I hope it's worth losing your career over then because that may very well be what happens. We're done here, then, I suppose." He stands up. "You won't be practicing with the team. I'd recommend you do more of those visits to children's hospitals like you did last week. The optics are much better in the press. You're going to need the public on your side if you're going to beat these charges. And God knows if we have any chance of winning the Super Bowl this year, we'll need you."

I stand, nod somberly, and exit.

All the while, I can't get the image of Emma freaking Foster out of my mind.

I let myself get weak with her for a time.

It won't happen again.

Even though, as I drive home, I hold the steering wheel in my hand, all the while wishing it was her skin I was feeling instead.

THE FOLLOWING MORNING, I call up a sports lawyer who comes highly recommended and lay out the situation for him. He goes over the details and he says that, unfortunately, more than anything, my problem is one of what he calls 'optics'.

"Who cares about optics?" I bite out. "What about the word of the law, Chuck?"

Chuck *hmpfs*.

"Mr. Brewer, this is the world we live in now: it's mob rule. You're the number-one most hated guy in sports right now. Sports TV shows are running highlights, or should we say *lowlights*, of you going off the rails over the past eight years, with the title *Everett Brewer's Rage Explained Through 'Roids?* You're getting ripped apart. And the league has been losing money this year. They need to do something to appease the fans. There is a trending hashtag right now for #BootBrewer. I can, and will, move forward with an appeal. But these aren't constitutional guidelines. Far from it. The league commissioner will exercise severe bendability with these rules."

Great, so what he's saying is that I'm screwed.

31

EMMA

In college, when I would get stressed out, I would ride the red line train all the way south, get on it, and ride it all the way back up north.

Something about the constant movement would soothe me.

So, on Monday, when I wake up and check my Twitter feed, I see a headline that makes my heart almost explode with shame and guilt:

Everett Brewer Suspended; Denies Alleged Steroid Abuse

Jesus, this is all my fault.

Why did I have to identify Jason — whom I just barely recognized as stopping by Everett's — and implicate Everett? Even if it was accidental.

My heart hurts, too, that I'm getting the cold shoulder from Everett, *again*. This is the first time I feel like I deserve it, though.

After I get out of bed, I say hi to Jack, Eve, Pam, and the new nanny, who is staying in a side porch we turned into a room, for now.

They're all so immersed in baby world this month that

they don't notice — or even ask — about how work is going. I don't go to Everett's house to work all week. Instead, I go out and head to a coffee shop, not wanting to admit the truth of the matter to them.

Besides, I'm still getting a paycheck from Cal and Rich. Only now that Everett's being suspended indefinitely from the team, I'm wondering about my employment status overall, since Cal and Rich were the ones who got me in trouble in the first place.

After I have a good breakfast, I put on a jacket and walk to the red line, and ride it up and down, thinking about my next move.

Since the moment I saw Everett, even at the hot dog stand, he's made my skin prickle in a way that no other man has been able to do.

With Everett, despite his broodiness, his closed-off emotions, and sometimes hot temper, whenever I'm even in the same room with him, I feel as though I'm sitting across from a giant bonfire, getting all warm and hot from the inside out, so much so that he lights me up, as well.

I ride the red line all the way down to 95th, get off, and then ride another train up toward downtown.

I feel awful about my role in everything. Everett's right about a lot. But not about everything.

If only there was some way I could make him see what my true intentions are.

Or maybe I was wrong to take the job in the first place, and the only way to avoid a catastrophe like this would have been to walk right out of the office the very moment Cal and Rich offered me the job and explained what they expected of me.

But the money was so good and my sister and I needed it so badly. We still do.

Although, if I wasn't working, I could help out a little more and we'd let the nanny go. But then that's not fair to me, either. Damn, this is a lose-lose situation all the way around.

I frown at a random person on the train, then get off in Wrigleyville.

Before I know it, I'm walking close to the area of the city in Chicago where Rachel works.

I shoot her a text to find out if she's got some time to hang out before her shift this afternoon.

Part of me feels bad for being that needy friend, but I helped Rachel through some tough times our junior year of college, so I don't feel *so* bad that I've been leaning on her a little this summer.

And fall, I remind myself.

It's now fall.

As I pass through the streets of the city, they're quieter now. It's the Chicago Jaguar's last home game of the season and if this were summer, there would be a bunch of frat bros out here already getting after it. Instead, all I see is a few Napleton jerseys, Chicago's star pitcher.

I chuckle, because even the simple act of seeing a Napleton jersey on the street makes me think of Everett.

The memory invades my thoughts of when I was on a date with Josh and Everett decided just to ruin it, the cocky bastard.

I hated it as much as I loved it.

And now that feeling is gone, just like he is.

RACHEL and I meet up at a nice restaurant within walking distance of her house before she has to run to her shift.

"Drinks. Get the drinks over here, Roger," Rachel says to the bartender. It's 11 a.m. and we are opening up the bar inside of the restaurant. Since she works in the industry, Rachel knows practically all of the bartenders in the neighborhood.

Roger frowns. "Don't you have to work in like an hour?"

Rachel shrugs. "Of course. You're telling me you've never had a shot or two while you're on your shift?"

He nods. "Touché."

Rachel leans back into our conversation, and I continue with my train of thought as soon as Roger is out of earshot. Obviously, I can't run the risk of him overhearing our conversation.

"Was there any way I could have not ended up with Everett hating me?"

"You definitely should have told him everything earlier. Like as soon as you slept with him," she says. "But other than that, I mean, you struggled a lot with the decision to take the job in the first place, exactly because you thought it would go against your morals. And in the end, it did."

I take another sip of my Moscow mule. "I should have known it was too good to be true. Girls like me just don't make $120k straight out of college."

Rachel puts up a hand. "Stop yourself right there. Because I'm on pace to make $100k this year. And you're just like me."

My eyes widen. "Holy crap! You're making that much from just working at the bar? What are you going to do with all that?"

"Yep. You know me, I don't go out a lot, so I'm not the one spending the money on booze. I figure if I work here for one more summer and do as well, I'll be able to buy an apartment, pay off the mortgage, maybe start playing a little Monopoly with it."

"Aren't you just a regular entrepreneur," I say. "Well done."

"Are you still making money from your job?" she asks.

"I got my paycheck last week, but obviously I won't be going back to work at Everett's house. He's no longer on the active roster after his suspension, so I'm not sure the league will continue to pay for his PA. Plus, he hates me."

"You still care about him?"

My gut heaves with the question, and my buzz starts to kick in. I remember the very first time we kissed and how my body felt: warm, fuzzy, and tingly all over.

I nod. "I do, although I really need to start getting over him. This chapter in my life feels like it's coming to an end. It sort of feels like it was all a dream."

"Which part?"

I laugh. "Oh, I don't know. The part where I was making ten-thousand dollars a month, maybe. More than I've made all year. Or the part where my boss was a football superstar — not to mention my boss — and we had the best sex of my life."

She nods somberly. "Don't forget, you hooked your best friend up with one of his teammates."

I smile. "Best wing-woman ever!"

"So you haven't talked to Everett all week?"

"No, I haven't talked to him once."

"And he went dark on social media. He is getting absolutely destroyed. I kind of feel sorry for the guy. If everyone knew what you and I know, they might have a shred of sympathy for him. As it is, he's just a millionaire superstar who rants at poor hot dog-stand girls."

I laugh again.

"It's so ironic how that rant set in motion the initial butterfly effect of me leaving the hot dog stand to try and branch out. If Everett wouldn't have peeved me off that day, I might not have gotten out of my comfort zone this summer."

Rachel checks to make sure the bartender is far away, then lowers her voice.

"It's so funny how, after seeing his rant against you, I wanted to punch him in the face. But after knowing everything he's going through — thanks to your impressive spying skills — I think he feels things incredibly deeply. I mean, he was writing freaking *napkin notes* to his daughter." Yes, I shared the details about the napkin note with Rachel. I had to tell someone. "He's having anxiety for years based on something he did when he was a teenager. I wonder if there's a way you could explain it to him, somehow, and he'd understand where you were coming from."

"I should have never taken a job that sacrificed my principles. That's something Everett would never do."

We sit in silence for a few minutes, watching the warm-ups for the game.

"There's something I need to do," I say. "Hang on."

Pulling out my phone, I dial a number and call someone I should have contacted a long time ago.

"Who are you calling?" she asks.

Cal's secretary answers. Even their direct line has a secretary. "Yes, I'd like to speak to Cal and Rich Davis, please."

"Um, Miss, they're busy in a meeting right now, and they only take calls by appointment," she says.

"You tell those two that if they don't get on the phone with me right now, I'll be filing a sexual harassment lawsuit against Cal. I saw the way he was looking at me." I hate to throw in that low blow, but I need to talk to him. Also, if they want to play the game of subterfuge and manipulation, I'm going to have to fight back.

"Um, who is this?" she says, sounding nervous.

"Emma Foster," I say, articulating my name especially well.

"Alright. Hang on."

"Emma. What's the meaning of this?" Cal answers. "We're in the middle of something important."

"Yeah? Is it more important than ruining the life of your best player so you can...I don't know, *lose* the season? I don't understand why you guys decided to be such dicks to him. Worried about him, my ass! You were trying to set him up, and you set me up, too. You figured I was this naïve little girl you could manipulate into nefariously giving up your best player."

"Emma, I'd consider what you are implying highly inappropriate. I should remind you that we're still paying your salary."

I scoff. "Are you seriously trying to manipulate me like that? Well you know what, fuck you, Cal!"

I can practically hear his mouth gaping on the other end of the phone.

"Well, Emma, I never thought you would be so..."

"Self-advocating? Articulate? What word are you looking for, you no-good liar?! Why would you try and get rid of your best player anyway? Are you *trying* to lose the Super Bowl?" I ask, sarcastically.

"We had to give someone up, Emma, or else we'll risk a huge fine and investigation of the team! This was an order coming from on high."

"On high? Wow, from God Himself. I didn't know he was the commissioner."

"You're really pushing it right now for someone who was making hot dogs for people for a living, making a tenth of what we are paying you now," Cal bites out. "You haven't talked to any media outlets, have you?"

My skin prickles with goosebumps. Media outlets. "Is there something you're trying to hide with this story? Something even I don't know?"

"You can't discuss the terms under which you were hired, Emma. You signed a firm-as-rocks, nondisclosure agreement. Look, you're all fired up now. But I'll expect you to call back later today and apologize."

"I'm not apologizing for a thing. And you can't fire me, because I quit!" I bite out.

I hear some shuffling on the phone, and Rich's voice comes on.

"Emma! What's the meaning of this? We had a deal."

"Goodbye, Dick," I say, and click the *end call* button.

"Holy shit! That was awesome!" Rachel says.

Roger, the bartender, is also spellbound. I'd forgotten about them while I ranted away.

"Was that seriously Cal Davis, owner of the Grizzlies?"

I nod.

"That's wild. I've never heard anyone talk to someone in that high of a position like that."

"They're the worst kind of assholes," I add. "They seem so sweet up front, but on the backend, they're deceiving you."

I chuckle.

The exact opposite of Everett Brewer.

Everett is damn near impossible to deal with up front, but the more you get to know him, the more you love him.

Love him.

Do I love Everett?

No. Love can't happen in just a couple of months.

I brush past the thought, and a big crowd of patrons comes in and sits down.

"Hey, Roger, is it just you here?" Rachel asks.

"Yeah. We just had a bunch of seasonal workers quit and go back to college a few weeks ago. We've been surprisingly busy though. Management is looking for some new personnel."

Rachel slaps me on the back. "Well, my associate and I are looking for jobs. What do you say?"

"You're looking for a job? What about Country Mike's BBQ Barn?" I ask her.

"It slows way down once baseball season is over. This place is a little more upscale, which means the food is more expensive, which means the tips will be way higher."

Roger leans in. "You two seem like a riot. I'll let the manager know. Do you have serving experience?"

I grin. "Oh, yes. Haven't you seen the hot dog stand rant?"

Holy shit. "You're the hot dog stand girl! Well, don't worry. There's no tip jars here. People just give them freely."

32

EVERETT

The week rolls by and I brood, not wanting to speak to a soul. My house feels bigger and emptier than normal. The only slight repose I have are my daily workouts, where I go harder than I have, just to feel the pain of the burn and release some stress.

Other than that, I feel like I'm at the bottom of an empty beer can. When the lawyer starts to dodge my incessant calls because he apparently is unable to make the appeal in this case, I sincerely wonder for a little while if I should call up Gates and try to dig up some dirt on the higher-ups in the commissioner's office. I entertain the idea and eventually nix it, because I don't want to stoop to their level. Making some clearly innocent man a fall guy. My agent tries to pull some strings, too, but the terms are ironclad. And being able to kick players off a team due to illegal substance use was one of the major concessions the players gave to the owners. So, it truly looks like I am S.O.L.

~

It's the following week on a Tuesday morning, and I'm at the lowest of lows, when I hear the doorbell ring.

It's...guess who?

"Heyyy, brother!" Jocko grins. I don't think the man has an off-day when it comes to appearing at my place.

"Seriously? You're doing the morning pop-in *again*?"

He breezes past me. "Bro, I've never seen anyone get ripped apart on Twitter like you are right now. Fans are *pissed*. What the hell happened? I know you're not popping steroids, so I needed to get the answer straight from the source."

As much as Jocko often annoys me, I'm happy to have him here today. We make coffee and breakfast and go sit outside on the patio.

I decide then and there that it's probably time to come clean with everything.

At this point, what do I have to lose?

I'm already going to be forfeiting the greater portion of my ten-million-dollar contract, so I might as well put it all out there.

Jocko is, for once in his life, left without words as I finish telling him the saga about the high school one-night stand that haunted me, Samantha's adoption, and then of course, Emma's betrayal. I tell him about the letters I wrote to her over the years that did nothing to mend my heart. And I tell him the details about the cancer, and how seeing her made me both the happiest and saddest I've ever been in my life.

When I'm done, Jocko sits back, puts his hands behind his head and watches the red and yellow leaves on the trees in my backyard rustle.

Jocko is a nonstop joker, but he does have a seldom-used serious side. And I can see that side on his face right now as he brings his eyes back to me.

"Why didn't you tell me, man? Tell one of us? You kept this a secret for so long. You know we wouldn't have judged you."

"It was my burden to bear," I say. "I was the one who messed up. I didn't need to bring anyone else in on it. Besides, after she told me Samantha had been adopted, there was nothing that could be done."

Jocko rakes a hand through his hair. "I was at that party. I remember you were acting weird the next few weeks, and you didn't say anything about the hook-up."

I shrug. "Not much that can be done now. Samantha's dying of cancer, and I can't save her."

Jocko squints. "Why not?"

"What am I going to do, just waltz up to the house where they live, and say, 'Hi, I know you don't know me, but I'm going to happily pay for all of your medical bills.'"

Jocko stands up. "Man, why are you resting on your fucking *laurels*? You're feeling sorry for yourself. And that sucks about Emma, man. I thought she was a gem. A real gem. You're adding fuel to the fire for me to remain a bachelor. That's why I don't like getting involved with women."

"You're fucking right," I say, slapping a hand on the table. "Why am I sitting here and taking this sitting down? So what if I get in trouble? Hell, they could take all my money, send me to jail for all I care. But I'm going to make sure Samantha gets the best treatment money can buy."

We head inside, and I grab my keys. "You coming?"

"Where are we going, exactly?"

"Samantha's parents' house. Gates gave me their address. So fuck it."

~

Jocko sits shotgun in my car on the drive down to the Lincoln Park neighborhood of the city. It feels good to have a partner in crime for this activity.

And that's exactly what he is: my partner in crime.

Because we are not supposed to intercede in the life of my adopted daughter.

Jocko comments, "Wouldn't it be funny if we got arrested for this, after all the stupid shit we did in high school without getting caught?"

"Hilarious," I bite out.

"Aw, sorry. Just trying to lighten the mood a little, man. My bad, though."

As I get off the exit and we head to Samantha's family's house, we open the windows. It's a gorgeous, late September day, and we can smell the cool breeze coming off from the lake.

Our drive takes us to Lincoln Street, right past the hot dog stand.

"There it is," Jocko says. "Wade's Weiner Shack. Wow. Business is booming. Maybe your little rant months ago gave them some free publicity."

A long line of people wraps down the sidewalk from the stand, and I wonder if Jocko could be right.

Slowing the vehicle, I look at the people waiting.

We even overhear one of them say, "Yeah, dude messed that tips girl up right here. But she *buried* him."

I guess my little rant is part of the Wade's Weiner Shack folklore, now.

Jocko purses his lips and looks at me. "For what it's worth, man, I went into the damn grocery store last week and they asked me if I wanted to leave a tip. I was like, no, why don't you just raise your prices and pay your employees more!"

"Preach, brother."

Eventually I turn onto a side street and we park.

We walk down the sidewalk until we stop in front of an old Brownstone building.

"Damn. This guy doesn't have the money to pay for his daughter's cancer treatment?" Jocko comments.

It's a very fair question. The house is in a very rich area of the city.

"Guy lost his job two years back. His wife works her ass off now, but he had a higher-up exec job that brought home a salary in the mid-six figures. She's a school teacher, so now they're living off her money and his savings. And he apparently lost a ton of money in the cryptocurrency crash of 2018," I say.

"Damn," Jocko says. "How do you know all that?"

"Gates," I say, simply.

He nods as if the man's name explains it all.

My heart thumps like crazy as we stand in front of the door.

"You think they'll be home?" Jocko asks.

I ring the doorbell, and we wait.

Every second that passes seems to take an hour.

We're just about to turn around when the wooden door opens.

On the other side of the screen door, the same man with gray and black hair whom I saw at the children's hospital, stands with wide eyes that have a little hint of meanness. Jocko stands down the steps and to the side, on the sidewalk.

"I'm—" I start to say, but the man cuts me off.

"I know who you are," he says, coolly. "When you started playing professionally, I had it verified that you were the same Everett Brewer who listed on Samantha's birth certificate as the father."

"I was reckless in my youth, and that's what I've come here to rectify."

"You're not rectifying shit," he says. "I'm not even going to ask how you got my address. But now it makes sense how you seemed to coincidentally show up at the children's hospital."

"I didn't mean to overstep any bounds."

"Didn't you, though? You knew her. And you knew that she was going to be talking nonstop for the next week about a visit from her favorite star player. She loves football. And now that she has a signed jersey, she's your biggest fan in the world. If she found out she was your daughter, we just don't know how that would affect her upbringing."

"Look, Ben, you're her father. Nothing is going to change that. I'm not looking to make some crazy stink about this—"

"Then why are you here, Everett?" The man's voice cuts me off. "What you're doing now is illegal. I don't care how big of a celebrity you are now. You're not just going to randomly step into Samantha's life. So I'll ask you kindly to please get off my property."

I give a humble sigh. "While I can't deny I would like nothing more than to be in her life, I understand where you're coming from. I heard about her cancer treatment, though. Do you have enough money to pay for it?"

His eyes shift back and forth. "We'll get by."

"Getting *by* is not an option. The only option is getting the best treatment that money can buy."

I notice he's uncomfortable, clenching his fists at his sides before he speaks.

"Like I said, I think it's time for you to go. We can pay it — we don't need Mr. Moneybags coming in to save the day."

I sneer. "Do you think this is about money? Thing is, Ben, money means nothing to me if Samantha doesn't live. I've had a hard-enough time dealing with the fact that I gave her up. If I don't do anything and everything in my power to help her, I'll regret that for the rest of my life."

Ben doesn't say anything, so I continue.

"Technically, you could sue me for intervening illegally in her life. Well, you know what, that's fine. I'll *give* you the money if it means you spend it on Samantha's treatment. I'll give you everything I have and live in a cardboard box for the rest of my life. I really and truly don't give a shit."

He runs a hand over his chin.

"Fine," he finally relents. "We'll figure out a way to do this. But I don't want you seeing her anymore."

My stomach curdles a little bit at that.

Having seen her just one time, I wanted more of that.

Shit, I wanted to see her every week, every day if I could.

Somehow.

But I hold my tongue, because right now, Ben holds the power in this negotiation.

"I won't see her. But you have to guarantee you'll use all the money for the best treatment."

We make lock eyes, and his gaze tells a story.

The main thrust of which being that he loves Samantha just as much as I do. After a pause, Ben opens the screen door and steps outside, and we examine each other closely.

After he takes off his glasses, he speaks.

"If you think I'd spend money on anything else, you're out of your fucking mind, Brewer. You have no idea what a blessing Samantha is."

My throat clenches up. I put my hand on his shoulder, and nod. "Let me know," I say, choking up. "Anything you need. Everything. And thank you for being her father."

A surge of myriad emotions rolls through me. I'm happy and sad, elated and melancholy all at once.

It's a complex emotion and situation to process. But in this moment, I realize the world has this amazing ability to make up for the shortcomings of one man with the heroic acts of another. I would never have been able to take care of Samantha if I became a father at age sixteen.

This man stepped in and became her — I can admit it, her *real* father.

"You were right to call me what you did," I say. "I'm just a sperm donor. And I'll always admire, respect, and yes, even envy you a little bit for being there for her."

Reaching into my pocket, I pull out a check.

"I don't know how much treatment costs, but you let me know if you need more."

I hand him a check made out to his name for one-hundred-thousand dollars, and his eyes widen.

He hesitates.

"Just take it," I say. "And in the notes area, I wrote down my phone number. I won't contact you again unless you make first contact. I see it in your eyes that you want only the best."

Nodding, he takes the check and examines it.

"I would say to tell Samantha she's loved, but I know you and your wife have given her all the love that she needs," I comment. "Take care, Ben. So long."

"Thank you," he calls when I get to the bottom of the stairs.

"It's nothing," I say. "The least I can do."

Jocko and I walk silently back to the car, him having just witnessed the whole thing.

"That's heavy, man," he says when we're back in the car.

"Yes," I say, looking at my watch. "Not even noon yet and I sure could use a drink."

"Damn straight. I'm still processing that you've kept this hidden for so long."

"I've always been the lone wolf of the family," I say. "No more."

As heavy as my heart is, driving off and thinking of Samantha, I feel as though a fourteen-year-old weight has been lifted from my chest.

Jocko says the names of a few nearby watering holes that he searches on his phone as my mind drifts off to the woman who set me down this path of self-realization.

I never expected her to have this effect on me, but she did.

Truth is, in spite of her betrayal, I miss her.

My hand shakes a little as I grip the steering wheel, and I tell Jocko to just tell me where to drive. He senses that I'm far away inside my mind, picks a place for us to go, and tells me which roads to turn onto.

I'm filled with questions as I drive.

Will Samantha's treatment go successfully?

Will I ever meet her?

Will she forgive me?

Funny how, even as I'm suspended from the league, concerns about football seem so far away right now when compared with real life-and-death conflicts.

I linger on the concept of forgiveness for a moment, and for some reason, a thing my old pastor back in Nebraska once said pops into my mind:

The act of forgiving isn't for the one who is forgiving. It's for the one who forgives, who has been holding on to something for so long.

When my life has seemed like I've been walking in a

dark tunnel for so long, it took Emma to guide me to the light.

If she hadn't entered my life, I wouldn't have taken the leaps I did this summer.

And how did I repay her? By pushing her out. Like I do with everyone in my life.

"Here," Jocko says, pointing to a semi-fancy-looking bar. He leans over and puts a hand on my shoulder. "Buddy. No matter what happens, I'm here for you. Got that?"

I nod, and a smirk tugs at my face. "Honestly, I feel about one-hundred times better after that talk. Well, maybe, ninety-ninety-point-nine."

"Ninety-nine, because Samantha still has to go through the treatment?"

"Yes. And, because this whole experience has got me thinking about Emma."

"Thought you were done talking to her?"

I heave a deep sigh. "I still want her."

Jocko pats me on the back as we head into the bar. "Let's talk about it, man. Guys can talk about this shit, too, you know."

I nod and we head inside the restaurant at eleven thirty-nine a.m., but it already feels like one of the longest days of my life.

And as I walk inside, I smell something familiar.

33

EMMA

"Dear God in Heaven, look at this tip I just got," my new coworker Deena says.

She shows me the receipt and I have to gape.

"One-thousand dollars?! That's insane."

"I know. Just two guys upstairs alone. All they had were a few drinks."

I silently curse myself for not taking the upstairs today. But it's a nice day outside, and I figured the patio would be busier. God knows I could use a big tip like that now that I'm off the Grizzlies' payroll.

"They still here?" I ask.

"Yes. They're just chatting. God, they are super-hot, too. And literally no one else is in the upstairs right now. You should go check them out," she winks.

"Sure. I'll pretend I'm filling the silverware station up there."

I grab two small handfuls of clean forks and walk up the stairs.

As the two men come into view, my heart stops for a full second.

Everett and Jocko sit with half-drunk pints of beer on their table, leaned in close with serious expressions.

With a pounding heart, I carry forth my plan to put forks into the silverware station and flip my hair to the side so neither of them can see my face.

It's a risky maneuver since they might recognize me, but my curiosity is piqued too high right now.

What are they doing here, of all places?

And why is Jocko in on a Tuesday? Shouldn't he be at work?

I say a silent prayer that neither of them will recognize me with my silly server uniform of blue jeans, a gingham shirt, and black apron.

With my back to them, I listen to their conversation reverberate throughout the room.

"So you think you're in love with her?" Jocko asks.

Well, fabulous...I have picked quite the time to hone in on their conversation.

"I don't let myself go around women. You get that," Everett says. "But she got to me. I don't know if I even know what being 'in love' means."

I open the drawer and reshuffle the forks repeatedly, throbbing with curiosity. Who is the woman in question?

Unless Everett had a secret lover, he'd have to be talking about me, wouldn't he?

"I've had fleeting moments of love," Jocko says. "But for some reason, I always knew it wasn't meant to last. Do you think you and her could last?"

"You mean, *if* she'll even talk to me. I didn't give her a chance to explain herself to me. I just cut her off."

"That's what you do. You're a cutter-offer," Jocko says. "But no man is an island."

"You sound just like Mom, ya know. Besides, you're one to talk, Mr. Bachelor-until-forty."

"That doesn't mean I haven't had meaningful relationships. And, don't tell anyone this or I'll kill you, if the right girl came along, who knows, I might reevaluate that stance. But it's unlikely. I don't know anyone who could make me change my mind."

"Not even your googly-eyed co-worker?" Everett smirks.

"She's got a *boyfriend*, dude. They're serious. They've been dating for five years. Wait, why are we talking about me right now? This is about you and Emma, for God's sake."

When Jocko says my name, I freeze up with a handful of forks.

"I still do like her. Maybe love her, fuck, man, I don't know. I never expected it would be someone like her, though."

"What did you expect?"

"I don't know. She's kind-hearted and loving, but she's got her shadowy parts, too. And maybe..." Everett pauses, clearing his throat. "Maybe she fucked up by accepting a job to spy on me. She's not perfect. But who am I kidding? Neither am I. And I still can't stop thinking about her."

I hear someone's chair push out. "Well, then, fucking call her! Christ, man! What are you waiting for?" Jocko says. "You haven't spoken to her in how long now?! Every day you don't speak with her, you lessen your shot at bringing her back!"

"I have no clue where she even is now," Everett says. "How would I even find her to talk to her in person?"

"Hold that thought," Jocko responds. "I'm going to hit the head."

I hear him walk to the second-floor bathroom behind us.

Drawing up courage, I turn around and flip my hair behind my back.

"Everett," I call out.

His body seems to slacken in his chair. "What the..."

Standing up, he strides toward me. "What are you doing here?"

"This is my new job," I shrug. "I quit the Grizzlies. The paycheck was nice, but fuck those guys. They got me in over my head on purpose. And I'll never forgive myself for what I did to you."

He eclipses the space between us in what seems like ridiculously long strides.

"Yes, you will," he says, and his hand on the small of my back has never felt so hot. "Because I forgive you."

He doesn't let me get another word in before his lips come crashing down on mine, swallowing up my response.

And I don't hate it.

A surge of raw energy rolls through me. Like I'm a car and he's the gasoline, I feel my body rejuvenating itself with the words I never expected a man like him to say after the shit that we've been through.

I forgive you.

He pulls back for a moment. "How much of that conversation did you hear?"

"Oh, I dropped in right at the moment when you were debating if you loved me or not."

"Shit," he says, holding my hands but turning his body slightly. "You weren't supposed to hear all of that."

I rake a hand through his hair. "It's okay."

"I don't want to freak you out. I might not be ready to say the three words to you...not yet, at least."

"I know you're not," I say. "I don't expect you to be."

He kisses me again, his hand traveling down to my ass. "I

thought I recognized you," he growls into my ear. "I thought I had to be hallucinating, though."

I moan and he lifts me up onto the server station.

I really shouldn't be doing this during my first week of work.

But *screw it.*

What's one more mistake on the job?

Through a foggy mind, I hear Jocko's steps when he comes out of the bathroom. "Oh, wow! Jesus, she made it over here fast. I'll, uh, wait for you two outside. Damn. Wow. Well, thanks for picking up the check, bro. Good to see you, Emma."

I have to giggle. Freaking Jocko.

Jocko leaves and it's just Everett and me. I feel the heat growing between my legs. Everett presses into my hips and I wrap my legs around him.

His hand runs up the side of my shirt. I pull back. "So that tip you gave to Deena was you? Not Jocko?"

His expression is perplexed. "She told you?"

"Of course. A thousand-dollar tip is a big deal." I smile. "Glad you finally learned how to tip."

"Thanks to you."

I smile on the inside, loving how much he's changed since our first encounter. I wonder which was the *real* him, and I like to think that as ruthless as Everett can be, that note showcased his kindness on the inside that was begging to escape.

We kiss again, both ravenous. His lips press hot against mine.

"As much as I'd love to fuck you right here on this countertop, I don't want to get you fired," Everett says.

"You sure? No one comes up here..."

"Hey, Emma, just wanted to check on..." It's Deena's voice as she walks up the stairs, not yet able to see us.

I push Everett away, and we frantically re-situate ourselves so we're standing with our clothes and hair straight like we were actually *not* just considering having sex in the workplace.

"—the rollups. Hi, Mr. Brewer!" Deena says, waving when she gets to the top. She pinches her forehead, seeing how we are standing awkwardly, not saying anything, an arm's length apart from one another. "Do you two know each other or something?"

Everett and I exchange a knowing glance.

"You could say that," Everett growls. Shrugging, he grabs me and kisses me on the lips.

"I'll give you two some, ah, time. Just let me take this box of fresh rollups and...have fun!"

"How late are you working today?" Everett breathes.

34

EMMA

After my shift, I drive over to Everett's house. The door is unlocked, and I head inside but don't see him anywhere.

It feels surreal to be here, and it almost feels as though I'm entering the front door for the first time.

When Everett's nowhere to be found on the first floor, I head up to the second floor, then peek inside the office. He's sitting there, looking at a stack of old letters.

"Hey," I say, tipping my forehead toward him. "Feeling sentimental?"

He glances up at me from his desk and grins softly. "Oh. You're here. Sorry, I was off in my own world re-reading some of these."

Standing up, he approaches me, then wraps my hips up with his big hands.

"I had an epiphany just now while I was going through all of the letters."

My eyes widen. "Tell me about it."

His lips hover inches from mine. "I did make a mistake. Yes, I was young, but it was a mistake. I wish I could have figured out a way to love Samantha. But realistically — and just logistically — it would have been incredibly difficult for me to raise a child. I was a teen, for goodness sake."

"This is what I've been saying all along."

I wrap my hand around the back of his neck. There's a glint of life and hope that I haven't seen before behind his normally very-pained eyes.

"Yes, you have. But I've learned there's a difference between saying the words out loud, and truly forgiving myself." His voice is low and gravelly. "And today, while I was going through those letters, I realized, truly internalized, that there was no chance I would ever be able to love Samantha the way I wish I could have, as her true father."

His jaw twitches, and he pauses for a beat before he locks his eyes on me. "But I realized today, that while it's true I'll never be able to correct my past actions, I don't have to deprive myself of love anymore. Because the one I want to love is right in front of me. It's you, Emma."

Chills wash over me.

"You got over your fear of saying the L word that quickly?"

He shrugs. "You're the most amazing woman I've met in my entire life. Emma, you're beautiful, you're smart, you're so kind and loving when it comes to your sister. From the moment I laid eyes on you, I've had to try *not* to love you. Yes, you took the job to work for me under faulty pretenses, but I don't blame you. Plus, you never ratted me out. How were you supposed to know that Jason Brennan was part of the biggest steroid scandal to rock the football world in years? Hell, I didn't even know he was dealing steroids. That's not your fault. At the end of the day, I was searching for a way I could fall out of love with you, rather than deal with the consequences of falling hard. But guess what?

Nothing could stop me from falling hard for you. Because I love you, Emma Foster."

My jaw hovers open. "I...don't really know what to say, Everett. I wasn't expecting to have this conversation right now."

He grins, his hand sliding down my hip to my thigh. I can feel the heat of his body emanating onto mine.

"Me neither. And you don't have to reciprocate. I realize this is a lot to handle."

I giggle, sliding my hands down his muscled back. "*You're* a lot to handle."

A mischevious grin creeps onto his face, and he presses himself into me.

"All this talk about *handling* has me riled up," he says.

"That makes two of us."

His lips crash onto mine and I let out a purr of a moan into his mouth. I can feel his weight pressing me into the wall in his office.

As we kiss, it's as if all of the tension that was building since the moment we met is seeking release.

I'm ravenous as I run my hand through his hair. He lifts me up, connecting his hands underneath my butt. I raise my legs up off the floor and wrap them around him, and he carries me over and sets me on his desk.

Dramatically, he swipes everything off of his desk — a laptop, a cup of pens, some papers — to create room for him to lean me back.

Once I'm on my back on the desk, he lowers himself onto me and I love how weighty he feels on top of my body. We kiss again and I arch my mound up and into his leg, the heat building between my thighs.

"I've missed this," he growls. "I missed you."

"I missed you, too," I moan back.

His mouth finds my neck and his hand deftly undoes the top button and zipper of my jeans. When his fingers run over my panties, I feel myself start to float away. Just like that, with his one touch.

I lift my hips to help him peel my jeans off of my body. He takes off his shirt, revealing his sexy, rippling upper body.

"Yes," I say, running my hand over his abs. "I've definitely missed these."

He lowers his body back onto me, and I grip his arms, which land on either side of my head on the desk.

"Goddamn you're sexy, Emma," Everett whispers. "Inside and out."

I'm about to try and craft a coherent response, when I feel his finger slide underneath my panties and onto the flesh of my clit.

Arching my back, I let out a huge moan.

God, he's good with that thing. Just the little pressure he gives, applied perfectly, whisks me away. My body burns with pent-up desire and pleasure for Everett and what he can do to me.

Reaching a hand down, I lay it on top of his wrist, just to feel how he feels me.

"Yes," he whispers, nibbling my ear. "I love when you put your hand on top of mine like that."

I run my free hand over his jeans, feeling his thick length pressing against my hand. A little clumsily, I unbutton and unzip his jeans.

Getting down off the desk for a moment, he pulls them off, and his boxers go down along with the jeans as his dick springs free.

Before I can react to that visual, he scoops me up off the desk, and the next thing I know, we're in his bedroom.

He helps me get my shirt and bra and panties off in in a blur of ravenous lust. Now we're both totally naked, romping on top of the covers, skin against skin.

Everett's touch is electric, and every time he palms my ass or cradles the back of my head, I get a new surge of butterflies that courses through my stomach.

His hard length rubs against my opening, bringing me ever closer to orgasm. I'm so worked up, I think I might even come without penetration.

And then, gripping the back of my neck, he pushes himself inside me.

"Oh, Everett," I moan.

After a few minutes of slowly adjusting to him, he speeds up and I buck to his rhythm.

It's sensory overload: his hands on my ass, the way he tugs at my hair, how deep he reaches inside of me.

When he thumbs my clit at the same time as he thrusts, I pulse and rock back and my first orgasm rips through me.

"Damn, I want you so bad, Em," he growls in my ear. "I love being inside you. And I love you, too."

The pleasure is almost too much. It's hard to think, but I realize it takes a lot to tell someone *I love you* when they're not saying it back.

We switch positions so that I'm on top, riding him. Another orgasm spreads through me, warming my entire body. Everett grips the back of my neck, pulls me down into him and kisses me, then licks my cheek from ear to mouth.

I bite his ear, then whisper, "I love you, too, Everett."

I didn't even know those words were just below the surface, aching to get out. What I've said seems to spur him into the next level of animalistic instinct, and they do the same for me, too. He grips my hips and steers himself somehow deeper inside of me, hitting a spot that causes my eyes to roll up in the back of my head.

Gripping my ass, he rolls our bodies back over so he's on top, and fucks me with such reckless abandon that I forget where I am, which way is up, and maybe even what my name is.

I wrap my legs around him as he comes, and I feel the warmth of his hot cum shooting inside me.

As we come down, I rest my head on his chest. He runs his hand through my hair.

"Did you mean it?" Everett asks.

I nod. "Yes."

"It wasn't just the sex you love? Or my gigantic cock" he asks on a smirk.

I smile. "I do love you. I was a little hesitant to say it. But, screw it. It's true."

EPILOGUE: EVERETT

Five Months Later

AN OLD JESSE FULLER blues song, *San Francisco Bay Blues,* plays in the background as I stare out at the skyline of San Francisco as I sit on the rooftop patio of Emma's and my new place, sipping a glass of whisky. A warm breeze wafts over me and I reflect on all of the events from the past few months. So much has changed.

My team, my city, my relationship status.

Cal and Rich truly believed I was doing illegal substances to compete at a higher level. They had to cover their own asses, which is why they hired Emma. They thought a young, naïve employee would tell them everything they needed to know.

But their jaws dropped after we explained to them, in a sealed meeting, everything that had happened and how I had been experiencing deep pangs of psychological guilt over the child I didn't know that I had fathered when I was a teenager. It was, without a doubt, the most difficult conversation I ever had in my life, but Emma was there at my side throughout it all. Even though the league reinstated me, I couldn't stay in Chicago without experiencing a constant media firestorm, so they traded me after my contract was live again, for both of our sakes.

And Samantha? Well, her cancer quietly went into remission, which made me so doggone happy I cried.

I've been a lone wolf for so long, I never knew the immense reserves of strength that could be drawn on when having a partner like Emma, someone who believes in you to your core and, yes, loves you.

I'm not one to get all mushy. I never believed that a woman could 'change' a man.

Emma didn't change me. But she did hold a mirror up to me, allowing me to see the deep scars that were tying me down. She's like a magnet that brings certain qualities in me to the surface that I didn't know I had.

Kindness, warmth. The desire to protect. The desire to provide for her and her family.

The whisky coats my throat and a smile eases across my face. I hear Emma singing in the kitchen through the open screen door.

After Chicago traded me to San Francisco this fall, I asked Emma to come out with me. She said yes, but only if Pam and her family were able to come out, as well.

Luckily, I was able to find us a gorgeous three-flat just east of San Francisco. Not only was I fine with having her sister around, but I was also very happy to have more 'family' since the only relative I have on the west coast is my brother, Maddox, who lives in Southern California with his new girl Sherry.

Now, Emma and I live on the third floor and Pam with her two kids just moved into the second-floor apartment this past January.

Some of my new teammates even helped Pam move in, and one of them asked for her number.

I think she's going to do just fine in this new city. She was even saying how happy she was to have a fresh start in a new place with a new energy.

I head back inside, and Emma is so in her own world, humming and getting dinner ready, that she doesn't notice me sneak up behind her.

I wrap my hands around her hips, pull her ass into my crotch, and give her a soft kiss on her exposed neck.

"Wow," I growl into her ear. "That smell."

"I know," she answers. "I think these just might be the best garlic mashed potatoes I've made in my life. Something about the air here."

I spin her around so she has to face me. She's still got an apron wrapped around her.

"I was talking about you. You smell amazing." I lean my nose between her ear and her shoulder and inhale so she gets the idea.

"Oh."

She grins and I kiss her, pulling her hips into me. "I mean, the garlic mash smells amazing, too."

"Mmm. And you smell like whisky."

We kiss once more, and I glance at the bottle of red wine on the kitchen counter.

"Wine?" I ask her.

"Oh. I meant to open that bottle. I distracted myself singing and forgot about it," she laughs.

I open up the bottle and pour two glasses, then drink with her and keep her company and wash a few of the dirty pots and pans while she finishes cooking the meal.

Fifteen minutes later, we sit down outside on the patio to our delicious meal of salad, steak, garlic mashed potatoes, and red wine.

"What are you thankful for?" she asks before we dig into our food, raising her glass. It's our new ritual: before we bite into our food, we name one thing we appreciate about the day or just life, in general.

As I look out over the city, I can't help but smile. "I'm thankful I finally feel like everything is working out just the way it was meant to."

Emma grins and puts a hand on my forearm. Her hair blows in the wind a little and she looks damn beautiful with how the city lights light up her face.

"In what way?" she asks, swirling the wine in her glass.

I glance away from her for a moment, then look back into Emma's eyes. "The Team. You. This apartment. Your new job, and the fact that you got into one of the top programs for counseling in the entire country."

She blushes. I read the essay she wrote, which was about her own upbringing and how she was going to make sure her sister's children would live better lives than her family.

"And you?" I ask her.

"I'm appreciative that Pam's move-in went well, and that you'll be around to be a father-figure to Jack and Eve."

I nod a little stoically and we clink our glasses together and sip our drinks.

The look Emma and I exchange contains more than a thousand words ever could.

Over the past couple of months, Emma, Pam, Eve, Jack, and I have all operated as one big family unit. Now that it's February and I'm done traveling for the season, I've actually taken on the role of watching Jack and Eve during the day when Pam is at work and Emma is volunteering at a local unit for drug rehab, part of her preparation for going to the University of California, Berkeley next year.

"I was too young to be a real father figure to Samantha. But I can be there for Jack and Eve as Uncle Everett in a way that they need, at least until Pam decides to start a relationship again and maybe bring a partner around the kids."

"Yes, you were too young then. I'm glad you finally see that now. And as for Pam, well, she's had George Fontereli's number pinned to her refrigerator for a few weeks now."

"I know. She stares at it but she's scared to call him."

"Isn't it a little strange that he gave her his number, and not the other way around?"

I shake my head. "George knew about Pam's situation with getting over Jack, and he didn't want to be too pushy. I filled him in."

"That's gentlemanly. I really hope she calls him. Even if they just go on one date."

"I'll remind her," I wink.

We make small talk during dinner, and I have a realization that I smile more during dinner with Emma than I did for the entire year before I met her. It's a good feeling, and makes me certain that the decision I've made for tonight is the right one.

"I'll be right back," I say, getting up. "I have to go to the bathroom."

"Wait," she says, pointing to her lips. "Give me a kiss first."

I give her one, gladly, and then head inside to our room.

Okay, I lied, I *don't* actually have to go to the bathroom. But this is a worthy lie.

I pull out the ring from the ring box and, with my hand

shaking, I slip it into the small, stylish-looking white box of lingerie I picked out for her earlier this week.

Just as I'm about to go outside and do the deed, my phone buzzes on my dresser and I can't help but see Jocko's name as he's FaceTiming me.

Hell, what's one more interruption from my brother at a key time like this? At this point, a call from him is good luck.

"My brother, what's up?" he says, and I can see his shit-eating grin through the phone.

"Just about to do the damn thing," I say. "I picked up the ring last week."

"Holy shit, man! Damn! Well, good on you. Maybe Mom will let up the pressure on me to get married if she knows you're doing it."

"Nah," I say. "She's most worried about you. I doubt she'll ever stop badgering you as long as you are Mr. 'not-getting-married-until-forty.' You're her favorite. So, what's up?"

"Right. Well, I, uh, just wanted your advice."

A chill washes over me. Jocko rarely asks for advice. "Go ahead."

"There's this girl at work. And she asked me to be her date for a destination wedding. I'm debating whether I should go with her or not. As friends, I mean."

"Wait...is this what's-her-face whom I saw you with at a work event this summer?"

"Allie. Yes, that's her," Jocko says.

"I knew it!" I grin. I knew those doe-eyes weren't looking at Jocko like just any old friend.

"She wants to go with you...as friends."

"I swear. We're just friends."

"I'd hope so. I mean, being that she has a boyfriend and all."

Jocko clears his throat. "Actually, they broke up."

My forehead wrinkles. "Oh. Well, that's an interesting development."

"Anyway, man, I'm just curious, do you think it's a good idea for me to go with her to the wedding as her friend?"

"Why do you keep saying 'as her friend'?"

"Because Allie and I are just friends."

"Just friends and she *just* broke up with her boyfriend. You're not going to make a run at her, like a rebound?"

"No, I will not be *making a run* at her. Well, actually, that's what I wanted to ask you about. I refuse to dip my pen in the company ink, so to speak. You think that's a good policy on the whole, right?"

I chuckle. "My man, you are asking the wrong guy. A romance with my assistant is the best thing I ever did. So, whose wedding is it that you're going to?"

Jocko laughs. "Peyton O'Rourke and Maddy Cooper. It's in Cancún."

My stomach curdles. "Holy shit."

"Yeah, I guess Allie knows Peyton from college."

"Well, I'll be damned. Small world. That should be a blast."

Jocko has a penchant for getting himself invited to parties. But damn, the Super Bowl champion's wedding?

"Let me get this straight...you'd be staying for five nights with Allie...in the same room. And you'd be just friends. No funny business."

"Exactly."

I laugh. "Man, good luck with that from the way she was looking at you."

I hear Emma's voice calling out to me. "Look, man, I gotta go," I say.

"Good luck! Hope she says 'yes'."

I hang up, toss my phone back onto the dresser, and head back to the patio.

Emma is leaning back in her chair, smiling. "You okay? I was worried you had fallen in for a second."

"I just got caught up," I say. "But I've got a surprise for you. You ready?"

Emma's eyes light up when she sees the white box. I hold it out and she takes it.

"Mmm. I like red." She pulls out the red lace bra and panties. It's nothing too fancy or elaborate, but then again, Emma looks good in everything.

"I like red, too." Leaning into her, I kiss her cheek, and then whisper, "I can't wait to fuck you in these, then get you out of them."

When I run my hand over her arm, I can feel the goosebumps. "Jesus, that's hot. Thank you," she says. "So, what's the occasion?"

"Maybe you should look a little harder in the box," I say.

Right as her eyes find the shiny ring inside the box, I get down on one knee. I can tell she sees the ring because puts a hand over her mouth and a tear rolls down her cheek.

"Em, when I first met you, I hated you for holding a mirror up to my own problems. Then, I wanted you, for being absolutely gorgeous. And, finally, I loved you for being able to call me on my shit. Maybe it's quick, but I already know no one else will ever be to me what you are. I love you, Emma Foster. Make me the happiest man in the world and say 'I do'."

Her eyes soften. "I do, Everett. I definitely do."

I put the ring on her finger, kiss her, and as she moans into my mouth, I think about the advice I once heard from someone who said that a woman can't actually change a man.

"I'm so happy, Everett," she says.

"Me, too, babe, so damn happy."

And when I compare the misery I felt last year to the joy of this night, I have to disagree.

I'm the happiest man in the world tonight.

And I have a feeling there are going to be many, many more nights just as joyful as this one.

THE END

OTHER BOOKS BY MICKEY MILLER

THE LAKE HOUSE: Brewer Brothers Book 1

A summer fling with a younger man? Yes, please.

The story of Everett's younger brother, Maddox.

"The **perfect escape read** that ticked all the boxes!! **Off the charts hotness,** a fun and addictive story that I inhaled before I even knew it."

-Book Haven Book Blog

THE SUBSTITUTE - The story of Maddy Cooper and Peyton O'Rourke

Superstar Peyton O'Rourke swore he'd marry Maddy Cooper the first time he saw her, twelve years ago.

Well, he's finally back in town.

And he's ready to finish the job. No matter what she might have to say about it.

*This hilarious rom-com is now available on **AUDIO**, narrated by* ***Sebastian York and CJ Bloom!***

<u>The Lying Game:</u>

Living with a sexy-as-sin roommate in a luxury penthouse should be a fantasy brought to life, right? Not when the roommate is Carter Flynn--my gorgeous ex--who hates my guts.

<u>The End Game:</u>

Book 2 of this scorching, enemies-to-lovers Duet!

Ballers Romance Series:

It was supposed to be just sex. But it became so much more.
(Chandler + Amy's Book!)

I've always been the good girl. Until one night in Tijuana. When a gorgeous stranger struck up a conversation with me. He was so damn cocky, I decided to play a trick on him. So I made up a fake name. It was innocent, even if he was sinfully sexy.

The Blackwell After Dark Series:

I'm studying to be a sex therapist, and I haven't even had sex yet. Which is why I decide that Professor Hanks is going to be the one to take my virginity.

How to find a wedding date at the last second: 1) Overheat your car on your cross country road trip 2) Make sure it's storming 3) Have a one night stand with the sexiest mechanic you've ever seen

Sebastian Blackwell isn't only the sexiest man I've ever met. He's also my boss.

My best friend's sister. A tiny white lie to get a loan. A fake fiance?

<u>Others:</u>

No sex for ten dates, which sounds easy. Despite the biceps bulging through his shirt. Despite the tattoos I desperately want to lick-- I mean, know more about. Despite the hunger in his eyes when he looks at me. No, it won't be easy.

Remember, you'll get a free book here if you sign up for my mailing list:

https://dl.bookfunnel.com/mgr4nddhh2

Thank you for reading!

ABOUT MICKEY MILLER

Hi. I'm romance author Mickey Miller. I write light, hot, fast-paced romance that will make you smile and probably blush.

I've written five top 100 Amazon Bestsellers, including my Amazon Top 25 Hit ***The Substitute*** which is now available in audio featuring narrator Sebastian York.

The easiest and best way to stay in touch with me for news and new releases is to sign up for my email list here:

https://mickeymillerauthor.com

You can also find me on Instagram @mickeymillerauthor. Reach out and let me know what you think about my books! I love hearing from readers, so don't be shy!

Lots of Love,

Mickey

CHAPTER 1 - SNEAK PREVIEW OF THE LYING GAME

It's natural to think hate and love are opposites.

They're not.

Actually, indifference is the opposite of love, not hate.

And indifference is precisely what I'm feeling right now as I stare at the tall blonde I met last night, who is still in my apartment. She's been lingering this morning, sticking around and watching TV in my penthouse.

The time has come for me to kick her out.

"I have practice soon, so it's time for you to go," I say, nicely but without room for discussion.

She blinks a few times, and leans over on the kitchen island, letting out a slow breath. Trying to be cute. "I can just hang out here while you're gone. And be waiting for you when you come back." She lifts her eyebrows and tilts her head as she tries to tempt me.

Clenching my jaw, I stare her down.

Last night, we were enjoying ourselves.

But this afternoon, I don't feel a shred of desire for her.

All I feel is the distinct sensation of wanting this awkwardness to be over, and for her to leave.

Am I an asshole?

Yes. And I'm fine with that.

I was very upfront last night with Natasha about my 'no strings attached' policy when it comes to pleasure.

I don't do relationships. They're not for me. Maybe I'm paranoid, but when you're worth millions of dollars you never know how a woman might deceive you. Maybe she'll play the part of a perfect girlfriend up front, then after a year you'll find out she has a giant secret she's been keeping from you, lying to your face every day.

And yes, that's happened to me.

Natasha stares at me, squinting and giving me this 'Blue Steel' type of look where she wants to seem like she's not trying too hard, but I see right through it.

My eyes drift over to my bookshelf. I notice my copy of *The Great Gatsby* put on top of the shelf. Natasha must have been reading it.

My muscles quiver, seeing the tattered copy of the book that I read junior year of high school. My then girlfriend Lacy and I would read the passages to each other after school. I was so into her, I thought I wanted to spend the rest of my life with her. She asked me why I didn't press for sex, like the other guys were all doing with their girlfriends. I had this zen calmness back then. I just knew we'd be together forever, so what was the hurry?

It's funny the things you think you 'know' when you're seventeen.

I 'knew' I'd be with Lacy.

I 'knew' I was a relationship guy. Not a fuckboy.

Then Lacy broke my heart with a lie.

Little did I know back then, I would become the king of one night stands. And I thank Lacy for breaking my heart to show me that.

Like James Gatz himself, if I reached for a relationship, I'd only be a boat beat back against the current, in search of a green light that doesn't exist.

Shaking my gaze off from the book, I refocus on Natasha, my smirk returning.

I love my life these days.

I'm twenty-seven years old, just signed my first multi-million dollar contract with the Chicago Wolverines.

I enjoy my lack of responsibility when I'm doing anything besides playing professional basketball.

Noticing me drifting off, Natasha steps around my marble kitchen island and runs her hand along my shoulder.

"You look pensive. Everything alright?"

I swallow, suddenly thinking that maybe my slapstick version of Natasha isn't appropriate. At least she reads. Maybe I've underestimated her, maybe she is relationship material.

"I can be waiting for you . . . when you get back," she adds, her voice full of sultry suggestion. She runs her tongue over her upper lip.

I tense when her finger grazes me. "Look, Natasha. I think you're great. Last night—and this morning—was a lot of fun. But you don't want me, believe me. I have a lot of issues."

She furrows her brow, and a curious smile spreads across her face. "I like issues."

I run my thumb and forefinger across my forehead.

"You've never seen issues like mine, believe me."

"Doesn't seem to affect your, ahem, prowess." She lets her eyes drift below my belt.

I let out a slow exhale. This is probably most guys'

dream come true. A hot blonde begging to be nothing but a friend with benefits.

Taking a moment to assess, I search inside myself for feelings. After all, she's smart. Attractive.

But I feel absolutely nothing for her.

Just then, my phone buzzes with a text. Picking it up, I play like someone's calling me.

"Hey Chandler, what's up?" I say to no one on the line.

"Oh we have a team dinner after practice tonight . . . oh totally forgot about that . . ."

She sighs, and I smile as I nod into my phone like Chandler is continuing to talk to me.

It's not that I mind being more forceful with her and simply telling her we are done. It's more that I enjoy the thrill of the lie.

Just then, my phone rings. For real.

Natasha shoots me a funny look.

"Were you just . . . faking a conversation?"

"Call coming on the other line," I say, waving her off. "Hi Mom."

Rolling her eyes, Natasha walks away.

"How's the best son in the world?" my mom drawls sweetly.

"Hey, Mama. What's up?"

"Well, the reason I called is, you obviously know Mrs. Benson."

My heart does a tumble at the name 'Benson.' I hold the phone away from my face, clutching it hard.

"No, Mom, I completely forgot that you two went to wine night together every Saturday in high school after my games. Why do you ask about her?"

"Well Carter, I have a favor to ask. Lacy is moving to Chicago for a modern dance tryout."

My heart skips a beat. I can already feel my blood pressure rising.

"Lacy's going to be in Chicago?"

"You didn't know? I figured she might have called you or you would have seen her Facebook updates."

My jaw tightens, and I try not to bite down too hard on my lip. My mom has no idea Lacy and I aren't exactly on speaking terms, and haven't been for years. "She must have forgotten to let me know."

"So, do you think she could crash at your place while she's there? Tryouts are an unpaid thing. Mrs. Benson is worried about Lacy having to pay rent. We were casually chatting at dinner last night, and I mentioned your new place and how you have that extra room. Apparently Lacy's living arrangements fell through at the last second. And Lacy is too shy to ask for favors, you know how she is. So that's why I'm calling."

I move my mouth to start talking, but nothing comes out.

It's just past the first of June. It's the tail end of spring, and we're headed into summer in Chicago, after putting up with one hell of a winter. This is the first summer I'll be living all by myself, in a place that I officially own.

I've already declared the theme of this summer to be freedom.

The freedom I've earned with a lifetime of dedication to my sport, which culminated just a few weeks ago when I signed that monster contract.

Freedom doesn't mean spending a summer with my ex-girlfriend.

My mom can sense my silent resistance.

"And you two always get along so well, anyway. It's only eight weeks and then she'll be out of your hair."

I grind my teeth.

Only eight weeks.

She's got me between a rock and a hard place.

Lacy Benson always knew how to fuck with me.

Still does, after all these years.

As big of an asshole as I am, I can't say 'no' to my own mother.

"Just eight weeks?" I bite out.

"Just eight weeks, and she'll be out of your hair. I talked with Mrs. Benson. She says her audition is at the end of July."

My cat Smokey brushes my leg.

She licks her paw.

I can feel the tension on the other side of the line.

"Of course she can stay with me, Mom," I finally bite out.

"I thought you'd be fine with it. I mean, you two get along so well."

"Of course we do."

"She'll be arriving on the train tonight around seven-thirty. I'm sure she'll be tired. She left yesterday morning."

"That's great. Just great. I can't wait to see her," I lie.

My mom and I say some more pleasantries, then we hang up.

"Smokey," I growl. "Come here. I'm done playing games."

I stare her down.

Finally, she rolls her neck and jumps into my arms. Maybe she senses the anger emanating from me just thinking about Lacy's name.

Well, if Lacy's going to be here, maybe I can finally get some revenge.

Maybe it would be fun to make this summer a living hell for her.

Natasha walks back into the room in heels. She shakes her head, and puts her hands on her hip.

"How was your chat with 'your mom'?" she says, making air quotes.

I smirk.

"You're an asshole," she says, shaking her head.

I nod. "I know."

"I can handle asshole. But I can't handle a blatant liar. I'm leaving."

As the door slams, I feel nothing in my heart.

Not desire. Not hate or ill will. Just indifference.

The way my heart feels about Lacy Benson, however, is another matter entirely.

I'm not indifferent to her. I hate Lacy with every bone in my body for how she lied to me.

—

Available in Kindle unlimited!

The Lying Game:

Living with a sexy-as-sin roommate in a luxury penthouse should be a fantasy brought to life, right? Not when the roommate is Carter Flynn--my gorgeous ex--who hates my guts.

Made in the USA
Columbia, SC
02 August 2020

15113548R00174